WHISP ·

SP

TWO STRANGERS

*Recent Titles by Beryl Matthews from
Severn House*

BATTLES LOST AND WON
A DEBT FROM THE PAST
DIAMONDS IN THE DUST
A FLIGHT OF GOLDEN WINGS
THE FORGOTTEN FAMILY
HOLD ON TO YOUR DREAMS
A NEW DAY
THE OPEN DOOR
A TIME OF PEACE
TWO STRANGERS
THE UNCERTAIN YEARS
WINGS OF THE MORNING

TWO STRANGERS

Beryl Matthews

Severn House Large Print
London & New York

This first large print edition published 2015
in Great Britain and the USA by
SEVERN HOUSE PUBLISHERS LTD of
19 Cedar Road, Sutton, Surrey, England, SM2 5DA.
First world regular print edition published 2014 by
Severn House Publishers Ltd., London and New York.

British Library Cataloguing in Publication Data

Matthews, Beryl author.
  Two strangers.
  1. Slums–England–London–Fiction. 2. Poplar (London,
  England)–Social conditions–20th century–Fiction.
  3. Great Britain–History–George V, 1910-1936–Fiction.
  4. Large type books.
  I. Title
  823.9'2-dc23

  ISBN-13: 9780727872913

Severn House Publishers support the Forest Stewardship Council™
[FSC™], the leading international forest certification organisation. All
our titles that are printed on FSC certified paper carry the FSC logo.

Typeset by Palimpsest Book Production Ltd.,
Falkirk, Stirlingshire, Scotland.
Printed and bound in Great Britain by
T J International, Padstow, Cornwall.

One

1920 Poplar, London

'You will do as I say, girl!'

Victoria Keats faced her father's wrath without flinching. He always called her 'girl', taking every opportunity to remind her that she wasn't the son he wanted so much. 'I won't go and work for that man. Everyone knows why he takes young girls into his house.'

'That's just rumours spread by jealous people. He's rich, and he's willing to give you a job.'

'No!' Vicki glanced at her mother, hoping for help from her, but it was hopeless. Years of miscarriages and abuse from her husband for not producing a son had drained the spirit from her. Vicki doubted that this argument even registered with her. It was heartbreaking to see her in such a state. No one was going to do that to Vicki – not ever!

'Don't you defy me, girl!' Eric Keats yelled, clenching his hands into tight fists of rage. 'You're fourteen now and bloody useless, so you'll work like all of us have to.'

'I've been working since I was ten, Dad.'

He snorted in disgust. 'Running errands for shops ain't enough. It's time you got a proper job.'

'I'm trying, but it ain't easy for a girl to find work.'

1

'That's why you'll take a job when it's offered. I'll tell Mr Preston you'll start tomorrow, so no more of your nonsense.' He turned and made for the door.

'There's no point you going to see him, Dad, because I ain't gonna work for him.'

Eric Keats spun round, his face flushed with fury. 'Then you get out of my house, girl! I ain't feeding you no more. Get out! And don't you come back – ever!'

Vicki was stunned and swayed slightly with the shock. She had always known her dad had never got over his disappointment that his only surviving child was a girl, but she had never imagined he would throw her out. One look at his face told her he meant it, but she wasn't going to plead, or change her mind about working for that awful man. She knew what had happened to a couple of the girls he had employed, and there was no way she was going to allow that to happen to her. Once he had finished with them, they had been turned out to fend for themselves. She had no idea what had become of them or the babies they were carrying. They had just disappeared.

'I told you to go!' He stepped menacingly towards her. 'You think you're so good, don't you? Well, see how you get on out there in the street. It won't be long before you begin to think that a job with Mr Preston would be luxury.'

He thought that was funny, and Vicki was incensed. How dare he laugh! Well, he wouldn't be getting the money Mr Preston was offering for her, and that gave her some satisfaction. Of course, nothing was ever said about money

2

changing hands, but she knew it went on. She looked him steadily in the eyes, refusing to show the fear trembling through her. One day, I'll make him regret this day, she vowed silently.

'Clear off!' he snarled, pushing her roughly towards the door.

Dodging quickly out of his way, she fought back tears. She wasn't going to let him see how frightened she was so he could gloat over hurting her. 'Let me get my coat and say goodbye to Mum.'

'You can have your coat, and that's all. Don't bother with anything else.' He glanced at his wife who was fast asleep in the chair, quite unaware of the commotion going on around her. 'She don't want you here, either. She's expecting again and this one will be born without your disruptive influence around. And it will be a boy this time.'

Disruptive! Well, yes, he would see it like that, but all she'd done was try to help and protect her mum. And she had never been slow to tell this arrogant, selfish man what she thought about his treatment of the woman he had married. It was clear now that he had just been waiting for an excuse to get rid of her.

She ran out of the scullery and up the stairs. Her room was only big enough to hold a single bed and a small cupboard, but she'd done her best to make it comfortable. It had been her bolt hole where she had been able to find some peace to read, without insults being continually hurled at her. Taking deep breaths to calm her trembling emotions, she fought to clear her head. She must think clearly . . . As far as she knew, there weren't any family members for her to go to and she'd never had much time to make friends. When she wasn't running around trying to earn a few pennies, she was sneaking into bookshops to read. It didn't matter what it was; her thirst to know things was insatiable, she had been told. That was a good word and she'd had to find a dictionary to find out its meaning. All the kids around here thought she was odd, but that wasn't true. She just liked different things to them. So, it was no good thinking any of them would help her. The only person she could rely on was herself. She was alone. *Think, Vicki! What are you going to need?*

Warmth. She dragged the threadbare blanket off the bed, placed her one change of clothes in the middle with her hairbrush and wrapped it up into a manageable bundle. Then she slipped on her coat. Under the cupboard she kept a small rusty tin, and inside was all she possessed – tuppence farthing. Tucking that safely in the pocket of her frock, she sat on the bed, head bowed as she struggled to overcome the sudden feeling of sickness. It was four o'clock now, and, with so little money, it would mean spending the night outside. Thankfully, it was May and not too cold, but she wasn't daft and knew it could well be dangerous out there for a young girl alone.

Picking up her bundle, she edged towards the top of the stairs and listened. There wasn't a sound. Knowing her dad was on a late shift at the docks, she hoped he had gone and her mother was still asleep. A couple of stairs creaked badly and Vicki stepped cautiously over them as she made her way downstairs.

Much to her relief, the scullery was empty, and she didn't stop to wonder where her mother was as she quickly cut off a large chunk of bread and wrapped it in a towel with a piece of cheese. There was an empty beer bottle on the table which she filled with water. She put that in her coat pocket along with a small piece of soap. She also included the brush she used for her teeth. That dealt with the need for food tonight and a way to keep clean; now she needed something for protection. In the back of the kitchen drawer she found an old pair of scissors, slightly rusty from little use, so they wouldn't be missed. They also went into her coat pocket. Then she slipped out of the house.

Her stride didn't falter until she reached the end of the street. She stopped and glanced back at the row of dingy houses, wondering if she would ever come back here again. It hadn't been much of a home, lacking laughter and affection, but it was all she had ever known, and it was still hard to leave. But her dad had thrown her out, not caring what happened to her, so she had no choice. She focused her attention on where she was. Left or right? Did it matter? She had no one she could turn to for help and nowhere to go. The loneliness that hit her at that moment was almost unbearable, but she had to cope with it. If she didn't, then despair and hopelessness faced her.

No! No! That wasn't going to happen. She was only fourteen, with her life in front of her, and it would be what she made of it. The immediate future facing her was bleak, but if she was sensible and careful, she would get through it.

Vicki gripped her bundle firmly. She had food for tonight, and a blanket, but it would soon be dark and she must find somewhere to sleep. And quickly, because it looked as if it could rain at any moment. But where to go? She knew of a couple of places where the drunks and homeless gathered, but the thought of going to one of those frightened her. Fights and even killings weren't unusual.

Without realizing she had even moved, she found herself turning left and walking quickly in that direction. There was a derelict warehouse about a mile away. It had been empty for years and was undoubtedly already occupied by the homeless. But it was huge, so there was a chance she could find a spot away from anyone else. It was worth a try, and nothing else came to mind.

It was drizzling by the time she reached the building. The doors and windows were boarded up, but she found a small window round the back that had only glass. It was closed, but when she pushed, it shuddered open, and, clambering up, she managed to wriggle through it. The light was fading fast but it was still possible to see where she was, and she let out a ragged sigh of relief. It was a large room, littered with broken furniture and old benches, and no one else was there. The only door was closed, but the lock was broken. Opening it cautiously, she peered out, and then, catching the sound of men's voices, she eased it shut, not wanting them to know she was here. As quietly as possible, she began dragging anything heavy to rest against the door. Finally satisfied that the room was secure, she sat on an old piece of bench and surveyed her work. If anyone tried to open that door, it wouldn't move, so she could relax and try to get some rest. The bench was hard but it kept her off the cold stone floor. Before settling down to eat her meagre meal of bread and cheese, she wedged wood against the small window so no one else would open it from the outside. With all that done, she wrapped the blanket around her and settled down. Tomorrow there would be a lot to do because she didn't intend to live like this any longer than could be helped.

It had been a restless and uncomfortable night, but at least no one had tried to break into the room. Her stomach growled with hunger and she would have to find something to eat by using what little money she had and hope that she could replace it during the day. Brushing the dust off her crumpled frock, she grimaced; sleeping in her clothes had not been a good idea, but she had been too frightened to get undressed in case any of the undesirables had found her and she'd had to run. Staying clean and tidy was going to be difficult, but an absolute necessity, as it had always been for her. She had never believed that you had to be dirty just because you lived in the slums. She had been the one who had scrubbed and cleaned the dingy little house until it had been spotless, but it wouldn't stay that way now.

No point thinking about that, she told herself firmly as she shook out the blanket and rolled it up. There had been lots of people working here at one time so there must be an outhouse somewhere. Not wanting to dismantle her barricade, she picked up her towel and piece of soap and then squeezed out of the window. The yard was littered with rubbish, but there was another building a few yards away which looked promising.

The door was boarded up and the two windows were too small for even her to get through, but she was sure this was an outhouse. There was a heap of metal nearby and a search soon uncovered a hefty iron bar. Pleased with her find, she went back to the door and began to try to lever the boarding off.

'What are you doing?'

Vicki spun round, the bar held in both hands in front of her. She had been so intent on what she had been doing that she hadn't heard anyone coming up behind her. From the cultured sound of his voice, her first thought was that this was someone in authority, but he was too shabby. She waved the bar menacingly. 'Don't you come near me!'

A slight smile touched the corners of his mouth as he held up his hands in surrender. 'I only wondered what you were trying to do.'

'That's a stupid question! I'm trying to open this bloody door, of course.'

He glanced at the towel and soap she had put on the window sill. 'There might not still be running water in there,' he pointed out gently.

'I know that! I've got to see, though, haven't I?' The realization of her perilous situation suddenly swamped her, and her bottom lip trembled. 'I can't walk around dirty because no one would give me any jobs, and I need to earn some money.'

He sighed. 'What are you doing out on your own? You're only a child.'

'My dad threw me out because I wouldn't go and work for a nasty old man – and I'll be fifteen in a few months.'

He tilted his head to one side and studied her intently, his startling green eyes taking in every detail. 'And what is this man's name?'

'Preston.' She grimaced as she said his name.

'I've heard of him. You faced a difficult choice.'

'Weren't difficult. I won't be sold, and that's that, so I've got to fend for myself.'

He nodded. 'If you'd put down that weapon, I'll get the door open for you.'

She stepped back and let the bar hang by her side, still keeping a firm grip on it.

The slight smile appeared again. 'That will have to do, I suppose.'

She took another step back. 'Go on, see what you can do.'

In only a few minutes he had ripped off the boarding panels and forced open the door. Then he disappeared inside.

Vicki waited, amazed at how easily he had managed to get into the outhouse, and doubted she would ever have been able to do it by herself. Of course, he was a tall man and obviously strong. His voice was soft, gentle, and when he spoke he sounded educated, so what was a man like that doing as a down-and-out? And there was no doubt from his appearance that he was one.

He reappeared after some minutes shaking water from his hands. 'You're in luck. Everything in there is still working, and I've cleaned up as much as possible for you.'

'Oh, thank you.' She smiled with relief. 'You didn't need to do that – I'd have done it myself – but it was kind of you to trouble.'

He dipped his head. 'My pleasure. What is your name?'

'Vicki. What's yours?'

'Bill. Where did you spend the night, Vicki?'

She relaxed her guard a little. He didn't seem threatening. 'I found a room with no one in it, and I barricaded the only door. The window is too small for anyone bigger than me to get through.'

'That was sensible of you.'

She nodded and eyed the book sticking out of his coat pocket. 'You like reading?'

'Very much. Do you like books as well?'

She nodded again, enthusiasm showing on her face. 'I like reading and looking up words I don't know, but I can't always say them properly. You speak like a gent.'

Bill chuckled, a deep musical sound, making no attempt to answer her obvious curiosity. 'Go and have a wash, Vicki, and I'll keep watch to see you're not disturbed.'

'You're not to come in. I'm taking the iron bar with me.'

'I promise to stay right here. You can trust me

– but I have the impression there haven't been many in your life you could trust.'

Her laugh was devoid of humour. 'None is the answer to that. You can't be too careful.'

'Indeed. Go and clean up, Vicki.'

She gave him a suspicious look. How do I know you will keep your word and stay out here?'

He held out his hand. 'I found a key inside and it locks the door. Take it.'

Taking a cautious step forward, she snatched it out of his hand and quickly stepped back. 'Thank you. You needn't wait.'

The outhouse was surprisingly clean. All the rubbish was piled in a corner, leaving the sink and privy uncluttered. Vicki nodded approval. Bill had done well, but she still didn't trust him. She might be young, but the men she had grown up around never did girls favours unless they wanted something in return. She locked the door.

When she came out a while later, she was annoyed to see he was still there, leaning against an old machine of some kind, reading his book.

He looked up and smiled. 'Feel better?'

'Yes, thank you.' She locked the door behind her and studied the key in her hands. 'You found this, so do you want it back?'

'No, you keep it.'

She nodded, relieved, but still wary of this man. 'I ain't gonna give you nothing for being kind to me.'

With a sigh, he pushed himself up straight. 'I'm not helping you for a reward, Vicki.'

'Then what you doing it for?'

He thought for a moment, and then said, 'I like to start my day by doing someone a good turn.'

'Oh, mister!' she snorted. 'You don't expect me to believe that, do you? I might be from the slums, but I ain't daft! No one does things for nothing.'

'You may not believe it, Vicki, but some people take great pleasure in helping others – and expect nothing in return. You have obviously had a harsh life.'

'You could say that.' She looked down at the ground and kicked at an old piece of tin while she blinked the moisture away from her eyes. The last thing she must do is show weakness of any kind.

'What are you going to do now?' he asked gently.

'I'm gonna make something of myself and make my dad sorry he chucked me out!' When she looked up, her expression was fierce with determination. 'And don't you dare laugh!'

'I wouldn't dream of laughing at you, Vicki, but if you are to achieve your dream, we are going to have to do something about your speech.'

'*We're* not going to do nothing, mate! I'll manage on my own. What's wrong with the way I talk, anyway?'

'Your accent is rough, you use a double negative often, and it would sound better if you didn't say "ain't".' He pulled a small book from his inner pocket and handed it to her. 'This should help you understand.'

Curious, she took it, admiring the beautiful

leather-bound volume. 'English Grammar? Er . . . can I borrow it?'

'You can keep it.'

'What?' Her head shot up. 'I can't take this from you. It must be worth a lot of money. This looks like real leather.'

'I don't need it, and I would like you to have it.' He smiled. 'When you're rich and famous, you can return it to me if you want to.'

She giggled. 'All right, that's a promise, but you ain't . . . aren't likely to get it back.'

'Oh, I have a feeling I will.' He put his head on one side, his expression thoughtful. 'I have every confidence in you. Now, let me do one more thing for you today, and that is to buy you a good breakfast.'

'You're full of good turns, aren't you? Don't you think you've done enough for me already?'

'Indulge me, Vicki. I can afford to buy us both a good meal today.'

Her instinct was to refuse; her stomach had other ideas, however, because at that moment it growled in anticipation, so she nodded. 'I'll put my things in a safe place and see you out the front.'

Two

After making sure that Bill had walked away and couldn't see where she was going, Vicki squeezed through the window again, relieved to see her barricade was untouched. She changed into her other frock and rolled the rest of her meagre belongings in the blanket. She stowed it behind a sturdy cupboard and then piled wood against it, but the book she put in her frock pocket. That was too precious to leave here; anyway, it didn't belong to her, so she had to keep it safe.

Bill smiled when he saw her running towards him. As they walked together along the road, she glanced up at him, still puzzled why a man like this was homeless. Didn't he know how good-looking he was? If he was in trouble, he could have found a woman of means to support him, surely? That sort of thing did happen, she knew.

A deep laugh rumbled through him. 'I can practically hear your mind working, Vicki.'

She grinned at him. 'You don't miss much, do you? I'm just trying to make some sense of you. I like to get the measure of people, but I can't figure you out at all. Your clothes have seen better days, but I can tell from the material and fit that they had been expensive. What the devil are you doing sleeping rough?'

'It doesn't matter what background one comes from; anyone can find themselves in difficulties.' His ready smile appeared again. 'But, like you, I intend this to be temporary.'

She nodded. 'You'll make it back, and I'll try my hardest to get out of this mess, no matter how long it takes.'

'Whatever it takes, Vicki?' he asked.

'No! There's things I won't do. I won't sell myself, I won't steal and I'll try never to hurt anyone unless my life depends on it. I've seen too much of that kind of thing. And do you know—' she glanced up at him, her face serious – 'it don't do no one any good to be cruel and dishonest. It always seems to come back on them somehow.'

'I agree.' He stopped and turned her to face him. 'I want you to promise that, no matter how tough things become, you won't drop those standards.'

'There's no fear of that.' She tapped her chest. 'Them feelings are deep in here!'

'Promise me, Vicki.'

'I promise.' She frowned. What a strange man he was. It sounded as if he really cared what she thought and did, but that was daft. He didn't even know her. 'It was sticking to what I feel that got me into this mess, but I'll get out of it my way.'

'Good girl.' The smile was back. 'Are you going to read and study that book I gave you?'

'Of course. Is that another promise you want me to make?' she teased.

'No, I'll take your word for that.' They began walking again. 'We're nearly at the cafe I use. Hungry?'

'Starving!' In fact, she was so hungry she was prepared to spend her few precious coins on a good meal. Bill had said he would pay for her, but she doubted he had enough money for the both of them. And, anyway, she couldn't take whatever money he had. It wouldn't be right when he was in the same situation as her.

It was a workman's cafe and busy at this time of the morning. Bill held the door open for her

15

as if she was a real lady, and the gesture made her feel good. Much to her surprise, Bill was greeted by some of the men who obviously knew him.

'There's a table by the window, Vicki,' Bill told her as he led her to the only vacant seats in the place.

When he held her chair for her, a broad smile crossed her face. 'You got lovely manners,' she said.

'There is no need to drop my standards just because I am in changed circumstances at the moment, is there?'

She shook her head.

'Hello, Bill.' The owner came up to them, all smiles. 'The usual, is it?'

'Yes, please, Frank, and the same for my guest, Vicki.'

'Nice to meet you, Vicki. The food will be right up.'

She watched Frank weave his way through the tables, and then turned her attention back to Bill. 'You must come here a lot because they all seem to know you.'

'I eat here quite often. The food is good and the helpings are generous.'

When a plate was put in front of her, she gasped, seeing what he meant. There were two eggs, fried bread, bacon and even a large sausage. She watched in astonishment as a pot of tea and a plate of bread and butter were also put on their table.

'Eat up; don't let it get cold.'

'But . . . but . . . I can't afford grub like this!'

'I'm paying, remember?' Bill told her gently, seeing the distress on her face.

'But this feast will cost a lot, and I can't let you do this.' She fished in her pocket and slipped two pennies across the table towards him. 'That's all I've got, but it will help a bit.'

'Vicki!' Bill said sternly. 'I am paying for our breakfast. Are you going to insult me by refusing to eat it?'

'Oh.' She was taken aback by his tone. 'I don't mean to do that, but I'm not happy that you might be spending your last bit of money on feeding me.'

'I know.' He smiled then, the gentleness back in his voice. 'But I can afford our meal, so you keep your money. Now eat up or Frank will think you don't like his cooking.'

The smell of the food was too much for Vicki. She put the coins back in her pocket, picked up her knife and fork, and began eating. She was ravenous, and there was enough food here to fill her up for the rest of the day.

They worked their way through everything on the table, and, when they had drained the teapot, Vicki sat back sighing contentedly. 'I've never had so much to eat at one meal,' she told Bill. 'There was enough food there for a week.'

'Would you like another helping?'

'Oh, no. That was more than enough! I enjoyed every mouthful, and it won't matter if I don't have anything else today. If I can earn some money, I'll buy you a meal next.'

'I won't be around, Vicki, because I'm moving on today.'

'Are you?' The stab of disappointment she felt surprised her. Why should she care if he was going to disappear? They had only just met. But, of course, she knew why. Bill had been kind to her, and that was something she was not used to. 'Have you got somewhere to go, then?'

He nodded, stood up and walked over to the counter. Vicki watched as he paid for their meal and talked to Frank; then they both came back to the table.

'When you need something to eat, Vicki, come and see Frank. He will see you are all right.'

Frank nodded and smiled at Vicki. 'Bill has told me of your plight, so it doesn't matter how much money you've got, I'll see you have something.'

'Thank . . . thank you.' She didn't know what to say, feeling quite overwhelmed by such kindness. However, she knew she wouldn't come in here begging for food, no matter what Frank said. No, there would have to be enough money in her pocket first. She knew her stubborn pride was daft, considering the situation she was in, but that was how she was.

'You mustn't starve.' Bill looked at her sternly as if he could read her mind. 'You're a growing girl and need regular food.'

She nodded, quite lost for words that these two strangers should feel any concern for her.

Vicki and Bill then left the cafe, and she looked up at him. 'Good luck, wherever you're going, Bill.'

'The same to you, Vicki. It's been a pleasure meeting you. Take care of yourself.'

She watched him stride away and had the feeling she could have liked and trusted him if they'd had time to get to know each other. Perhaps it was just as well, though; it would be silly to start depending on anyone. She had always been alone, and it was best if it stayed that way.

Right! If she was not going to starve, she had to earn some money. That had been a good start to the day – better than she could have hoped, thanks to Bill. But that wasn't going to happen again; it was up to her now. She turned and headed towards the market where she knew some of the traders.

The street was busy. Many traders had already set their stalls ready for the day, but a few were still unloading. Vicki made her way along, looking for any opportunity.

'Doris!' she called, when she saw the woman struggling on her own. 'Do you want help with those boxes?'

'I could use some, Vicki,' she answered, straightening up and holding her back. 'Ted ain't too good today, so I'm on my own.'

Vicki hurried over. 'You look worn out, Doris. Sit down and I'll soon have this done for you.'

'Thanks.' Doris sat on an old rickety chair, sighing with relief. 'I'm glad you came along. Stay with me for the rest of the day and I'll feed you, and give you a bob for your trouble.'

'I ain't got nothing else to do today.' Vicki couldn't believe her luck. Food and a shilling at the end of the day would be wonderful. If she did well, then Doris might even want her tomorrow, too.

With a smile on her face, Vicki began hoisting the heavy boxes of goods, unpacking them and arranging everything in neat sections. Ted and Doris sold just about everything, except food. There were curtain materials, tools, household items and many more odds and ends.

Vicki soon had the job done and stood back to survey her handiwork. 'Is this how you want it, Doris?'

'Lovely and neat, lass.' She nodded her approval. 'All we want now are the customers. I couldn't miss a day's trading, but I didn't know how I was going to manage on my own. Now, before we start getting busy, go to the cafe and get us both a mug of tea. I'm gasping for a nice strong cuppa. Oh, and make it a bun each, as well.'

Vicki wasn't hungry yet, but she wasn't going to say no to any food. It could be wrapped up and saved for later, she thought, taking the money from Doris and then running across the road to the little cafe all the traders used.

By the time she was back, the market was starting to throng with shoppers, and the sounds of traders shouting their wares began to fill the street. Determined that she was going to earn her keep this day, Vicki stood in front of the stall, doing her utmost to entice customers.

Doris was smiling as she served the people Vicki had persuaded to stop.

Trade was steady, and the day went well. After they had packed everything away, Doris gave Vicki the promised shilling. 'Will you need help tomorrow?' she asked, hopefully.

'I expect Ted will be all right by then, but come along, just in case.'

'Thanks. I'll do that.' Happy that she had been able to get work for the whole day, Vicki ran across to the cafe. Now that she had more money in her pocket she felt able to spend the tuppence Bill had refused to take. She bought a pie for her supper, and the owner kindly filled an old bottle with water for her. The pie and the bun she had saved would fill her stomach nicely for the night.

Arriving back at the warehouse, she was relieved to see the small window hadn't been touched. She checked that she wasn't being watched, then squeezed through the window and rushed over to inspect her barricade, letting out a sigh of relief to see it was still in place. She should be safe again tonight and, hopefully, she would be able to get some sleep because after such a busy day she was tired. Before settling down, though, she would read some of the book Bill had left with her. She had promised him she would, and as he had been so kind to her, it would be wrong not to try to do what he had suggested. If she spoke better, she might be able to get a proper job.

Vicki glanced around at the squalid surroundings and pulled a face. She must try very hard to get out of this awful place. Pulling the book out of her pocket, she propped herself up against the wall under the window to get the best light, and began reading.

An hour later she gave up. Not only was it now too dark to see clearly, but she hadn't been able to make any sense of what she'd read. Clutching the book to her, she bowed her head and muttered, 'Oh, Bill, whatever made you think this would help me? I'm just a kid from the slums, with poor schooling. I know I was way ahead of the other kids, but the teachers didn't even try to give me harder lessons. They only worried about the slower ones, so I never got any further, and they threw me out at twelve.'

The book was put away safely, and Vicki sat munching her food, deep in thought. It was going to be hard, but she would keep trying. If she gave up, then the life in front of her would be bleak, and probably short. There were many damaged men back from the war roaming around, and she would never be safe living like this. She had to get out of here as quickly as possible.

The early morning sun was streaming through the window when Vicki woke up. Not wanting to miss the chance of another day's work, she washed quickly and ran to the market.

It was a terrible disappointment to see Ted there. Not that she wanted him to be sick, but she had hoped he would take another day to rest.

'Hello, Vicki.' Ted smiled. 'Thanks for helping Doris yesterday.'

'That's all right. I'm glad you're feeling better. Do you need help today?'

'No, we can manage, lass.'

Vicki smiled, waved to Doris, and began to walk through the market to see if there was work at any of the other stalls.

Three

It was sheer luck her hiding place hadn't been discovered for so long, but that was where her good fortune ended. The bitter March wind was ripping through Vicki's thin coat and she was so cold she could hardly move. To add to her misery, it was beginning to snow again. She looked up at the small window and wondered where she was going to get the strength to pull herself through. She knew she must, though, because if she collapsed out here it would be the end.

It was with sheer desperation that she managed to struggle through, and, with the last reserves of her strength gone, she fell on to the concrete floor. That was where she stayed for a while, gasping with relief. After that first hopeful day, things had become more and more difficult. In the struggle to earn enough money for food, ten months had slipped by. Her fifteenth birthday had come and gone unnoticed, and now her situation was frightening. She was so weak and scruffy that no one would give her a job. To her shame, she had started begging at the railway station. Several times she had stopped outside the cafe Bill had taken her to, but just hadn't been able to make herself go in and ask for something to eat. The man had said she could, but she couldn't go in there looking like this, and she wasn't sure if he'd only said that because Bill was there. If she went in begging for food and got thrown out, then that would be the end of her. No, she just couldn't do it.

Forcing herself to stand up, Vicki went over to the small fireplace and knelt down in front of it. She had resisted lighting a fire because she hadn't wanted to draw attention to her hiding place, but if she was going to see the spring, then she had to take the chance.

There was plenty of paper and wood in the room and it didn't take her long to have a fire ready to light. She had been lucky today when a passenger running to catch the train dropped a match box. Vicki had pounced on it. There were only six matches still in the box, but if she was careful they might last her a while. With shaking hands, she struck a match and held it to the paper. Luckily, everything in the room was dry, and the wood soon caught. She watched anxiously, hoping there wouldn't be too much smoke pouring out of the chimney. She carefully fed small pieces of wood on to the fire and there was soon a good blaze going. She began to thaw out. The relief was overwhelming and, in her fragile state, she began to cry in great gulping sobs. When her dad had thrown her out and she had found this warehouse, she had been confident that it would only be a temporary place to stay, but she was still here. Where had her hopes and dreams of making a good life for herself gone?

More composed after a while, she wiped her face dry and munched the bun she had managed to buy today. As she gazed at the comforting flames, her mind began to clear. There had to be a way out of this desperate mess, but everywhere she went they turned her away, saying they only wanted boys . . .

Boys . . . boys . . . The word kept running through her head as she finished the last crumbs of her meagre meal. Then she nodded to herself. If that was the only way to get a job, then she would have to pass herself off as a boy. It shouldn't be too hard. If she cut her hair and changed her clothes, it should be possible. Getting hold of trousers, jacket and a shirt wasn't going to be easy, though, but she would find a way. The railway station would be her best bet. Even though she hated begging like that, it had to be done. If she was lucky, she would get enough money for what she needed. There was a stall at the market selling cast-off clothes, and they were cheap.

The tears had drained her, but now that she was warm, had a small amount of food inside her and a purpose for tomorrow, she felt better. She banked up the fire for the night and settled down to sleep.

The next day the bitter wind had dropped, and there was only a light covering of snow on the ground. When the sun came out, Vicki lifted her face to the brightness. It was too early in the year for there to be any warmth in it, but it was welcome, just the same. She was terribly weak and had to walk slowly, but she did feel a bit stronger after a night resting by the fire, which was a relief because she had to get some money, even if it took all day.

25

The station was already busy when she settled by the door. Taking a deep breath, she braced herself to beg from everyone who came on to the platform, pleading desperately. There was a small tea room close by, and she could smell the food cooking. It was agony, and the tears she was shedding were genuine. She had to succeed today, or it would be the end for her. Soon she wouldn't even be able to stand.

A smartly dressed man stopped and studied her, shaking his head. 'How long is it since you've had a decent meal?'

'I . . . I had a bun yesterday, sir,' she said.

'I said a *meal*!' His tone was sharp.

'Not for a long time, sir.'

'No, it doesn't look like it. Come with me.'

He ushered her inside the cafe, made her sit at a table and then went to the counter. Vicki swiped the tears from her face. She cried too easily these days, but she didn't seem to have enough strength to stop the flow. It disgusted her because she had never indulged in self-pity. But she had never been in such a dreadful state before. She quickly wiped her face with the back of her hand and watched the man walking back to the table. He had a slight limp and was leaning on a silver-topped cane for support.

'What is your name?' he asked as he sat down, leaning the cane against the table.

'Vicki, sir.' She noticed the cane had a dog's head on it.

He sighed again. 'And where is your family, Vicki?'

'They live in Poplar, sir.'

'And why aren't you with them?'

'My dad threw me out when I wouldn't go and work for a nasty man. Girls weren't safe around him, and I wouldn't do that.' She didn't even consider lying.

'So you ended up begging.'

Vicki nodded, the tears trickling down her face again.

He handed her a pristine handkerchief, sighing deeply once more. 'Can't you find work in a decent household, or even a shop? You speak well and sound educated.'

That remark surprised her. She hadn't realized that the hours she had spent on the lessons in Bill's book had actually improved her speech. She wiped her face and managed a rare smile. 'Thank you, sir. I've been trying to get work, but I'm such a mess now they won't even give me a chance.'

'How long have you been fending for yourself?'

'Nearly a year. I don't like begging, but I'm desperate now, sir.' She held out the handkerchief to him, but he refused to take it back.

'Ah, here is your food. I want to see you eat every scrap.'

When Vicki saw two slices of toast piled high with scrambled egg, she nearly burst into tears again. She managed to fight the feeling off. This man had kindly brought her in here so she mustn't embarrass him.

He never said a word as she worked her way through the food and two cups of steaming tea.

'Would you like another helping?' he asked when she had finished.

'Oh, no, sir. I'm full right up. That was very generous of you, and I'm grateful.'

He gestured to the man at the counter who immediately came and put a large brown paper bag on the table and then went back to work.

'There's enough food in there to see you through the day, and this is to buy yourself some decent clothes.'

Vicki stared at the money on the table, mesmerized. Ten shillings! 'No, no, sir. The food I'll take because I'm starving, but that's all.' Her eyes showed suspicion when she looked at him. This wasn't right.

'I mean you no harm, young lady. I do not want anything from you. My only reason for doing this is to try to help you.' He stood up. 'Take the money, and give me the satisfaction of believing that I might have saved a life this day.'

'You have, sir.'

He gave a slight nod of his head he walked out, and Vicki watched him get on the train just about to leave the station. When it had steamed away, Vicki turned to the man who had served them. 'Do you know his name?'

'Never seen him before.' He studied her, a deep frown on his face. 'He was angry to see such a young girl obviously starving to death. I gathered from the little he said that he had served in the war – an officer, by the look of him – and had seen enough suffering. If you have a family somewhere, then you had better go back to them before it's too late.'

Vicki stood up, steadying herself on the table, and shook her head. 'My dad threw me out and told me never to come back. He doesn't change his mind when it's made up, so I've got to survive on my own.'

'Well, you're not doing a very good job of it. Look at you! You can hardly stand.'

'I know I've got to do something to get out of this mess, but do you realize how difficult it is to get work? Even men who have returned from the war can't find work, so what chance do you think a mere girl has? Will you give me a job? I don't care what it is.'

He shook his head.

'No, I didn't think so. Well—' Vicki gathered up the bag of food and the money – 'thank you for caring.'

The sun was still shining when Vicki walked back to the platform, so she sat on a seat, trying to gather enough strength to tackle the long walk back to the market. She now had enough food for two days if she was careful, and money to buy the clothes she needed. Then she would go back to the warehouse, cut her hair short and scrub herself until she was spotless. A bar of soap had better go on her shopping list.

She lifted her face to the sun, forcing herself to think clearly. Having a full stomach after such a long time had made her sleepy, and she began to drift off . . .

The noise of another train arriving woke her suddenly, and she sat up straight. She couldn't sit here all day. There were things to do. She stood up and walked out of the station. Should she spend some of her precious money on a bus? Her decision was soon made and she began walking, knowing she had to be careful with every penny she had been given.

That evening Vicki lit a fire again, needing the comforting blaze for warmth and to dry her under-clothes. As she watched the flames leap into life, she marvelled, not for the first time, that she had managed to keep this hiding place to herself all these months. It was a stroke of good luck she didn't take for granted. She could always hear others in the building, but no one had ever bothered her.

She held her hands out to the blaze, trying to stop them shaking. She was exhausted, but the clothes had been bought, her hair chopped off short with the old scissors she had brought with her, and she was clean. Tomorrow she would clamber out of this room as a boy. She had to get a job – any kind of a job!

Pulling her knees up, she bowed her head towards them. She had been given a lifeline today, and it mustn't be wasted. She owed that to the kind gentleman, and to Bill – two strangers who had reached out to help her. She couldn't let them down – and she mustn't let herself down!

Four

The day was overcast but thankfully not too cold, because the clothes Vicki had bought, though neat and tidy, were not very warm. They had been the cheapest she could find, because she had to keep as much as possible for food. There was no telling how long it would take to find a job, and it was important that she regain her strength. Being so weak was frightening.

There had been enough food from yesterday for her to have a cheese sandwich for breakfast, and it was helping. She wasn't quite so shaky and in danger of falling down.

When Vicki reached the High Street, she leant against a wall, taking deep breaths to steady herself. Her head was spinning after the walk, and she must look bright and lively if anyone was going to take her on. Also, she was so nervous that her heart was thumping. She had done her best to look like a boy, but had she succeeded well enough to fool others?

Tucking the remains of her hair under the cap she had bought, she straightened up, fixed a bright smile on her face and began to study each shop, looking for any sign that they needed help. She would soon find out if her disguise was going to pass scrutiny.

It quite quickly became evident that no one was advertising for help, so the only thing to do was go in and ask. After she had tried a hardware shop, a gentlemen's outfitter and a butcher, all without success, she found a low wall and sat down to rest. They had all turned her down, but they had appeared to accept her as a boy without question. That made her more confident, but she was now so tired her hands were shaking again. She couldn't continue like this. There had been a small cafe down a side street a little way back, and it was time to use some of her remaining money. What she needed now was food and a chance to rest. A nice strong mug of tea would also prepare her to continue her search. She was absolutely determined to do all she could today, even if she collapsed with the effort.

The cafe was small but cheap, and as it was around the middle of the day there were quite a few people already in there. Vicki found a vacant table in the corner.

'What can I get you, lad?' a rather scruffy man asked as soon as she sat down.

'The cheapest meal you've got, and a mug of strong tea, please.' She smiled. He had called her 'lad' without hesitation.

'That'll be a small piece of fish and chips. All right?'

'Fine. Thank you.'

In the comforting warmth and with the enticing smell of food, Vicki closed her eyes, the chatter of other customers slipping into the distance. A hand on her shoulder made her jump.

'Here, drink your tea, lad.'

'Oh, thanks.' She nodded as he put the mug and a plate of food in front of her. 'It's nice and warm in here, and I nearly fell asleep.'

'Tired, are you?'

'I'm looking for work and have been walking all morning,' she offered as a reason for her exhaustion. She smiled. 'The fish and chips look lovely.'

'I've given you a few extra chips, and if you need more tea just give me a nod. No extra charge.'

'Thanks a lot.'

By the time she had finished her meal and downed two mugs of steaming tea, Vicki dragged herself out of the seat and went to the counter to pay. While waiting for change from the two shillings she had handed over, the scruffy man came over.

'Did you say you were looking for work, kid?'

'Yes.' She looked at him eagerly. 'Do you know someone who might hire me? I don't care what I do.'

'Well—' he rubbed his hand over the stubble on his chin, making a rasping sound – 'there's a barber two doors down from here. You could try them. I'm sure I heard Bob say he could use a willing lad in the shop.'

'Oh, did you? I'll go there now.' Vicki pocketed her change and hurried out, desperate not to miss any opportunity of work. The glimmer of hope gave her a much needed burst of energy.

There wasn't a notice in the window, but it was a nice shop, and quite busy. That was a good sign. Straightening her cap, she walked in.

The middle-aged man cutting a customer's hair looked up. 'Can I help you, young man?'

Vicki politely whipped off her cap. 'I'm looking for work, sir, and the man from the cafe said you might need someone. I'm a hard worker and will do anything, sir.'

'Hmm.' He looked her up and down, and then called, 'Flo!'

A homely, but smartly dressed woman came from the back of the shop and smiled at Vicki.

'This lad is looking for work. Have a word with him, Flo, and see if he will suit us. And

33

while you're at it, for goodness' sake cut his hair. It looks as if it's been chopped off with a blunt knife!'

She smiled broadly. 'Had a go at it yourself, did you?'

Vicki nodded, not knowing what to say.

'Well, we'll soon put that right. What's your name, son?'

'Er . . . Jim . . . Jim Keats, madam.' This was something Vicki hadn't given any thought to, and she said the first name that came into her head. She had said her real surname, though. It was too complicated to change that as well.

'All right, Jim Keats, come with me and we'll have a talk.'

The back room was warm and comfortable. There was a fire burning in the grate, two armchairs, a small black leaded stove and a table and four chairs. The curtains were dark red with small roses embossed in the material, and a door opened on to a neat yard with a flower bed in the middle. Vicki thought it must look lovely in the summer, and her orderly mind noticed how clean and tidy everything was. Oh, she liked this place!

'Sit down, Jim, and tell me about yourself.'

Vicki clasped her hands tightly. She was lying about being a boy, but she refused to do more than that. Anything she told this nice woman would have to be the truth, as far as possible, of course. 'I'm fifteen, and willing to do any kind of work, madam.'

'You can call me Mrs Howard, Jim. And where do you live?'

'My mum and dad live in Poplar, but I've been on my own for nearly a year. My dad threw me out.'

'And why did he do that?' she asked, frowning.

'I didn't do anything bad,' Vicki hastily added. 'He mistreats my mum, and I stood up to him. He didn't like it and told me to get out and never come back.' Vicki drew in a silent breath, hoping she hadn't ruined her chances. She had done her best to smarten herself up, but it was still obvious to anyone that she had been living rough.

Flo looked angry. 'And where have you been staying?'

'I found a safe place in an old warehouse.'

Flo surged to her feet and swept into the shop to talk to her husband. Vicki felt the tears gathering. Any hope of getting this job had just disappeared. They wouldn't take on a vagrant – and that is what she was. Why hadn't she come up with a believable lie? She was a fool!

When Bob came back with his wife, Vicki stood up, ready to leave quickly before disgracing herself by bursting into tears. Her weakness disgusted her, but if she was going to survive for much longer, she desperately needed a job.

The barber stood in front of her, blocking the doorway, so she would have to stay and listen while he told her she had wasted his time.

Flo had opened another door, and her husband waved a pair of scissors in that direction. 'There's a bed in there, and an outhouse just outside. I will expect you to keep your room and yourself clean. You will eat with us. I will give you half a crown a week for pocket money, and you can keep any tips you receive from customers. I shall expect you to be polite and cheerful to anyone who comes into the shop, and be prepared to work hard.'

Vicki stared at him, unable to believe what he was saying. 'Do . . . do you mean I can have the job and live here?'

'Those are my terms, young man. Do you still want to work for us?'

'Yes, please, sir! I'll keep everything spotless and work hard for you, sir!' Her head was swimming with relief, and she grabbed hold of the back of a chair to steady herself. A job and a safe place to sleep! It must be a dream!

'Sit down, Jim, before you fall down.' The barber shook his head. 'It is evident that you have had a rough time, but it is also very clear that you have been very brave. You speak well, and your manners are good. I believe you have the qualities I have been looking for.'

'You won't regret taking me on, sir.' Vicki's voice was husky with emotion. 'I'll be the best worker you've ever had.'

'We shall soon see. I want you to go and collect whatever belongings you have and come straight back here. We will get you settled in today, and you can start in the shop tomorrow.' Her nodded to his wife. 'Give Jim a strong cup of tea and something to eat now, Flo. And for goodness' sake, cut his hair before he leaves the shop. He'll give us a bad reputation looking like that.'

Vicki watched them laughing together at the shared joke and marvelled that a husband and wife could look so happy together. It was not something she was used to seeing.

'Have a look at your room,' Flo said, when her husband had returned to his shop.

Vicki followed her on trembling legs. She had given up all hope of getting the job and, suddenly, she had more than she could ever have hoped for. The room was just large enough for a single bed, a small wardrobe and a cupboard beside the bed, on which a clock ticked rhythmically. The cover on the bed was a mass of tiny blue flowers, with matching curtains at the window. It was spotlessly clean and, to Vicki, looked like heaven. She closed her eyes tightly for a moment to keep control of her emotions. Then she managed a tremulous smile. 'It's perfect.'

'Good, that's fine, then. Now, I'll make some tea. What would you like to eat?'

'I've had my lunch, Mrs Howard, at the cafe up the road.'

She studied Vicki, a deep frown on her face. 'You're far too thin, Jim. We've got to build you up. Could you manage egg on toast?'

Vicki nodded. She really wasn't hungry – a rare feeling these days – but it would be rude to refuse.

Flo smiled with approval. 'Eat first, and then I'll cut your hair properly. When we've done that, you can go and collect your things. I'll come with you if you need any help.'

'That's kind of you, Mrs Howard, but I can manage. I haven't very much.'

'No, I don't suppose you have,' she said sadly. 'I want you to come straight back so we can get

37

you settled in, and then there will still be time to show you the work you will be doing in the shop.'

'I can get to the warehouse and back in less than an hour.'

'That will do nicely. Sit down, son. It won't take long to cook you an egg and sort out your hair.'

There wasn't anyone around when Vicki reached the warehouse, and she was able to squeeze through the window unnoticed. She didn't want to give away her hiding place, as much as she hated it here, because she might need it again at some time in the future. She shuddered at the thought, but if Mr and Mrs Howard found out she was really a girl, then they would turn her out. This had been a safe place, and she didn't want anyone else to find it. When her few possessions were wrapped in the old blanket and secured with a piece of string, Vicki tossed it out of the window and followed. She then put the pieces of wood across the window, making sure they were secure. The key to the outhouse she kept, just in case. All the exertion and excitement suddenly took its toll and she was very sick, her stomach not used to so much food. Propping herself against the wall, she waited for the sickness to pass. After ten minutes or so, she felt steadier, picked up her bundle and headed back to the shop, knowing she mustn't be late or show any sign of weakness. Nothing must spoil this stroke of good luck!

She had to stop and rest twice on the way, but when she reached the shop she walked in, a bright smile on her face. They weren't going to know she could hardly put one foot in front of the other. Regular food and a real bed to sleep in would soon get rid of these awful feelings.

'Ah, good, you're back.' Flo was waiting in the shop. 'Put your things in your room, then we'll have a nice cup of tea and an hour in the shop.'

Still smiling, Vicki did as ordered. Her room! It was hard to take in what had happened, but she must be very careful or she could find herself back in that nightmare. The bundle was tucked under the bed, out of sight. They mustn't see that because it had all her girls' clothes in it. As soon as there was time – and a little money – she had to buy more shirts, and perhaps a pair of pyjamas.

Flo already had the tea brewing when Vicki came out of the room. The barber and his assistant, Sid, joined them, and they all sat down together. After drinking the tea, Vicki began to feel better and even managed to eat a biscuit.

The shop bell rang and the two men went back to work. Flo studied Vicki carefully. 'Do you want another cup, Jim?'

'No, thank you, Mrs Howard.'

She nodded. 'At least you've got a bit of colour in your face now. You were as white as a sheet when you returned. Are you sure you feel well enough to run through your duties in the shop?'

'Oh, yes.' Vicki stood up, smiling. 'I'm fine, and looking forward to finding out what I will be doing.'

The next hour took every ounce of her concentration as she made herself move with speed when the floor needed sweeping. She gathered the towels and put them in the basket ready for washing, and helped customers on with their hats and coats when they were preparing to leave. The fog of fatigue was draining what little strength she had, but she would not give in or show any outward sign that she wouldn't be capable of doing this job.

'Well done, Jim,' Flo said. 'That will do for today.'

Vicki smiled and took the towels out of the basket. 'I'll wash these ready for tomorrow, shall I?'

Flo took them out of her hands and put them back in the basket. 'We'll deal with these later. We have plenty of clean ones. Now, you go and have a rest. Dinner will be in an hour.'

By the time Vicki went to her room, she was shaking badly and threw herself on to the bed. It felt wonderful after the hard stone floor of the warehouse, but she was too tired to cry. This time, though, they would have been tears of relief. She had a job with nice people and a lovely place to stay. And she had managed to get through the day without collapsing. That was quite an achievement, and now she had an hour to gather her strength. She drifted off to sleep with a smile on her face.

Oh, she did hope this was real . . . and that the dream would last.

Five

'I hope we've done the right thing, Flo,' Bob said later that evening as his wife cleared away the dishes.

'Only time will tell. There was such a heart-breaking look of desperation in his eyes, I couldn't turn him away.' She smiled sadly. 'But I also believe he is an honest boy and will work hard for us. He didn't try to hide the situation he was in.'

'That's true, but there's something about him that doesn't set right with me.' Bob shook his head, puzzled. 'I can't fathom it at the moment, but I have the feeling he's guarding a secret of some kind. Something he's frightened we will find out.'

'I know what you mean, but with the life he's been leading he's bound to have things he doesn't want to talk about.' Flo patted her husband's hand. 'Well, whatever it is, we've given him a chance, and all we can do now is wait and see how he works out. I'll just pop down and see if he's settled in all right. He's so frail it worries me.'

There was no sign of Jim, but the back room was tidy, and, to her amazement, the dirty towels had all been washed and were strung across the stove to dry. The door to the outhouse was locked and bolted, so the boy wasn't out there. Flo

41

wandered into the shop, thinking he might be there, and looked around. The chairs had been straightened, all shelves cleaned and everything arranged neatly. Clean towels were also stacked ready for use. On closer inspection, she saw that the combs and brushes had been washed. The shop was spotless and ready for the next day.

'My word,' she murmured, 'the lad could hardly stand up, yet he's obviously been working hard. What determination.' But where was he? The poor little devil must have gone to bed exhausted. Returning to the back room, she listened at his door and heard a muffled sound – like someone crying softly.

Alarmed, Flo rushed upstairs. 'Bob!'

He jumped to his feet. 'What's happened?'

'You've got to see what Jim's done! I don't know how he managed it. He was so weak it was an effort for him to get through an hour in the shop. He's in bed now and I'm sure I heard him crying. What should I do, Bob? Should I go in and see if he's all right?'

'Slow down, Flo.' Bob tried to calm her down. 'First, show me what you're talking about.'

They went into the shop and Flo watched her husband inspect everything, noting his nods of approval.

'Excellent. I've never seen the place look so pristine, but he didn't need to do all this tonight. Did you tell him to?'

'No.' Flo shook her head. 'He's done this on his own. I told him to rest after dinner.'

Bob pursed his lips, walked into the back room and listened by Jim's door, and then he stepped back and motioned Flo to follow him back upstairs again.

'Well?' she asked, once they were in the sitting room.

'Not a sound from him now. He's probably fast asleep, so it's best if we don't disturb him, Flo. The kid's got problems, and that's probably the first proper bed he's slept in for some time. I expect it all seems a bit overwhelming at the moment. He's obviously going to work hard to keep this job, but I'm worried that we might have taken on a load of trouble with him.'

Flo shook her head. 'He'll settle in as soon as he gets his strength back, and we will discover we have found a treasure.'

'I've always trusted your judgement, my dear, but don't you think you might have allowed your emotions to take over this time?'

'A bit, I suppose, but I still think he's right for us and will be a hard, loyal worker.'

'Not like some we've had, eh?' her husband joked.

'No.' Flo laughed softly. 'The lazy tykes.'

Vicki was up, washed and dressed when Bob and Flo came downstairs. The towels left to dry overnight were in a neat pile on the table. She had also made her bed and tidied the room. She was still feeling weak, but, after the first sound night's sleep she'd had in a long time, she was feeling a little more energetic.

'Good morning, Jim.' Flo came in with a bright smile on her face as she studied Vicki intently. 'Did you sleep well?'

'Yes, thank you, Mrs Howard. The bed is lovely and comfortable. Is there anything you would like me to do now?'

'Not until we've had breakfast. Anyway, you did it all last night. Now, what would you like to eat?'

'Anything – a piece of bread . . .'

'That's not enough for a growing lad. Give him a fry-up like we all have, Flo, and perhaps some porridge first.'

Remembering the sickness the day before, Vicki knew she must eat sparingly until her stomach got used to regular food again. 'Please, sir, that will be too much. I haven't had much to eat for some time, and I can't seem to manage a lot at the moment.'

'Sit down, Jim.' Bob motioned to a chair. 'We didn't have much time to talk yesterday, so now tell me just how bad things have been for you.'

Vicki clenched her hands together tightly under the table. She was well aware how thin she looked, so there was no point in telling lies. 'I was starving, sir. I had to get a job or I wasn't going to last much longer.'

'You said you had something to eat at the cafe up the road. How did you have enough money for that?'

'A kind man gave me a little money, and I needed to eat if I was going to keep looking for a job.'

'And who was this man?'

'A stranger, sir. He saw me when he was about to catch a train. I was . . . I was there . . . begging.' Vicki looked down in shame, gulping

44

back emotion. 'He bought me a meal at the station, and then gave me some money. He said he hoped he had saved a life that day – and he had, sir.'

'And then he caught his train?'

Vicki nodded. 'He never even told me his name, but I owe him a lot.'

'At least there are some decent people around.' Bob looked furious when he turned to his wife. 'Flo, give Jim whatever he wants. A little and often might be the best for a couple of days.'

'Of course. Could you eat a bacon sandwich, Jim?'

'That would be lovely. Thank you, Mrs Howard. Would you like me to cook breakfast for you?'

'No, thank you, son. You sit there and get ready for the busy day ahead.' She smiled, looking amused. 'Can you cook, then?'

'Oh, yes. I used to do all the cooking and cleaning at home.'

'Really? What did your mother do?'

'Not much.' Vicki only just stopped herself from saying that she was always pregnant, trying for a son. 'She . . . er . . . wasn't all that well.'

'If you did so much for her, she must miss you.'

Vicki shook her head, not liking this conversation. 'I don't think she cared if I was there or not. Oh, there's the shop bell, sir. Shall I go and see who it is?'

'That will be my first appointment – Mr Knight. Go and tell him I'll be right there,' Bob told her, quickly drinking his cup of tea. 'I'll eat when I've finished, Flo.'

Vicki rushed into the shop, relieved to get away from the awkward questions. 'Good morning, sir. Mr Howard will be here in a moment. May I take your hat and coat?'

When he nodded, she helped him off with his coat and hung it carefully on the stand, then turned with a smile on her face. 'Are you having a haircut today, Mr Knight?'

He ran a hand over his chin. 'And a shave.'

'Very well, sir. If you would sit here, please.' She placed a gown on him, as she had seen the barber do, and then put clean towels on the stand.

When the barber came into the shop, everything was ready for him to start straight away, and Vicki watched his expression anxiously, hoping she had done the right thing. She breathed a sigh of relief when he gave her a brief nod of approval.

The two men were talking as the barber set to work, and it was obvious to Vicki that this was a very regular customer. She waited with the broom in her hands, ready to sweep the floor as soon as needed, desperate to make a good impression. She watched every move the barber made, fascinated by his skill with scissors and a cutthroat razor.

At a nod from Bob, she stepped forward and swept the fallen hair away from the chair, careful not to leave even a small shaving there. Then she stood back again.

When the customer stood up, Vicki was there at once to help him on with his coat and hat. While he paid his bill, she collected the used towels and tidied the barber's tools. She noticed that the razor was by the sink and decided to

46

leave that until she could ask Mr Howard what he wanted done with it.

'You did well, Jim,' the barber told her. 'Mr Knight said you had looked after him well. He left this for you.'

Vicki gazed at the threepenny piece being held out to her, then looked up in amazement. 'For me?'

Bob laughed at her expression. 'Take it, Jim. He's a good customer and he said it was lovely to be greeted by such a bright, well-spoken young man.'

'Oh, thank you, sir.' She put the money in her pocket. 'I've cleared everything up, but I'm not sure what to do about the razor.'

'I don't want you to touch that. It's too dangerous, and I like to see to that myself.' He smiled. 'Now let's go and eat before anyone else arrives. We've got a busy day today.'

They had barely finished breakfast when the barber's assistant, Sid, arrived, and he was immediately followed by a steady flow of customers. It didn't take Vicki long to realize that this was a well-respected establishment, and that Sid was nearly as good as Mr Howard. She knew she was so lucky to have got this job, and she would do everything she could to make sure she kept it. She swept, cleared up and made sure they always had a fresh supply of towels without being told. It was a nice bright day and the towels were drying quickly as they fluttered on the line in the yard.

During the afternoon, two young women came in and Flo greeted them. There was a section at the end of the shop where a curtain could be pulled across to make it more private for the ladies.

'Go and help my wife, Jim. We'll be all right out here for a while.'

'Yes, sir.' The girls these days were wearing their hair short, and Vicki couldn't take her eyes off them as they had their hair cut and waved. They looked so lovely and happy when admiring their finished styles. She also looked at Mrs Howard with fresh eyes. She was as talented with hair as her husband.

'Thank you, Jim, you were a great help,' Flo said as she pulled back the curtain.

'I enjoyed it.' Vicki smiled. 'You're very good, Mrs Howard.'

'My husband taught me. More and more young ladies are having the latest styles.' She smiled. 'Let's go and have a cup of tea. We deserve it.'

'Oh, I must go back to Mr Howard now.'

'No, you need a break. We're taking fifteen minutes, Bob,' she said to her husband.

He nodded. 'We'll join you in a minute. There's half an hour before our next customers.'

'Any of your famous fruit cake left?' Sid asked, winking at Flo.

'I think you have hollow legs, Sid. Don't worry, I made one last night.'

When Vicki went to pick up the kettle, Flo stopped her. 'You sit down, son. I'll make the tea. You can take over the job when you've found your way around.'

Grateful for the chance to rest her legs, Vicki sat at the table and watched Flo, noting where everything was kept. She would insist on doing the tea from tomorrow, but now she was so tired her entire body was beginning to shake. It had been a very busy day, and there were still two hours to go before they closed.

The two men arrived, laughing about something, and Vicki couldn't help smiling. It was a sound that had been sadly lacking in her life, and it gave her a glow of pleasure.

Flo joined in as she served them all with tea and large slices of fruit cake. Vicki didn't really listen to what was being said; the words and laughter just flowed around her like a comforting blanket.

'Jim.'

She looked up at the sound of the name she was still getting used to.

'You were miles away,' Sid joked. 'What do you think of your first day in the shop?'

'I've enjoyed it very much, thank you.'

'And you've done very well,' Bob told her. 'You're always there when needed, and the customers like you. Keep that up, lad, and you'll do well.'

'Thank you, sir.' Vicki smiled with relief at the praise. They were pleased with her, and that made her feel more secure.

'Would you another slice of cake?' Flo asked her.

'Er . . .' Vicki looked down at her plate and was surprised to see it empty. 'Oh, no thank you, Mrs Howard. That was lovely.'

'I'll have another slice, Mrs H.' Sid grinned and held out his plate.

Five minutes later the shop bell rang and the two men went back to work. Vicki also stood up and said, 'I'll do the washing-up later, Mrs Howard.'

'No need, son. It won't take me a minute, and I haven't got another customer today. Off you go.'

By the time the shop was closed, dinner over, and Vicki was in her room, she was so tired she could hardly stand. But that didn't matter. She had got through the day and been praised for her work, and she was so happy. Running her hand over the soft pillow, she let the tears trickle down her face, knowing that this tendency to be emotional would stop as she regained her strength.

What a day it had been! She dived into her pocket for the tips she had received and spread them out on the bed. Six whole pennies! On Sunday she would be able to buy another shirt and might even manage to afford a pair of boy's pyjamas – at the second-hand stall, of course. If she was careful, she wouldn't have to touch her wages because she wanted to save as much as she could. With some money behind her, she would never have to go back to that terrible life she had been leading. The thought of that made her feel sick, but she soon recovered as she put the money safely away in her purse. Sighing deeply, she looked around her room.

Her room!

Six

The sun was warm, the birds were singing, and the bustle of London seemed miles away in this pleasant patch of garden. Vicki took a deep breath and smiled contentedly, lifting her face to the sun. She had been working for the Howards for two months now and couldn't remember when she had been so happy. They were more like family to her than her own had ever been. The fact that she was deceiving them still rankled with her, but if she hadn't pretended to be a boy, she would never have been given a job with them. Because of that, and because she had become very fond of them, she worked extra hard. They never failed to show how pleased they were with her, treating her more like their own child than just someone who worked for them. She was even being allowed to shampoo customers now, and Flo was teaching her how to style hair. If she had a skill like that, she would never go hungry again.

As the memory of that nightmare lanced through her, a shadow fell across her face and she opened her eyes. 'Hello, Mrs Howard, isn't it a lovely day? Can I do anything for you?'

'No, Jim, it's Sunday and your day off.' She sat beside Vicki on the old wooden bench. 'That's a beautiful book you're reading. What is it?'

Vicki closed it and ran her hand lovingly over

the binding, and then held it out to Flo. 'This was lent to me on the day after my dad threw me out. I was trying to break into an old outhouse in the hope I could clean myself up. A man came and helped me, and then he bought me breakfast. He said I could increase my chances in life if I improved my speech. He told me to study the book.'

'So this is why you speak so well,' Flo remarked, turning the pages.

Vicki nodded. 'I've studied it from cover to cover many times, and practised the lessons diligently, trying all the time to imitate the way he spoke. He was a kind man.'

'And where is he now?' Flo handed the book back to Vicki.

'I don't know. After we'd had breakfast, he walked away, and I've never seen him again.'

'That is a valuable little book, Jim. When you were desperate, didn't you consider selling it?'

'Oh, no!' She looked at Flo, horrified at the suggestion. 'It doesn't belong to me, and somehow, someway, I want to return it to him.'

'That will be difficult if you don't know where he went. What do you know about him?'

'Nothing really. He said his name was Bill, but that was all.' Vicki gazed into space, remembering. 'He was obviously a real gentleman. Well educated, I would say, with an upper-class accent and beautiful manners. I couldn't help wondering why a man like that was living rough. His clothes had seen better days, but I could see that they had once been expensive, and made for him because they fit perfectly.'

'Perhaps he'd been in the forces. Many poor souls have had a hard time adjusting after that brutal conflict.'

Vicki sat up straight, eyes wide. 'I never thought of that! He was about the right age to have fought in the war. He was tall and had an air of authority about him. He could have been an army officer.'

'Maybe, but if you don't know his surname, it could be impossible to trace him.'

'I'll find him.' Vicki nodded with determination. 'Someday I'll find him – and the man at the station, if I can. I owe so much to those two strangers, and I want to let them know how much they've helped me. Let them see that perhaps I was worth helping.'

'I'm sure they knew that.' Flo stood up and smiled. 'We think you have the talent and enthusiasm to become an excellent hairdresser. Probably better than both of us. In a couple of years, customers will be flooding in to have their hair styled by you.'

'That's kind of you, Mrs Howard,' Vicki laughed, 'but you are both masters with a pair of scissors. I'll try my hardest, but I could never hope to match both of you.'

'We'll see,' Flo said, as she walked back to the house.

'Been enjoying the sunshine?' Bob looked up and smiled when Flo walked in.

'Jim's in the garden, and I sat with him for a while. I was intrigued by the book he was reading. It was a small, leather-bound volume, and he let me have a look at it. The cover was beautiful blue leather, and it was clearly an expensive edition.'

'Oh?' Bob frowned. 'Did the boy say where he got it?'

Flo nodded and then related their conversation in full, leaving nothing out.

'He would rather starve than sell the one item he possessed of value?' Bob asked, astounded.

'That's what he said, and I believe him. The book obviously means a great deal to him, and he wants to return it to the man who gave it to him.'

'How on earth will he be able to do that? From what you say, he only knows the man as Bill. Was there anything in the book to indicate who it belonged to?'

'Nothing . . . except . . .' Flo shook her head. 'It probably means nothing.'

'What?'

'Well, there was a coat of arms embossed on the book.'

Bob shook his head. 'If the man was a down-and-out, he could have got it from anywhere. That won't be any help at all.'

'You're right, of course, but you must admit it's a strange story, Bob.'

'And getting stranger the more we learn. My God, Flo, that boy's been living a dangerous life. He's far too innocent to be cast out on his own like that.'

'I agree, but he had enough sense to find himself a safe place to sleep. He told me the only way into the room at the warehouse was through a tiny window – only big enough for him.'

'Thankfully, he does seem to have his head screwed on all right, but what's happened to him is criminal. I'd like to meet his father and give him a piece of my mind.'

'You'll have to stand in line behind me!' Flo told him.

They looked at each other, their expressions serious, and then Bob stood up. 'Put the kettle on, Flo. I'll just pop down and see if Jim would like a cup of tea with us – and I'd like to take a look at this mysterious book.'

While her husband was downstairs, Flo quickly made some sandwiches with a nice piece of boiled ham and got out the rock cakes she had made in the morning. Jim was eating better now – he'd finished all of his lunch today – but she still liked to see he had food at regular intervals. That gaunt look had gone, thank goodness, and he was beginning to put on some weight at last. The poor little devil had been stick thin when he'd arrived, and that had worried her. But the change in him now was very noticeable. When she'd cut his hair that first day, it had been limp and lifeless, but now it was glossy, with a tendency to curl, and had a glint of golden red in the dark hair, blending in with his startling amber eyes. She smiled to herself in amusement. What would the young ladies of today give for such colouring?

Monday was, as always, a quiet day for the barber, and, seeing that Jim was keeping himself busy cleaning out the stock cupboard, Bob removed his apron. 'Will you hold the fort, Sid? I'm going to pop out for an hour.'

His assistant looked up from the newspaper he was reading. 'Of course, Bob.'

√ 'Thanks.' Bob found Flo upstairs making one of her delicious cakes. 'I'm going to see Harry Butler. He's very knowledgeable about history, as you know, and I thought he might be able to help with that coat of arms on Jim's book. I've made a rough sketch.'

'I thought you said it wouldn't mean anything.'

Bob shrugged. 'It probably doesn't, but I'm intrigued, Flo. Why would that man give away such a valuable book? It was a first edition, as well.'

'Was it? I never noticed that.' Flo smiled at her husband. 'Well, you haven't visited Harry for a while, and he'll be pleased to see you.'

'Won't be long.' Bob kissed his wife and left by the side door, whistling as he walked up the street. He didn't know why he was bothering with this, but there was a mystery surrounding that boy, and it had caught his interest. Anyway, it would give him something to do on a slow afternoon.

Harry was a retired teacher and always happy to see Bob. He smiled broadly when he opened the door, and ushered Bob into the front room. 'What a pleasant surprise. What brings you out during shop hours?'

'It's very quiet today so I thought I'd take the chance and pop round. I've got a mystery for you, Harry.'

'Good, good. Sit down and tell me all about it.' Harry poured them both a beer, sat down and leant forward in his chair, eager to hear what Bob

56

had to say. 'All right, tell me what this is all about.'

Bob gave him a brief outline of Jim and the book, and then he took the sketch he'd made and handed it to Harry.

'Ah, you haven't got the book, I suppose?'

'No. It means a lot to the lad, and I didn't like to ask if I could borrow it. And I haven't told him I'm here.'

'Hmm.' Harry took a large book from a shelf near him and began turning the pages, referring often to the sketch as he did so.

After about fifteen minutes of silence, he jumped up and sorted through another pile of books until he found what he was looking for. He thumbed through that for a while and then looked up.

'Have you found something?' Bob asked, noticing the excited gleam in Harry's eyes.

'I think so, but I need the book to be certain. Any chance of that, do you think?'

'I'm sure Jim won't let it out of his sight, but why don't you join us for dinner one evening? We could bring up your interest in old books, and he will probably let you have a look at it.'

'Good idea. And I never turn down a chance to have one of Flo's dinners.' He grinned. 'What about tonight?'

Bob laughed. 'You are eager. All right. Now, will you tell me what you've found?'

'Not until I've seen the book.' Harry closed his large reference volumes. 'Want another beer?'

'Are you going to leave me in suspense?' Bob held out his glass.

'I want to be sure before saying anything.' He refilled both their glasses. 'Tell me what the boy said about the man. Every detail.'

They had a guest for dinner! Vicki paused in the doorway, not sure what to do. 'Er . . . I can eat downstairs, Mrs Howard, and I'll come and wash up when you've finished.'

'There's no need for that, Jim,' Flo said, leading Vicki over to the man who was studying her with a deep frown on his face. 'Harry, this is Jim.'

'Ah.' The serious expression disappeared and was replaced with a smile. 'You're not quite what I expected. I'm pleased to meet you . . . Jim.'

Vicki didn't miss the pause before he said her name, and her insides churned with fear. She was well aware that now she was filling out it was becoming harder to pass herself off as a boy, and she had the uncomfortable feeling that this man had seen through her disguise. As she shook his hand, she looked him straight in the eyes, silently beseeching him not to give her away, and when he gave a slight nod of his head – and the hint of a wink – she relaxed. 'And I'm pleased to meet you, sir.'

'Sit down,' Flo ordered, 'and eat while the food is hot.'

During the meal, Vicki listened with interest. Harry was a knowledgeable man, and his account of historical events was fascinating. She remained silent for most of the time, speaking only when spoken to, but when the conversation turned to more recent times, she ventured a couple of questions about the war. She knew it had been terrible, of course, but she wanted to know what it had really been like for the men and officers. She had seen for herself how so many had been damaged, physically and mentally. Her dad could never tell her anything because hadn't joined the army – flat feet, or something.

The things Harry told her brought a lump to her throat, but she managed to hold her emotions in check – boys didn't cry. And when he said the casualty rates were very high among the young officers, Vicki wondered if Bill had been one of them.

'I believe you feel you might have met one of those young officers?' Harry asked.

'I'm not sure, sir. I'm only guessing.'

'Bob told me about the book the man gave you. Would you let me have a look at it?'

'I don't think it will tell you much, sir. It's only a little book.'

'Oh, you never know.' Harry smiled. 'I'd like to see it, though. If you don't mind?'

'I'll get it.' Vicki glanced at Bob. 'May I be excused for a moment, sir?'

'Of course, lad. Harry has a passion for old books.'

It only took Vicki a couple of minutes to return with the precious book, and Harry took it from her eagerly.

They watched the older man study it with great care, using a magnifying glass to make out every detail of the embossed coat of arms. Then he quickly turned the pages of a large book he had brought with him.

'Hmm. Interesting. I believe you said the man

59

was well-spoken, Jim. This book might have belonged to him – or his family. Would you like me to see if I can find out anything about it?'

Vicki hesitated. She knew this was a kind offer, and he obviously loved delving into anything historical, but she couldn't start her search for Bill while she was still pretending to be a boy. It was most unlikely Harry would turn up anything of use, but she couldn't take that chance yet. Her life had to be straightened out first. She reluctantly shook her head. 'Thank you for your generous offer, sir, but the time isn't right yet.'

'Oh.' Harry raised his eyebrows in query. 'And why isn't the time right?'

She shuffled uncomfortably. 'I have things to sort out first. I . . . er . . . promised him I was going to make something of myself, and I haven't done that yet.'

'I see.' Harry smiled. 'Well, when you do feel the time is right, come and see me.'

'Thank you, sir. I will certainly do that.'

'Good. That's settled, then. Take good care of that book, and I'll have another look at it when you're ready.'

When she had helped Flo to clear up after the meal, Vicki went downstairs again, her mind in turmoil. Had he guessed she was a girl? And, if he had, would he tell Mr and Mrs Howard? After all, he was their friend, and he might not like them being deceived like this. Vicki was all too aware that the deception couldn't go on much longer, but the thought of owning up frightened her. She was happier now than at any time in her

60

life, and it would break her heart to leave the Howards and the shop.

Keeping busy was the best way to calm her worries, so she went into the shop to make sure everything was ready for the next day.

'Is your name Victoria?'

Vicki started at the voice behind and dropped the towels she had been holding. Trying to remain calm, she picked them up and turned slowly, her face ashen.

'Don't look so alarmed,' Harry said gently. 'I haven't said anything to your employers.'

'How did you know?'

'After Bob told me they had taken in a young boy who had been thrown out of his home, I was so appalled by the story I made some enquiries. I have friends who live in Poplar and they told me a young girl had been turned out to fend for herself, but they didn't know of a boy. The moment I saw you, I knew you were that girl. Tell me the reason for your deception.'

Knowing there was little point in hiding anything from this man, she began at the beginning. By the time she had finished, he was nodding his head. 'So this was the only way you felt you could survive.'

'I didn't know what else I could do, sir.' She cast an anguished look at him. 'Are you going to tell Mr and Mrs Howard?'

'No. That's for you to do when you're ready. But don't leave it too long. They are not fools.'

'I know, sir,' she said earnestly. 'They have been so kind, and it worries me that I'm telling them lies, but I'm terrified they will make me

61

leave.' She turned her back on Harry, shaking with emotion and fear. 'I'm so happy here, and if I have to go back on the streets . . . Well, I couldn't stand that again, sir. I couldn't!'

'That is unlikely to happen again, my dear. I gather they have become very fond of you. You have friends now, and that includes me. So I want you to come and see me when you need help. Will you do that?'

'Thank you, sir. You're very kind.'

'I can hear a "but" in your voice.'

Vicki took a deep breath. 'I have had to rely on myself most of my life, and I find it hard to do anything else, but I will promise to see you when it is time to try to find Bill.'

'Good.' He smiled. 'I look forward to seeing you then. Take care of that book, because I will need to study it again.'

As he walked away, Vicki felt a huge surge of relief. He wasn't going to reveal her secret. She had a little longer.

Seven

How quickly this year had flown! They had been such happy months, but Vicki knew she couldn't put off telling Mr and Mrs Howard the truth about herself any longer. Christmas was only two weeks away and she had decided that the New Year would be the right time to own up to her deception. The Howards had welcomed her into their home and made her feel safe and cared for, for the first time in her life, so she wanted to buy them each a little present to show her gratitude. She wandered round the busy Christmas market, wondering what they would like. She mustn't spend too much, of course, in case she needed money later. Her insides clenched in pain at the thought of being out on her own again, but it had to be faced. Harry had kept his word and not told them who she really was, but the deception was becoming very difficult to maintain. She looked like a girl. There was no getting away from that fact now, and she was too fond of the Howards to deceive them any longer. She had been saving hard, so she would at least have some money for a while, but how she prayed that she wouldn't have to survive out there on her own again. Even so, she wouldn't blame the Howards if they were angry and told her to leave.

She swiped a tear away from her eyes and took a steadying breath. But there was Christmas to enjoy first.

'We're getting more and more ladies wanting their hair done.' Bob smiled at his wife. 'And it's all down to your skill, Flo. Word is spreading fast, and using part of the barber's isn't good enough.'

'I agree. It can get a bit crowded, but I don't see what we can do about it.'

'I might have the solution.' Bob pulled out a chair from the table. 'Sit down and we'll talk about it.'

'I know that look in your eyes.' Flo smiled as she sat down. 'Just what are you planning?'

'What do you think about expanding our business?'

'Well, we're certainly getting a lot of trade. But we haven't got the space to expand.'

'The shop next door will be vacant in January, so how about opening a ladies' salon?'

'I'd like that, Bob,' Flo told him eagerly. 'And that place would be perfect.'

'That's what I thought you'd say.' He gave a knowing smile. 'I've already said we'd take it.'

Flo laughed. 'What if I'd said no?'

'Then I would have had to talk you into it. Now, you'll need a young girl to train and help you.' Bob pursed his lips. 'The choice is obvious, and that means I'll have to advertise for a lad for the shop. Doesn't it?'

'Ah, you've noticed.'

'Of course I have.' Bob shook his head. 'And so has everyone else, but we've kept our mouths shut. I believe she's sixteen now, and it shows. How desperate the poor little thing must have been. How are we going to get round this, Flo?'

Flo sighed. 'I don't know. I've felt several times she was on the point of telling me, but each time she's backed off. Let's leave it a while longer and see if she comes to us. The last thing I want us to do is frighten her and make her run away. If she does that, we might never find her again, and I couldn't bear that to happen.'

'Nor me. I think it would help if we make it clear we are offering her a job with you in the new shop. But it would be easier if she came and told us herself.'

Flo nodded. 'I believe she will.'

'I hope you're right.' Bob stood up at the sharp rap on the side door. 'That will be Harry. I asked him to drop round.'

'Just in time for lunch.' Flo smiled in amusement. 'I swear he can smell the cooking right up the road. Good job I always cook too much.'

'Well, he might have to pay for his dinner this time because I'm thinking of asking him to help in the shop until I can get a new lad.' Laughing, Bob went down to let his friend in.

'Smells lovely in here,' Harry said, kissing Flo on the cheek as soon as he walked in.

'Yes, you can stay for lunch.' Flo poured him a cup of tea from the ever-ready teapot. 'Sit down and tell us what you've been up to.'

'Thanks.' Harry looked round. 'Isn't your little helper in today, Bob?'

'Gone to the market to do a bit of Christmas shopping, but he'll be back in time for lunch. He isn't in the habit of spending money, though. We know he's been saving every penny possible.'

Harry nodded. 'Terrified about being turned out again, I expect.'

'That will never happen,' Flo declared forcefully. 'We were never blessed with children, and we've come to love her like our own.'

Harry narrowed his eyes. 'You said *her*. Has she spoken to you, then?'

'That was a slip of the tongue. I must be more careful.' Flo regarded Harry with suspicion. 'How long have you known?'

'The moment I set eyes on her. As soon as Bob told me about his helper, I went to a pub I know in Poplar and got talking to some of the locals.

When I brought up the subject of a young boy who had been turned out to fend for himself, they hadn't heard of one, but they told me about a fourteen-year-old girl. Evidently, her brute of a father just kicked her out. As soon as I saw her I knew she was that girl.'

'Why didn't you tell us, Harry?' Bob demanded.

'Because deceiving you is worrying her, and she intends to tell you herself.' Harry drained his cup, put it down and sighed. 'I asked her why she was doing this, and she said it had been impossible to get a job because she was a girl, so she did the only thing possible and dressed as a boy. She was desperate.'

Bob's mouth set in a grim line. 'The kid who came into our shop that day was just skin and bones, and could hardly stand up. But what courage! We saw what it took for her to just stay on her feet, and it was a relief to see her slowly gain in strength. How could a man do that to his own child?'

'There are some bastards around. From the tales I was told about her father, he must be nothing short of a monster.'

'I don't doubt that, Harry.' Flo refilled their cups. 'For the time being, though, we must go back to thinking and referring to her as Jim. When he's ready he will tell us, and until then we mustn't even give a hint that we know.'

'That's best,' Harry agreed, 'but remember, that kid is very frightened. He thinks the world of you both, and is sure you will be angry at his deception. He expects to be turned out again.'

'Never!' Flo and Bob said together.

66

'We have plans, and that includes all of us – even you, Harry.'

'Uh-oh, I don't like the sound of this, but tell me anyway.' Harry listened intently while Bob explained about the new shop.

'That's a wonderful idea.' Harry was nodding enthusiastically. 'And I'll certainly help you out for a while if you're stuck, Bob. Explain all that to . . . er . . . Jim, as soon as possible.'

'We intend to.' Flo listened as the door downstairs opened and closed. 'Change the subject now. He's back.'

Flo and Bob smiled at each other when they heard Vicki running up the stairs, full of life and energy. They well remembered when every step had been an effort. They had longed to help, but the determination on her face told them not to. She had been fighting to hide her weakness as much as possible, and they had watched with admiration as she struggled. Now it was a joy to them to see the difference.

'Hope I'm not late, Mrs Howard?' Vicki burst into the room, cheeks glowing from the cold wind blowing that day. 'The market was so crowded you could hardly move.'

'Lunch won't be for another half an hour yet, and Harry will be joining us.'

Vicki nodded. 'Hello, sir. It's chilly out there, but it hasn't stopped people doing their shopping.'

'I expect they're all rushing to buy their last-minute gifts. Did you manage to get what you wanted?'

'Yes, sir.' Vicki smiled, and then turned her

attention to Flo, her eyes shining with excitement. 'I saw a girl with an amazing haircut. It was very short, perfectly straight, and framing her face. Like this.' She tried to pull her own hair into the shape, and giggled. 'My hair is too wavy to show you, but it was almost like a cap, and so black it shone blue in the pale sunlight. She looked beautiful.'

'I think I know what you mean, but will you draw it for me? Then we can try it out on one of our clients.'

Vicki nodded excitedly. 'I'll do that. Can I help you with lunch?'

'Thank you.' She smiled fondly. 'What would we do without you? You've become part of our family now. It was a lucky day for us when you walked into the shop.'

'I was the lucky one,' Vicki said, her voice husky with emotion. She remembered that day so well. 'You gave me a chance, and I'll always be grateful to you for that.'

'Ah, you don't owe us a thing,' Bob said. 'You've worked hard, and we're going to promote you next year.'

'Oh.' Vicki stopped what she was doing and spun round quickly.

'Yes.' Bob was smiling broadly. 'We're opening a ladies' salon in the shop next door, and we want you to be Flo's assistant.'

'But . . . but . . .' Vicki looked from one to the other and then said in a whisper, 'Won't you want a girl for that, Mrs Howard?'

'What I need is you. You have a real flair for ladies hair, and I'll train you to become a stylist.'

Tears began to stream silently down Vicki's face.

'What's the matter, dear?' Flo asked anxiously. 'Don't you want to do that? You can stay in the barber's if you'd rather.'

'Oh, no, it isn't that. I would love to work with you and learn how to become a good ladies' hairdresser, but I don't deserve to be given such a job.'

'Now, that isn't true,' Bob declared. 'You've earned the chance. What on earth makes you believe you don't deserve it?'

Vicki looked down at the floor, unable to meet their eyes. 'Because I've been lying to you all the time. I intended to tell you after Christmas, but this changes everything. I wanted a few more happy weeks before you threw me out.'

'Nothing you've done will every make us do that.' Bob was on his feet now and made Vicki sit down. 'Why don't you tell us what's troubling you?'

Wiping the tears away from her cheeks, she took a deep breath, her heart heavy with fear. 'I'm really a girl . . .'

'We already know that.' Flo patted her hand and smiled. 'Victoria, isn't it?'

She nodded and glanced up at Harry.

He held up his hands. 'I never said a word. It's obvious to anyone now that you're not a boy.'

'So you see, Victoria – or do you prefer Vicki?' Bob asked.

'Vicki, please.' She felt overwhelmed with disbelief. They didn't mind? They already knew? They hadn't told her to get out!

'Right, well, Vicki, we understand why you dressed as a boy. It took a lot of courage to survive your ordeal, and you did the only thing you could. We respect you for that. You didn't ask for pity – you wanted to work your way out of the disaster you were in, and that showed a sound character.'

'And that's what we recognized when we saw you.' Flo poured Vicki a cup of tea and placed it in her hands. 'There was something about you that made us believe you were worth helping, and I guess that was what made those two strangers reach out to you.'

'Yes,' Harry nodded. 'Does this mean I can start a search to see if I can find them? You mustn't hold out too much hope, Vicki. We have precious little to go on.'

'I know that, sir, but anything you can find out would be helpful. Thank you, sir.' Vicki didn't know whether to laugh or cry now – the relief was enormous. Everything was going to be all right! She could hardly believe it. All these months of worry and guilt had been unnecessary.

'So, now that is out of the way, do you want to work with me in the new shop?' Flo asked.

'Oh, yes, please! Oh, but what about the barber's? They need someone as well.'

Bob laughed. 'I've roped Harry in to help until I can get a young lad.'

'You'll enjoy that, sir. The customers are all so nice.' She gave him a dimpled smile. 'They are very generous with their tips.'

'I don't know about enjoying it, but I'll try to

70

do as good a job as you. From what I've heard, though, that will be close to impossible.'

'Oh, sir, you are funning me.'

Flo grinned. 'I'm taking you shopping tomorrow, Vicki. I can't wait to see you in pretty clothes and style your beautiful hair. We'll go to Weston's, up the road.'

'Oh, but they're expensive. I can't afford clothes from there.'

'Some new clothes will be our Christmas present to you.'

The clothes with which Vicki had left the house in Poplar no longer fitted, no matter how much she pulled and breathed in. She had grown quite a lot, and, anyway, they were far too shabby to go into a ladies' shop with Flo. The frock was torn from squeezing in and out of the tiny window, and the coat was in a dreadful state.

There was a knock on her door and she opened it, her expression worried. 'I can't come out with you like this. I'll be a disgrace to you, and I can't wear the boy's clothes where we're going. I'll go and get something from the market. They have a stall selling used clothes. They are cheap, but some garments are quite nice if you search through them.'

Flo was shaking her head as she studied Vicki critically. 'No, no, I won't have you wearing second-hand clothes. But I do agree that you can't go out like that. Take those things off and throw them away. I'll see if I have anything upstairs to fit you.'

'I don't mind them, Mrs Howard. I've only ever had second-hand clothes.'

71

'Well, those days are over. Our ladies' salon is going to attract a good class of customer, and we are going to look as smart as they are!'

Vicki watched Flo leave and hurry up the stairs, and then she sat down on the bed with a thump, unable to believe what was happening. Her mind had been in a whirl since yesterday, and a lump came to her throat as she gazed around her room. And it was still *her* room! She had been terrified about losing this security, and, even worse, it would have broken her heart to leave the Howards. But that nightmare hadn't happened. In fact, the Howards seemed pleased she was really a girl, and her deception didn't bother them at all. Vicki had never known such kindness and under-standing existed, and she was having a job taking it all in. There had been no doubt in her mind that she would lose all this for lying to them. It was unbelievable, and she loved them for that. And that was another emotion she had never experienced before.

'Here we are.' Flo returned with an armful of clothes. 'Let's see if we can make some of these fit you. They're on the tight side for me, so we might be able to do something with them. I've found you some proper undergarments as well. It wouldn't do to have you wearing a boy's vest and pants.'

Half an hour later, with the aid of some hasty stitching, Vicki looked respectable. She stared in the mirror in disbelief. She had been thinking of herself as a boy for months now, and it was disconcerting to see a young girl looking back at her.

'That will have to do until we can get you better clothes.' Flo nodded, holding a brush in her hands. 'I'll have a quick go at your hair, but it will have to grow before we can style it properly.'

When they were ready to leave, Vicki said, 'I have a bit saved up, so I can pay towards the clothes.'

'No need for that.' Flo chuckled. 'Bob's given me instructions to see you are dressed fashionably – and he's given me the money – enough for both of us. So, let's go shopping!'

The proprietor of Weston's greeted them warmly, and Vicki recognized her as one of Flo's regular customers. This made her even more nervous in case she remembered her as the boy who had shampooed her hair on many occasions.

'And what can I do for you today, Mrs Howard? New stock arrived yesterday, so I'm sure we can find something stylish for you.'

'I want a complete set of clothes for my niece, Victoria, and perhaps a frock for myself.'

If the shop owner wondered why Mrs Howard had a niece no one had ever heard of, she was too professional to let her curiosity show. Vicki quickly realized that Flo had introduced her like this to avoid questions. After all, it wouldn't seem strange that she was buying clothes for a relative, would it? Whatever the reason, Vicki was relieved the woman had not shown any sign of recognizing her as Jim. She gazed longingly at the racks of lovely clothes and stifled a sigh of pure pleasure. How she was looking forward to being herself again!

After nearly two hours, Vicki felt as if she had tried on nearly everything in the shop, and there were a lot of items piled on the counter waiting to be parcelled up.

'Try on this amber frock,' Flo told her, holding out the most exquisite and fashionable garment Vicki had ever seen.

She stepped close and whispered, 'You mustn't buy me any more. I only needed one frock and a coat. Anything else I need I can get at the market. They do sell new clothes as well.'

'Just try this on, and that will be the last, I promise – apart from a pair of shoes, of course. You must have those.'

From the look of pleasure on Flo's face, Vicki knew it would be hopeless to argue, and she couldn't do that in the shop. There were other customers as well, and they all seemed to know Flo.

The frock fitted perfectly, and when she stepped out of the fitting room there was complete silence in the shop. Everyone was staring at her, and she fidgeted nervously. 'It's all wrong for me, isn't it?'

'It's lovely.' Flo made Vicki turn round and round. 'Oh, my dear, you are such a beautiful girl. You must have that frock. It brings out the colour of your eyes.'

'You'll have to watch her, Mrs Howard,' one customer said, laughing. 'You'll have all the young men in the district after her.'

Vicki glared at the woman who had spoken, making her fall silent, and then looked away. 'Oh, no, they won't,' she said under her breath. 'I don't want this frock! You've spent too much on me already,' she added hastily, realizing that she had spoken too sharply.

'All right, my dear. I think we've bought enough, anyway. I just wanted you to have something special, but if you don't like it, then we'll leave it.'

Vicki quickly changed, and she was relieved to be away when they left the shop. Flo quickly ushered her into a shoe shop, and finally the shopping was finished.

As they walked back, loaded with bags, Flo asked, 'Why did that woman's remarks upset you so, Vicki?'

'I don't want men after me! I'm never going to marry and end up like my mum.'

'Not all men are cruel, my dear. Look at Bob. He's the kindest man you could ever wish to meet. We've been married for twenty-three years, and I've never regretted one of them. We're very happy together.'

'I know you are. From what I've seen, though, there are more unhappy marriages than happy ones. I'm not going to risk it.

'You'll change your mind when you fall in love.'

Vicki shook her head vigorously. 'Never!'

Eight

The day they were given the keys to the shop next door was very exciting, and they couldn't wait to start turning it into the elegant salon they had planned so carefully. They had talked of little else over Christmas, and it had been the happiest one Vicki had ever experienced and she had savoured every moment. There had been so much laughter and joy at the giving of presents, and she had helped Flo prepare and cook a large chicken with roast potatoes and all sorts of vegetables. Then they'd had a Christmas pudding, and at tea time a trifle and Christmas cake. There had been so much food that Vicki had wondered how they were going to get through it, but there were so many people dropping in and nothing went to waste.

There was an almost permanent smile on her face now as she gazed around the shop. It was in a terrible mess, but they couldn't wait to get started on the transformation. A local handyman was going to help clear the place of rubbish and put up shelves, and then a plumber would fit two sinks. They had spent a long time deciding on the kind of chairs they wanted and other necessary pieces of furniture. They had chosen peach and white for the towels, and the same shade of peach for smart salon aprons.

It was hard work, but after only a week they were ready to open.

Flo sat in one of the chairs and looked around with obvious satisfaction. 'All we need now are customers. How are we doing with bookings?'

'Quite good.' Vicki opened the large appointment book. She had been given complete charge of this side of the business, and she was proud and determined to be the most efficient assistant any hairdresser could have. 'We have twelve for next week, so far, starting from Tuesday, and

I've asked each of your regulars to spread the word.'

'That was a good idea, and twelve isn't bad for a start.' Flo stood up. 'We'll give ourselves Monday to finish off the final details, and then open for business on Tuesday. I don't know what I would have done without you, my dear. You're a good organizer. Do you know that?'

'I enjoy arranging things.' Vicki smiled, pleased with the compliment. Christmas and the work to get the salon ready had been a joy, and adding to her joy was the relief of not having to pretend any more. She was also delighted to be wearing feminine clothes again. The Howards had taken her deception with understanding, and for the first time in her life she felt secure and cared for. It was a heady feeling, and, looking back, it seemed worth all the suffering she had gone through, abandoned and hiding in that terrible warehouse.

When Bob, Sid and Harry walked in to inspect the work they had done, Vicki's thoughts turned to the two strangers who had reached out to her with kindness. She was happy – but were they? What had happened to Bill? She had often wondered if he would turn up again, but he never had. And when she tried to remember every detail about the man at the station, she had the impression that he had been tense and harassed, and yet he had taken the time to stop and help a young girl in desperate need. She worried about them.

'My word,' Sid turned slowly to study everything, 'you girls have worked hard.'

'They certainly have.' Bob nodded his approval.

'It's all very tasteful, and the colour scheme has a calming effect.'

'The colours were Vicki's idea,' Flo said, 'and I'm pleased the way it has turned out. We have the look I was aiming for. The bookings are already coming in, so we are going to open on Tuesday.'

While the opening was being discussed, Vicki went over to Harry. 'Have you been able to find out anything yet?'

'I haven't had much time, but the coat of arms on the book belongs to the Ashington family. George Ashington was born in 1796 and made his fortune in trade. As far as I can discover, he had three ships carrying cargoes of all kinds. His descendants inherited great wealth, and I'll start looking into this further as soon as Bob finds a lad for the barber's.' Harry spoke loud enough for everyone to hear, making them laugh.

'I'm trying,' Bob told him, 'but why don't you just admit you're enjoying yourself in the shop?'

'Can't look gloomy, can I? I'd never get any tips if I scowled at the customers.' He gave Vicki a sly wink. 'As I was saying, the Ashingtons' home was sold some years ago. Perhaps the contents were sold as well and that was how your stranger got hold of the book, but I'll try to find someone in the family. It won't be easy . . .' He glanced across at Bob. 'And it will take time!'

Bob just smiled and said nothing.

The first two days of business were slow, but, as the week went by, they became busier and busier, and when they had locked up at the end of

Saturday, Flo and Vicki collapsed into chairs, smiles on their faces.

'What a week!'

Vicki agreed, her smile broadening. 'And the appointment book for next week is filling nicely. Your shop is going to be a success.'

'*Our* shop, my dear. This is *our* shop.' She laughed softly. 'Two customers have said they want their hair cut like yours. You're setting a new trend, Vicki.'

'What? A short back and sides!'

'It has grown a little. Another month and I'll really be able to do something with it.'

'Are you girls going to sit there all night?' Bob asked, looking through the door. 'We're starving so Sid has gone to the chippie. It's going to be fish and chips all round this evening.'

'Oh, good.' Flo sighed with relief. 'We're too tired to cook.'

'You both deserve a night off. Come on, up you get.' Bob pulled his wife out of the chair. 'Harry's laying the table and making the tea.'

Over the next few weeks, the business of both shops steadily increased, and Flo had decided that Vicki was proficient enough to cut and set hair. She was even beginning to get a few of her own clients. That promotion meant that they had to employ a young girl to help in the shop. Her name was Annie, the daughter of someone the Howards knew, and she was eager and working out well. Bob hadn't had any luck finding a suitable boy for the barber's, and Harry was still working there. He groused about being kept so

79

busy at his age, but no one took any notice because he was obviously enjoying himself. He had led quite a solitary life in his retirement, lost in his books, but now he was talking and laughing with customers, and appeared to be happy. However, working in the shop left him little time to help Vicki track down the two strangers. But she, also, had been too busy to give it much thought. In the quiet moments, though, they were never far from her mind, and her desire to trace them never wavered. The happier she became, the more determined she was to find them one day.

Another busy week was coming to an end, and as Vicki was showing a customer the back of her hair after cutting it, she heard a voice she had never expected to hear again.

'So, this is where you've bloody well been hiding yourself!'

Vicki spun round, horrified, and nearly dropped the hand mirror. He was in his usual state after work – drunk!

'Quite the young lady,' he sneered, 'and doing all right for yourself. Well, you can forget all that. And you can hand over the money you're earning. We need it more than you.'

There was only one thought in Vicki's mind, and that was to get the belligerent man out of the shop. They were finishing up, but there were still three customers, and they were looking at him in disgust.

Although shocked at seeing him again, Vicki was determined to face him as she always had, with courage and without flinching. She took a moment to put the mirror down and apologize to her customer, and then she strode over and pushed him out of the shop.

'Don't you push me around, girl!' he shouted. 'Get your things. You're coming home with me.'

'This is my home, and I'm not going anywhere with you. And stop shouting. You're making people stare.'

'Let them!' He glared at the small crowd and then turned his attention back to Vicki. 'You heard what I said.'

'And you heard my reply. Go away, and don't come back here again. If you do, I'll call the police and have you removed.'

'Don't you talk to me like that, girl!'

He moved so quickly that Vicki didn't have time to duck, and the blow made her stagger back, her head ringing so much she nearly lost consciousness.

Someone caught her and held her firmly so she didn't collapse on to the pavement. When her vision cleared, she could see Bob, Sid and Harry surrounding her attacker; Flo was the one holding her from behind.

'You will not touch our girl again!' Sid was a tall, well-built young man, and his tone was threatening.

'I'll do what I like with her! She's my kid, so mind your own bloody business.'

'It is our business,' Bob said. 'She is my daughter.'

'Don't be daft!' he snorted. 'She might be dressed posh and speak proper now, but she belongs to me, and she's coming with me.'

Vicki watched the scene with horror, not taking in what was being said. All she could think about was how Bob and Flo must be feeling. They had taken her in, lavished her with kindness and understanding, and now she had brought this disgraceful scene to their doorstep. 'Oh, I'm so sorry . . . so sorry,' she gasped.

'You've no need to apologize, my dear,' Flo said gently. 'We'll see that this obnoxious man doesn't come near you again.'

'But the shame . . . and outside your lovely shops . . . Oh, no, now a policeman has arrived.'

'It's all right. We sent Harry to find him.'

Vicki turned her head to look at Flo. 'But why? It will only make things worse. Look at the crowd gathering to watch. It will harm your business.'

'I doubt that. Most of the onlookers know and like you, Vicki. That man needs to be dealt with for hitting you like that. We won't have you treated so badly, my dear, and certainly not by that monster. He threw you out and disowned you. He has no rights to you now.'

'What's the trouble here? Stop shouting, sir; you are causing a disturbance.'

'That's my kid, and they're stopping me from taking her home. She ran away and I've been looking for her.'

'Liar!' Pulling herself away from Flo's supporting arm, Vicki faced her father, furious now. 'He's lying, officer. He threw me out when I was fourteen and told me never to come back. I'm sixteen now and he can't tell me what to do any more!'

'That's the truth,' Bob told the policeman.

'Victoria is our daughter now, and we want him arrested for assaulting her.'

'She's my kid, and I can hit her if I want to.' He swayed as he tried to focus on the policeman before turning his attention back to Vicki.

When he lifted his hand to hit her again, she stood her ground, as she always had done in the past, never allowing him to intimidate or frighten her.

Sid's hand shot out and blocked the blow, and there was menace in his tone when he said, 'Don't you dare hit her again! This man is drunk and out of control, officer. Do you need any more proof that he is violent?'

'You can come with me to the station and sober up.' The officer took hold of his arm. 'We'll sort this out when you're more coherent.'

'I ain't coming with you. I ain't done nothing!'

'Come along now. We'll lock you up until you've calmed down.'

'I'll come with you,' Sid offered.

'Thank you, sir.' The policeman looked at the Howards. 'I'll expect you all to come to the station tomorrow and give us the full story. The young lady, as well.'

'We'll be there,' Flo assured him.

They watched them until they turned the corner of the street, then Flo took hold of Vicki's arm. 'We must see to your poor face. That was a savage blow he gave you, and your lip is badly cut.'

Vicki looked down and saw the blood dripping down her pristine salon apron. 'Oh, this will be ruined. I didn't realize it was bleeding.'

'Don't worry about that. A good soak and it will come out all right.'

She was led back to the house and sat patiently while her injuries were dealt with.

'Good, the bleeding has stopped,' Flo said gently. 'Put the kettle on, Harry. We all need a strong cup of tea to calm our nerves.'

Still terribly worried about the Howards being drawn into that disgraceful scene, Vicki said, 'I can go the station on my own tomorrow; I can deal with him. I don't want you involved in this.'

'We're already involved.' Bob gave a wry smile. 'Did you see Sid's face? He really wanted to knock the daylights out of him.'

Harry nodded, and there was an amused smile on his face. 'I don't know how he stopped himself, but it was a good job he did or he would have been arrested as well. That copper was in no mood for more trouble.'

When they all laughed, Vicki gazed in wonder from one to the other. They didn't seem to be at all troubled that an unpleasant scene had taken place right outside their shops. 'But . . . but . . . it wasn't good for your business.'

'On the contrary, people will be flocking in to find out more details. Don't you worry about a thing.' Flo smiled and squeezed her hand. 'You are not facing this alone.'

It was a long night as the events outside the shop filled Vicki's mind, denying her any sleep at all. She couldn't understand why her father should have demanded that she return home to them after all this time. And she couldn't believe he hadn't known what was happening to her. She would have been seen and recognized by someone in the area, and word would have got back to him. It just didn't make sense. He hated her; she had never had any doubt about that, so what on earth had he been shouting about? He was drunk – that was obvious – so perhaps he didn't know what he was saying.

As the first glimmer of morning light filtered through her window, she had come to a decision. Washing her bruised face carefully, she dressed and went upstairs. Bob and Flo were already up, and the smell of cooking bacon and eggs filled the kitchen.

'Oh, my dear, you've got a nasty bruise there. Did you manage to get any sleep?'

'Not much,' Vicki admitted.

'Let me have a look at your lip.' Flo gently examined the swollen injury, a concerned frown on her face. Finally, she nodded. 'At least the cut hasn't opened again, but it must be painful. I want you to try to eat some breakfast, but chewing might be painful. Do you think you would be able to manage some scrambled eggs?'

'Yes, please.' To be truthful, she wasn't feeling much like eating, but they were concerned and she didn't want to upset them more than necessary.

'Has that man hit you before, Vicki?' Bob asked, sitting next to her.

'He's always been handy with his fists when he's had a few beers, and he'd obviously been drinking. If he hadn't, I don't think he would have stopped, but I can only think he must have been furious to see me looking so well.'

'A man like that doesn't deserve to have children!'

'It isn't children he dislikes; it's only me. If he'd had a couple of boys as well, he could have ignored me. He wants a son.'

'What does it matter?' Flo shook her head. 'He'd been blessed with a lovely, intelligent daughter. He should have been grateful to have you.'

'Gratitude and love don't belong in his vocabulary,' Vicki told them. 'I don't think he even knows the meaning of the words.'

'Well, he never wanted you, but we do, Vicki.' Bob smiled. 'From now on, you are our daughter. That's if it's all right with you, of course?'

'I would be honoured to be called your daughter,' Vicki told them, her voice full of emotion.

'Good. Now try to eat something, and then we'll go to the police station. Sid and Harry are going to meet us there at ten o'clock. We'll give our report, like they asked, and then we're all going to have a nice lunch out.'

Vicki took a small amount of scrambled egg and let it slip down without causing too much pain. Then she put the knife and fork down and turned to Bob. 'I have decided, for my mother's sake, that I won't have him charged with assault. All I want is for him to be warned to stay away from me, and if he doesn't he will be charged next time.'

'Of course we'll do what you want, but are you

sure, my dear?' Flo took her hand and held it.

'Yes, I'm positive. I've had all night to think about it.'

Bob nodded. 'Then we won't file any charges against him, but he doesn't deserve your kindness.'

Vicki gave a lopsided grimace. 'Nevertheless, I want to do this – not for his sake, but for mine. There has been enough unkindness, and it's got to end.'

Nine

The police were thorough, taking statements from each of them. Vicki was taken to a room by two officers who wanted to know everything from the time she was turned out to fend for herself. She kept it brief, not wanting to go into details about the horror of that time. Even after all these months, it still turned her stomach inside out to bring it all to mind.

When she had finished, the senior officer nodded. 'That's what Mr and Mrs Howard told us. They also said that when you came to them you were so weak you could hardly stand up. Is that right?'

'Yes, sir,' she admitted. 'I was starving. They saved my life.'

'And after the way your father has treated you, you still don't want to charge him with assault?'

'No, sir. All I want is for him to go away and

87

leave me alone. If he goes to prison, it will only cause my mother more grief.'

'And was your mother kind to you?'

'No, sir. She didn't care what happened to me, but it wasn't her fault. She's too tired and worn out trying to have a son, but something like this will only add to her problems. I'm with people who are kind to me, and I'm learning to become a hairdresser. The Howards are my family now.'

'Very well. We'll warn him to stay away from you or he will be arrested again.'

'Thank you, sir.'

With the interview over, they returned to the front desk where the others were waiting.

'Bring Mr Keats from the cells,' the officer ordered the desk sergeant.

Vicki knew her father's every mood and was struck by the change in him. A night in the cells had frightened him. The belligerence had been replaced by a subdued man who was visibly scared of being sent to prison.

'Mr Keats, because of the kindness of your daughter, no charges are being made against you. However, you are hereby warned to stay away from her and the shops owned by Mr and Mrs Howard. If you disobey this order, you will be arrested again. Is that understood?' the officer asked.

'Yes.'

'Then you are free to go.'

Without giving any of them even a glance, Mr Keats was out of the door as fast as his legs would carry him.

'He didn't even thank you, Vicki,' Bob remarked in disgust.

'For all his bluster, that man is a coward,' Sid said. 'He didn't have the courage to look at his daughter.'

'We don't think you will have any more trouble with him, Miss Keats, but you call us if you do.'

'Thank you, sir.'

It was with profound relief that Vicki walked out of the police station. She had done the right thing and now felt it was time to put the past behind her – if she could. That man was no longer her father, and he had no claim on her from now on. She was free.

'Right. Where are we going to eat?' Sid wanted to know as they walked along. 'I'm starving after that.'

They all laughed, the tension broken. Sid was always hungry.

'There's a nice little place just along here,' Flo told him. 'They do a nice roast on a Sunday.'

'Good. Ah, but will you be able to chew properly?' Sid asked, studying Vicki's damaged face.

'I'll manage.' The way they were heading took them past the railway station, and Vicki paused; the place held bad memories for her. Memories of shame and despair, but one stranger had taken the time to stop and help her. Who was he?

Harry stood beside her, 'Are you now ready to start your search for those two men?'

She nodded. 'Yes, I think it's time to see if I can find them.'

'Then we'll look into it. I've been holding off, Vicki, because I didn't feel you had quite reached

89

that point. After today, though, things have changed for you, haven't they?'

'I do feel as if I'm free at last,' she sighed. 'I would like to put the past behind me, but I don't think I can until I've tried to find my two strangers. Without them, I wouldn't be where I am today.'

'Then that unpleasant scene with your father has done some good. Can you remember what day it was when you met this man at the station? Was it a weekday, or a weekend?'

'I'm not sure. The days didn't mean much to me then.' Vicki frowned in concentration and turned to Bob. 'Can you remember what day in the week I came to your shop?'

'It was a Thursday, wasn't it, Flo?'

'That's right.'

'That means I must have seen him on a Tuesday, because it took me a day to get the clothes I needed. At least, I think it was only a day.' Vicki shook her head. 'I'm sorry, but it's hard to remember.'

'Never mind, my dear.' Seeing Vicki's bottom lip tremble, Flo took hold of her arm and led her away from the station. 'You can try different days, and Harry will come with you. Won't you, Harry?'

'Of course. I was going to suggest the same thing myself. Now, where did you say we are going to eat?'

'The Lombard cafe is in the next road.'

'Perfect.' Harry took hold of Vicki's other arm and smiled down at her. 'Let's forget about unpleasant things for a while and enjoy a good

90

meal together. Bud Lombard does a lovely steak and kidney pudding, or a hearty roast. That, and a good strong pot of tea, will do us all a power of good.'

As they walked the short distance to the cafe, Vicki struggled with her emotions. How did she get so lucky? The change from a starving, home-less girl to this was unbelievable. She was no longer alone, fighting to stay alive. That terrible time was behind her, and now she was cared for. These wonderful people were her friends, and they cared what happened to her, rallying round and standing beside her when trouble came. It was a heady feeling and not easy to come to terms with. Her home life had been wretched, and the time she had spent in that warehouse was a nightmare – best forgotten. She drew in a ragged breath. But it was most unlikely she would ever be able to do that completely. It was a part of her now and would always colour her life to a certain extent. *Is that how* you *feel, Bill? Does what you endured still haunt you?*

'Here we are.' Bob held open the door for them. 'There's a table by the window, Flo. You all sit down and I'll order our meal. Steak and kidney pudding all round?'

Everyone nodded agreement, and Vicki did the same, smiling. They were all in a jolly mood, and she wouldn't do anything to spoil their enjoy-ment, so she pushed away any gloomy thoughts and settled down to relax with her friends. Her father had been dealt with and could no longer cause her any trouble. This was her life now, and she could look forward to a future she never dreamed possible. Although he didn't realize it, her dad had done her a favour making her leave home, and she had done him a favour today by refusing to make a complaint against him. She felt right about that.

'Here we are. Enjoy.'

Vicki gazed at the plate in front of her and gasped. 'It's a *huge* steak and kidney pudding!'

They all laughed at her astonishment, and Bob said, 'Let's see how much of that you can eat, Vicki.'

The next couple of months were hectic as the business increased. Much to Vicki's relief, there had been no sign of her father again. He had obviously taken the police warning to heart.

'It's time you and Harry took a couple of days off,' Bob told Vicki at the end of another busy week.

'We can't do that,' she protested. 'You are busy, and our bookings are full. We're having a job to fit everyone in.'

'I know you girls have made a huge success of the salon, but you've never even had one day off since you came to us. You're growing up now and don't have any time to yourself. You should be out dancing and having fun like all the other young girls today.'

'That's right,' Flo said. 'When the shop closes, you deal with the books and the money, not to mention all the cleaning and washing of towels. I can manage for a couple of days, my dear. Our apprentice is coming along nicely and can tackle more jobs now. We've already told Harry, because we know you want to start your search for the men who helped you. He's eager to get going as well, but neither of you have had the time to spend on it.'

'I know,' Vicki sighed, 'but we can't leave you to cope on your own.'

'Yes, you can, and you must.' Bob smiled at his wife. 'We're old hands at this and will manage. We want you to do this, Vicki, so we won't hear any excuses. We have the feeling you will never really be able to put the past behind you until you find these two men.'

'We know it's important to you,' Flo told her gently, 'and that makes it important to us as well. Take the time, my dear, and find them, if at all possible.'

'It could be an impossible task,' Vicki admitted.

'That's true, and something you will have to face, but at least you will have tried. You will stand a better chance of success with Harry's help. This is just the kind of thing he loves, and he doesn't give up easily.'

Bob laughed. 'That's right, Flo. Once he gets going, no stone is left unturned. Do it, Vicki, and if you can find these men, we want you to bring them here so we can thank them as well. Harry wants to start on Monday morning.'

'All right.' Vicki began pacing the empty shop, and then she smiled. 'Thank you very much. I'll go and see Harry tomorrow so we can work out a plan of action.'

'I think he's already started on that, and he's expecting you. He said to tell you he'll be in all day. He's so eager to get started he couldn't even stay and talk to you himself. I told him he'd better succeed or I'll dock his pay for the two days!' Bob said, laughing.

'Oh, and he's also expecting you to bring him back for Sunday lunch.'

'Of course he is!' Vicki shook her head in amusement. 'He's practically moved in here.'

'He likes the company – and Flo's cooking. And I don't blame him. That house of his is much too large for one man. And although he never admitted it, I think he's been lonely there since his wife died four years ago.'

Vicki nodded. 'I expect he has. I'll go round early in the morning.'

They decided to go to the station straight away. Even though it was Sunday, they were still hoping they might be able to gain some kind of clue to the man's identity.

As soon as they stepped on to the station platform, Vicki stopped, crying out in despair. 'Oh, no!'

Harry swore under his breath when he saw what she was looking at. He caught hold of her shoulders to steady her as she swayed alarmingly with distress.

'That's where I stood! We've got to do something.' She struggled to get away from Harry's firm grip.

'Easy, Vicki. We'll help him.'

She looked up at Harry, tears brimming from her eyes. 'He's so young – younger than I was. Can we do something for him?'

'We'll talk to him first. You never know, his

94

family might have sent him out to beg for them. It does happen.'

'I know what goes on, Harry, but that is not the case with him.' She shook her head, walking towards the youngster. 'I know the signs too well. That boy is hungry and alone.'

'Spare a penny, mister?' the urchin asked, looking at Harry. 'I ain't 'ad nuffin' to eat for two days.'

'Come with us to the station cafe, young man, and we'll buy you breakfast.'

'Cor, thanks, mister.' The boy ambled along with them, wiping his grubby hands on equally dirty trousers.

Vicki watched, noting every detail. She had tried to keep herself clean, but she'd had the outhouse Bill had managed to open for her. This boy obviously had nowhere to wash. Where on earth was he sleeping? From the look of him, he could only be around twelve years of age. It was hard to tell, but if that was right, then he was tall for his age. He was about her height, painfully thin and seemed to be all arms and legs.

'Do you want anything, Vicki?' Harry asked as they found themselves a table.

'Just tea, please.'

The boy was still trying to clean his hands, so he obviously cared about his dirty state. There was a half-empty glass of water on the table, and Vicki took a clean handkerchief from her bag, moistened it in the water and then handed it to him. Smiling, she said, 'Here, wipe that over your hands. What's your name?'

'Dave,' he told her, scrubbing his hands with

95

the wet cloth. He grimaced. 'Sorry, miss, but I'm filthy. I wanted to go to the public baths, but any money I get goes on food.'

'I know exactly the situation you're in. Not long ago, I was homeless, starving and begging on this station, like you.'

Dave opened his eyes wide, staring at her in disbelief. 'You was?'

She nodded, and he lent forward eagerly. 'How did you get like you are now? I mean, you're a real lady. Posh, like.'

'I was lucky.'

Dave sighed. 'I could do with a bit of that luck.'

'The food won't be long,' Harry told them as he came back to the table and sat down. 'Tell us how you got into this mess, young man.'

'Well, me dad was killed in the war, and me mum met this other bloke, but he didn't want kids around him, so they sent me to my mum's sister and her old man. They didn't want nothing to do with kids really, but I think Mum's new man gave them some money. The man is a brute. He would beat me for no reason at all, so I left.' He pulled up his sleeves to show vivid bruises. 'I got these all over me. Well, I couldn't take no more of that. I had to leave.' Dave looked at them imploringly. 'I couldn't do nuffin' else, could I? He'd 'ave bloody well killed me if I hadn't!'

'Won't they come looking for you?' Harry asked.

'Nah, I 'spect they're glad to be shot of me.' He turned his attention to a plate of breakfast put in front of him, looking at the food as if he couldn't believe his eyes.

Harry and Vicki drank their tea and watched in silence as the boy wolfed the food down and wiped the plate clean.

'Tell me your name and how long you've been on the streets,' Harry said, as soon as he had the boy's attention again.

'I'm called Dave – I already told the lady – and I've been fending for myself for two weeks. It ain't easy, but I don't know what I can do, or where I can go.'

'If someone gave you a room and food, would you be willing to work?'

'Oh, I would, mister!' Dave sat bolt upright, hope filling his eyes. 'I'd work real hard and wouldn't cause no trouble. Do you know someone who'd do that for me?'

'I might consider it.'

Vicki looked at Harry with interest, but said nothing.

Dave was on his feet. 'Oh, blimey, I'd be ever so grateful! To be honest, I'm scared out here on my own, and I'm desperate to find a safe place to live.'

'Sit down,' Harry told him gently. 'Would you like some more toast and tea while we talk about it?'

The boy nodded, hardly able to sit still.

When Harry left the table to make the order, Dave reached across and grasped Vicki's arm. 'Will he do it . . . will he? Is he the one who took you in?'

'No, but he's a good friend of the people who did. He's a kind man, Dave.'

'Oh, I can see that!'

Harry brought the tea and toast with him and then sat down again. 'How old are you, Dave?'

'Er . . . fourteen . . . nearly.'

'Nearly?' Harry raised his eyebrows in query. 'I want the truth, young man.'

'I'm twelve,' he muttered, a worried expression on his face. 'But I'm strong and can do any kind of work. I don't care how hard it is. Lots of kids work at my age.'

'I know, but that doesn't make it right.' Harry turned to Vicki. 'Do you think Bob would let him work in the barber's a couple of days a week? He can stay with me. There's plenty of room in my house.'

'We could ask him.' Vicki studied Dave carefully. 'We would have to clean him up and get him some better clothes. I kept the ones I used to wear, and there's a good chance they will fit him.'

Dave was looking puzzled, the food forgotten for a moment.

'Right, we'll do that, but don't mention it to Bob and Flo yet.' Harry turned his attention back to Dave. 'You can come back with us, young man, and we'll see what we can do for you. Vicki knows what it's like to be homeless, so she can help you.'

'She told me, mister. Can't hardly believe it, seeing her now. A real lady, she is, and talks like one.'

'She taught herself to speak like that because it would help her to get a job. I was a teacher and can give you lessons in English. It will give you a better chance in life.'

'Oh, I'd like that!' Dave smiled at both of them, and then continued eating the toast. 'I won't let you down, and I like learning. Not that I've had much chance.'

'On the days you've been at the station, have you seen a man who perhaps gave you a generous amount of money, or even bought you a meal? He's quite tall, has a slight limp and carries a silver-topped cane. He's around forty, I would guess.'

'Can't say I have. You're the first people to ever take any notice of me, but I've only been coming here for a few days.'

Seeing the plates and cups were now empty, Harry stood up. 'The stationmaster is on the platform. I expect he knows most of the regulars.'

They left the cafe, and when Vicki described the man to the stationmaster, he pursed his lips as he tried to recall a passenger like that. 'Well . . . I see a good many who could fit that description, but there is one I remember. He only comes now and again.'

'Any particular day?' Vicki asked.

'I think it's during the week – not weekends. Sorry I can't be more help.'

This was disappointing, but Vicki was well aware that this could be a futile search. However, she wasn't ready to give up. 'Can I ask you to do me a favour? If you see this man again, could you try to get his name?'

'Ah, well, you'll have to tell me why you want to know.'

'He helped me a while ago. If it is the man I'm looking for, he knows me as Vicki, and I

99

would like to see him. I work at the Howards' ladies' hairdressing salon.'

The man nodded. 'I'll keep an eye out for him.'

'Thank you very much.'

As a train steamed into the station, Harry said, 'We can't do any more here today, Vicki. Let's go back to my place and see what we can do with this young man.'

Dave ambled along, chatting happily to Harry, leaving Vicki to her thoughts. She hoped the stationmaster would keep his word and let her know if the stranger turned up.

Ten

'Turn round and show Vicki how well the clothes fit you.' Harry smiled as he shook his head. 'He's almost as thin as you were.'

'Er . . .' Dave looked confused. 'These are boys' clothes . . . but you're a girl.'

Vicki laughed at his expression. 'Did you think we were going to put you in a frock?'

He smirked. 'I was blooming well hoping you wasn't, but when you said you was going to get some of your clothes for me, I didn't know what to expect. You didn't wear these, did you?'

'Yes, I was desperate to get a job, and everyone wanted boys, so I cut my hair short and dressed as a boy. It worked and the Howards took me in.'

'Gosh! You're real clever, ain't you? I wouldn't have fought of such a thing.'

'It wasn't easy, and I couldn't keep it up for long.'

He smirked again. 'Don't 'spect you could.'

Vicki studied the boy carefully. Now he was clean and wearing decent clothes he looked quite presentable, except for his hair. That was a mess, but she had collected her scissors as well. 'Sit down, Dave, and I'll cut your hair.'

He sat patiently while she worked. When she had finished, Harry nodded his approval. 'Much better. Now, Vicki, didn't you say I was invited to lunch?'

'That's right.' She replaced the scissors in her bag, and then looked at Harry. He was enjoying himself, and she wondered just what he was planning to do about Dave.

'Then we'd better get going. Mustn't keep Flo waiting. Come on, young man, you'll enjoy Mrs Howard's cooking.'

'Er . . . me too?'

'Of course. I want you to meet your future employers.'

'Um . . . s'posing they don't want me?'

Harry visibly winced. 'We'll have to start work on your speech straight away. And of course they'll want you.'

Dave sidled up to Vicki as Harry headed for the door, and whispered, 'Are you sure this is all right? They might just chuck me out.'

'No, they won't, Dave. They took in a boy who was really a girl, and they didn't turn me out when they discovered I had been lying to them.'

She smiled and hurried the boy after Harry. 'And I'm still with them. They're good people, so don't look so worried. You'll be fine.'

'If you say so.' He still didn't look convinced.

Harry was the first up the stairs. 'Set another place, Flo. We've brought you a guest.'

Dave was trying to hide behind Vicki, and Bob walked over so he could see the boy properly. 'Those clothes look familiar. Come out, young man, so we can have a look at you.'

He shuffled out from behind Vicki, but still kept close to her.

'What's your name, young man?'

'D . . . Dave, mister.'

'Welcome to our home, Dave. I hope you're hungry, because my wife is the best cook in all of London.'

'Don't take any notice of him,' Flo laughed. 'I'm only the second best, really. Sit down, everyone. Vicki, will you help me to dish up?'

'Of course.' She followed Flo to the kitchen.

'Where did you find him?'

Vicki told her what had happened that morning.

'Poor little devil!' Flo shook her head, frowning in concern. 'How many more children are out there trying to fend for themselves?'

'Too many.'

'Terrible.' Then she smiled at Vicki. 'Well, we saved one; perhaps we can save another one.'

'Harry seems to have taken to him and is prepared to give him a room and food.' Vicki tipped her head to one side and looked at Flo. 'He's only around twelve, but he appears to be a willing boy. All he needs now is a regular job.'

'Well, that's up to Bob. We know Harry wants more time to himself, and we do need a boy for the barber's. He's a bit young, though, but perhaps he could do part of the week – the busiest days.'

'That sounds ideal. Could you suggest it?'

'Let's see how things go first. Now, they've had long enough to talk, so let's get this meal on the table.'

The two men were in serious conversation with Dave when they carried the food in.

'So, what do you think, young man? Shall we give each other a try?'

'Yes, please, mister!' Dave's head bobbed up and down. 'I'd like that and I'll work real hard.'

'I shall expect you to,' Bob said. 'Now, we can enjoy our meal, and then I'll take you to the shop and show you everything. Harry will work with you at first. You watch carefully how he treats the customers.'

Dave's head bobbed again. 'I'll stick to him like glue.'

The boy looked up at Vicki when she put his plate in front of him, and smiled. 'I ain't 'arf glad you come to the station today. I'd have been sleeping in a doorway somewhere, and probably starving hungry. Frightening out there, ain't it?'

'Yes, it is.' Vicki sat beside him. 'You do realize you've got to work well for Mr Howard, don't you? He can't have anyone in the barber's who isn't efficient and polite to the customers.'

'I know that well enough.' His expression clouded. 'I'll be good. I don't want to go back on the streets again. I want to be like you – make somefin' of myself.'

103

Vicki was pleased to see him smile again when she said, 'I am sure you will.'

While Flo and Vicki cleared up, the men took Dave down to the shop, and they could hear his excited chatter.

'I can help you in the salon tomorrow. There isn't much else we can do, and Harry will be busy from now on. All we can hope is that the stationmaster will see the man and let me know.' Vicki sighed.' I don't hold out much hope, though. In fact, I'm beginning to think my idea of finding both men is just a dream. I've involved Harry in an impossible task. If only I knew more about them.'

'Didn't you once tell me that when Bill took you to that cafe, they seemed to know him?'

'Oh!' Vicki's eyes opened wide. 'I'd forgotten that. He did speak to some of the men there as if he knew them. How could that have slipped my mind?'

'You had just lost your home, Vicki, and I expect it was a confusing time. Why don't you go there today and see if you can find out if they know his name?'

'I'll do that as soon as we've cleared up.'

'Take your two days off, my dear, and don't give up.'

Vicki hesitated outside the cafe, remembering the breakfast she had shared with Bill. That had been a time when she had been unaware of the horror of the months to come. Her stomach churned just as it had when she had tried to go in there later and beg for food. As desperate as she had been, she hadn't been able to do it. The thought of all those faces staring at her dishevelled state had sent her slinking away in shame. She wasn't begging this time, so there was nothing to be ashamed of, but the memories were vivid in her mind. Although her clothes were smart and she was clean, she could still feel the grime and dirt. She had sunk so low at that time, and if it hadn't been for the Howards, she didn't know what would have become of her. Seeing the place again had brought it all back to her, and it was disturbing.

Taking a deep breath, she opened the door and walked in, grateful that the cafe was nearly empty at that time of the day.

'Can I help you, miss?' a man asked, smiling.

She was relieved when she recognized him as the same man who had served them that day. 'I don't know if you remember, but around two years ago I came in here with a man called Bill. You seemed to know him quite well, and I wondered if you could tell me his full name or anything else about him?'

He was now staring at her in disbelief, taking in every detail of her fashionable clothes and appearance. 'You're that girl?'

She nodded. 'Yes, I'm Vicki.'

'Good Lord! I would never have recognized you.' He led her to a table. 'Sit down, Vicki, and tell me how you became such an elegant young woman.'

'It's a long story,' she told him, as he ordered his helper to bring them a pot of tea. 'I had a rough time for a while, but I was lucky.'

'I kept looking for you, but you never came

back, so I hoped you were all right. Why do you want to know about Bill?'

She then explained about the two strangers who had helped her. 'So, you see, I want to find both of them if I can. Especially Bill. He gave me a book which has helped me, and I want to return it to him.'

'Hmm, well, I don't think I can be much help to you. He came in here for a few months, but we only ever knew him as Bill. We knew he was living rough, but he always had money to pay for his food. By his manner and speech, he was obviously a gentleman, and we assumed he was another casualty of that damned war – you know, having trouble coming to terms with the terrible things they had seen and done.'

'An officer, do you think?'

'Without a doubt. We never saw him again after he walked out of the door with you.'

'He told me he was leaving.' Vicki sipped her tea, disappointed. 'I did so hope you would know more about him.'

'Sorry. He never talked about himself, and we didn't ask. Wish we had now, but it doesn't do to be too nosy. If a man wants to keep his secrets, then we respect that.'

'Of course. Thank you for talking to me. If he should ever come in here again, would you tell him I would like to see him? I live with Mr and Mrs Howard and work in their ladies' hairdressing salon.'

'I know the shop.' He smiled and nodded. 'I can see why you look so elegant. Bill would be delighted to know you've done well, so I will certainly tell him if he ever turns up again. I doubt if he will, though,' he told her seriously. 'It's been too long, but I will ask around and see if anyone else has more details about him. Not much hope of that either – as I said, he never talked about himself. With nothing to go on, how are you going to find him?'

'I don't know, but I won't give up.' Vicki took out her purse. 'How much was the tea?'

'That was on me.' He stood up and held out his hand. 'It was lovely meeting you again, Vicki. I hope you do manage to track him down.'

'So do I. And thank you for the tea.'

As Vicki walked away from the cafe, she stopped, turned and gazed at the shop, pleased she had returned there at last. She hadn't gained any new information about Bill, but she had faced another part of her past, and that made her feel good.

Eleven

When Vicki arrived back at Harry's, he was completely absorbed in searching through his books. He didn't even know she was there until she spoke to him, and he only then looked up and smiled. 'I didn't expect you back today.'

'I've just been to the cafe Bill took me to in the hope that they might know something about him, but they didn't, I'm afraid.' She sat down and looked around. 'Where's Dave?'

'I left him settling in his room. I've put him in the room at the top of the stairs.'

'Oh, right.' Vicki stood up again. 'I'll go and see if he wants something to eat.'

'Don't expect so,' Harry laughed. 'He's already polished off most of the cake Flo baked for me.'

'I'll see, anyway.' Vicki ran up the stairs and knocked on the door. When there was no reply, she opened it a crack and looked in, calling the boy's name, but the room was empty.

After a quick search of the house and garden, she went back to Harry. 'He's disappeared.'

'What?'

'Dave isn't in the house. When did you last see him, Harry?'

He studied the clock on his desk and said, 'About an hour ago. Are you sure he isn't here?'

'Positive.' Vicki frowned anxiously. 'I do hope he hasn't run away already.'

Harry closed his book and shook his head. 'No, I'm sure of that. He was so pleased with his room and said he couldn't wait to sleep in a proper bed again. Perhaps he has some personal things somewhere and has gone to collect them.'

'Maybe, but he should have told you.' Vicki wandered over to the window, and after a moment said with relief, 'He's coming down the street now, and he's got someone with him.'

Harry joined her and watched in disbelief. 'Where on earth did he find him?'

'Oh dear, Harry, I think you might have a problem.' She looked up at him, laughter in her eyes.

He grinned back. 'Well, I will say one thing. Life has become interesting since I met you.'

They hid their amusement as Dave walked into the room, pulling a reluctant young child after him.

'Who have you got there?' Harry asked.

'This is my brother, Alfie. He's eight. You bin so good to me, and when I saw that big room you said I could have . . . well. Two can sleep in that bed, easy. I couldn't leave my little brother with those terrible people, now could I?' He looked imploringly at Harry and Vicki. 'Can he stay with us, please? We won't be no trouble. Will we, Alfie?'

Alfie shook his head.

'He don't say much,' Dave explained. 'He got cuffed so many times for opening his mouth, so he just keeps it shut now. Can we stay? Please, Mr Harry. We'll be ever so good. Promise.'

'Of course you can,' Harry said gently. 'You can help me put another bed in your room for your brother.'

'Oh, thanks!' Dave's worried expression disappeared like magic and he stooped down. 'Do you hear that, Alfie? You can stay here with me and the kind man. You'll be all right now. Just you wait till you see our room. It's huge and ever so clean. You'll like that, won't you?'

The child nodded again, never taking his eyes off Harry.

The little boy was still holding tightly to his brother's hand. Vicki bent down to his level, recognizing the fear radiating through the child. 'We're very pleased to meet you, Alfie. Your

109

brother has brought you to a safe place, so there is no need to be frightened of us.'

'That's right,' Dave said. 'I told you I would find a good place for us, and I have. Those monsters won't find us here, Alfie.'

The boy was still looking around at everyone, but said nothing in response to his brother's assurances.

'Can he speak at all?' Vicki asked.

'Oh, yes, miss. He used to chatter a lot, but he's learnt to keep his mouth shut. It's safer, you see.' Dave pulled a face and sighed. 'It's something I was never able to do, and that's why I got covered in bruises.'

Appalled by the way these children had obviously been treated, and knowing full well what it was like, she held out her hand to the little boy. 'Will you come with me, Alfie? We'll go to the kitchen and make tea and some sandwiches while Harry and Dave get a bed ready for you.'

He edged away from her, not prepared to let go of his brother.

'It's all right,' Dave assured him. 'You can trust her, 'cause she's been treated rough like us, and she was chucked out to fend for herself. She understands, and she's ever so kind. Go on, she'll give you something nice to eat, and then you can have a sleep in a lovely bed. She won't hurt you, Alfie. No one here will hurt us. I've always told you the truth, haven't I?'

Still holding out her hand, Vicki could have cried in sorrow for this traumatized small child, but she managed to keep a smile on her face.

Never taking his eyes off Vicki, Alfie slowly

released Dave's hand and then took hold of hers.

She grasped it gently, pleased with this small victory, and smiled at Dave, who nodded his approval. 'Let's go and see what we can find in the larder, shall we?'

The child was shaking as she led him to the kitchen, and she desperately wanted to hug him and tell him everything was going to be all right. But that would only frighten him more, and she couldn't give him that assurance because it might not be true. The people these boys had been with might soon come looking for them, and there was no telling what Harry intended to do about that.

She sat the boy on a chair and opened the larder. 'Now, let's see what we've got here. Are you hungry?'

The only response was a nod again, but at least that showed he was listening and understood what was being said to him. 'There's a fresh loaf of bread, cheese and ham. Oh, and there's one of Mrs Howard's lovely cherry cakes.'

Alfie never took his eyes off her as she prepared the food, and she kept on talking to him, ignoring the silence from the little boy. Dave seemed to do that, and he knew his brother and what they had endured better than anyone. By the time the plate was piled high with sandwiches, Harry and Dave came downstairs and joined them in the kitchen.

'Cor, look at all that grub, Alfie,' his brother exclaimed, sitting beside him and smiling broadly. 'You've got a lovely bed all to yourself, but don't look so worried. We're in the same room. You won't be on your own. I won't never let that happen again. I had to leave you, you know that, but I'd promised to come back for you as soon as I had somewhere for us to stay. And I did, didn't I?'

Another nod.

Dave put his arm around his brother's shoulder and turned Alfie to face him. 'You mustn't worry no more. I'm getting a job so I'll be able to look after you, and no one's gonna take us away from here. I won't never let that happen. I'll fight anyone who tries to do that. You're safe now, Alfie.'

Vicki had been listening carefully to this conversation as she made the tea. Dave was very aware how troubled his little brother was, and was doing his utmost to make him feel secure.

She poured out the cups of tea and sat down at the table. 'I've made some cheese and some ham sandwiches, so everyone help themselves. What would you like, Alfie – cheese or ham?'

He just stared at her.

'Have one of each,' she said, putting two sandwiches on his plate, and then took the same for herself.

'Eat up, Alfie,' Dave said through a mouthful of bread. 'They're smashing.'

While the boys were eating, Vicki spoke quietly to Harry. 'What are you going to do?'

'Keep them.'

She had never seen Harry look so angry or so determined.

'But what if someone comes looking for them? Alfie is very young.'

'A friend of mine works on the local council, and I will damned well report this to him if it becomes necessary. They must never be allowed to go back to the people they were with. Do you know, they've hardly had any schooling! I can put that right.' Harry sighed deeply. 'I'm going to need help and I know just the two people for the job.'

'I'll do what I can as well,' Vicki assured him. 'I'll even move in here to help with the boys, if you want me to.'

Harry smiled. 'I've been used to looking after a school full of children, so I should be able to manage two. And I think you had better cut the cake.'

'My goodness,' she exclaimed. The sandwich plate was empty. 'You really enjoyed those, didn't you?'

The boys nodded, and Dave grinned. 'Alfie had four and has drunk all of his tea.'

'Well done,' Harry said, putting a slice of cake on the little boy's plate. 'You try that. It's the best cake in London. And another cup of tea, I think, to wash it down. Same for you, Dave?'

'Yes, please, Mr Harry.'

When it was time for the boys to go to bed, Dave insisted that Alfie could share his bath, and Harry agreed, knowing that would be the best for the little boy. He needed careful handling; he hadn't said a word yet, or even smiled.

As soon as Vicki got her hands on their clothes, she gave them a good scrub and then hung them in the kitchen to dry overnight. The boys each used one of Harry's shirts to sleep in. She would need to go to the market and buy them more clothes. They only had what they were standing up in. When they had run away, it hadn't entered their minds to bring anything with them.

After she had made sure they were settled in their beds, Vicki went downstairs again. Harry was in the front room, and she sat in an armchair, sighing raggedly. 'They are both tired, and I don't think you'll have a peep out of them tonight. You could be taking on a load of trouble, Harry.'

'Maybe. To be honest, though, I've missed the children at the school since retiring. I've been mulling over an idea for a while now, and this has helped me to make up my mind.'

'What idea?'

'There are too many children being mistreated and lacking a proper education, like those two upstairs. There are five bedrooms in this house, and an attic not being used. With a bit of work, that space would make another two rooms. I'm going to turn this house into a boarding school.'

Vicki gasped. 'But how will you manage? And where will your pupils come from?'

'I've thought it through very carefully.' Harry laughed at her astonished expression. 'My friends, Edward and Pearl Hunt, will jump at the chance to become involved. He was a teacher as well, and his wife is a cook.'

'That sounds ideal, but how do you know they would be willing to help?'

'Because I talked this over with them some time ago, and since then they've been urging me to do something about it. And to answer your other question, I'll get the youngsters off the streets if I have to.'

'But they won't be able to pay anything towards their keep, and it will be expensive.' Vicki was struggling to grasp just how Harry was going to do such an ambitious thing.

'I've got enough, Vicki, and I might as well put it to good use. If I get short of money, then we will have to run some money-making schemes.' Harry leant forward, his eyes shining with enthusiasm. 'If I can help just a few to have a better life, then I'll be a happy man.'

'Oh, Harry, I think it's a wonderful plan!'

He nodded. 'So do I. But this isn't going to be easy and there will be some difficult times ahead. It also means that, for a while, I might not be able to spend as much time as I would like on finding your two strangers. It might take a little longer than we'd hoped.'

'I'm not worried about that. Helping the children is more important. I've waited this long, and a delay won't make any difference. You just tell me if you discover anything that might lead to finding Bill, and I'll follow it up. You are going to have your hands full from now on.'

'I know I am, but there will still be quiet times when I can do a bit of investigating.'

When Harry smiled and relaxed back in the chair, she couldn't help noticing that he looked ten years younger. Retirement hadn't suited him, and now he had a purpose in life again. And that was doing something he loved – looking after and teaching children. She was happy for him and determined to give him all the help she could.

Her job at the shop and her loyalty to Bob and Flo would come first, of course, but from now on her spare time would be spent here. 'You're not going to be able to work in the barber's any more, are you?'

'I'll work that out with Bob when I bring Dave with me in the morning and explain what happened. I don't think Bob has made much effort to find anyone because he could see I was enjoying being useful again.'

'You'll have to bring Alfie with you, as well. He can't be left on his own.'

'I wouldn't do that. The poor child is traumatized enough, and at this point it would be cruel to separate him from his brother. Dave really cares for him. It must have been desperation that made him leave him behind when he walked out.'

Vicki sighed. 'Dave clearly didn't have any choice, but he went back for him the moment you said he could live here. Has he told you the name of the people he was living with?'

'Not yet, and I haven't pushed him, but he has given me a couple of clues without realizing it. He puts on a brave face, but he's still frightened they might be sent back there. It could take a while for that fear to go. I'll find out eventually and then I'll make sure the couple are dealt with. I'll do everything in my power to see that Dave and Alfie never go back to them. The way they've treated those boys is criminal.'

Vicki agreed, but she was still worried. 'You might not be allowed to keep them, Harry.'

'I know that, but I'll get my friends to move in here. As a married couple, they will have a

116

much better chance of being considered suitable to look after them.' Harry smiled. 'Don't look so worried. I know what I'm doing.'

'Of course you do.' She stood up. 'I'd better go. I'll see you at the shop tomorrow.'

Harry laughed. 'All three of us. Bob and Flo don't know what's facing them.'

'You should be on your way to Harry's,' Flo said when she found Vicki stacking the towels ready for use. 'You've still got another day off, remember?'

'Harry is coming here first so I thought I'd make myself useful while I waited. I've checked the appointments and you won't be too rushed today, but the rest of the week is booked solid.' Vicki walked to the window and looked up the road. 'The clouds are breaking and it looks as if it will be a nice day. Yesterday was dry, as well.'

'Vicki! You're chattering, and you never do that. Are you nervous about something? What's going on?'

Another glance up the road made Vicki smile. 'You are about to find out. I hope you're ready for a big surprise.'

Twelve

Bob and Flo studied the two nervous boys standing in the shop. Bob rubbed his chin thoughtfully. 'Dave we know, but who is this little fellow?'

√ 'This is Dave's brother, Alfie,' Harry explained.

'I see . . . And what are you doing with two children now, Harry?'

'It's a long story, Bob, but the short version is that I'm going to open that school I've been talking about for ages. It will be for children like these.'

'Ah. I thought that was just a dream of a man who wasn't happy with retirement.'

'It was, but now I'm going to make it happen. These boys have given me the push I needed. And coming to know Vicki and what she went through, of course.'

Everyone was lost for words, just staring at the children as if they couldn't believe their eyes, and Sid was laughing quietly at the scene. Vicki could see this was making Dave and Alfie very uneasy, so she winked at them and grinned. Alfie then edged towards her, pulling his brother with him, The little boy caught hold of her hand, clearly needing some kind of reassurance that everything was going to be all right. She grasped it, still smiling.

'Well, it's a good thing this is a quiet day, because we want to know what you've planned, Harry. And I suspect this is going to involve us as well.'

'Only as far as Dave is concerned, as we've already agreed. But I won't be able to work here full-time any longer, of course.'

'Of course.' Bob turned to his wife. 'Put the kettle on, Flo. This could take some time.'

'I'll do that,' Sid told them, already heading for the kitchen.

'There's an apple pie in the larder, Sid. Get that out as well. I expect these boys are hungry.' Flo then turned to the young child. 'Would you like a nice big slice of pie, Alfie?'

He tried to hide behind his brother without letting go of Vicki's hand. His reaction made Flo frown. 'You don't have to be frightened of me, Alfie.'

'He's had a rough time,' Vicki told her softly.

'I can see that now. Come on, young man, and tell me all about yourself.'

'He don't talk much,' Dave told her. 'He can, but he stopped because the people we was with sloshed him if he opened his mouth. They was always telling us to be quiet, so he don't say nothing now. But he'll be all right soon – won't you, Alfie?'

There was no response.

'Oh dear, Vicki,' Flo said under her breath. 'I know Harry has dealt with children all his working life, but I hope he fully understands what he's taking on.'

'I believe he does. He's good with them, and, whatever happens, these boys must not go back to the abuse they have suffered.'

'We ain't never gonna do that!' Dave's mouth was set in a grim line. 'I won't let those monsters get their hands on my Alfie again!'

Alfie whimpered. It was the first sound Vicki had heard him make, so she bent down to him. 'It's all right, sweetie, you're safe with us now.'

'You don't have to be afraid no more.' Dave

hugged him and ruffled his hair affectionately. 'I wouldn't never have brought you to anyone who was cruel. These are all kind, like I've already told you. Mr Harry's gonna look after us and teach us lots of things. We've got lovely beds to sleep in, we're clean and have full bellies, and Vicki's gonna see we've always got a good haircut.' He laughed. 'Won't you, Vicki?'

'Definitely!'

Alfie seemed to relax a little, so Flo smiled. 'We'd better go and get a piece of that pie before the men eat it all.'

When the two boys had eaten every scrap of pie on their plates, Bob looked at Vicki. 'I expect Alfie would like to see the shops. Why don't you go with Dave and open up for us? Customers will be arriving soon.'

'I'll do that. Come on, boys, you can help me.' Vicki stood up and held out her hand for Alfie. 'I'll show you where your big brother is going to work.'

The little boy didn't take her hand this time, but he did stay close to his brother as they made their way downstairs. Sid had already opened the barber's, so she took them through the connecting door to the ladies' salon. She could see that Alfie was looking very intently around as his brother explained everything. He was also near to tears.

'Why is he so upset?' Vicki asked Dave.

'I fink he's frightened I'm gonna be here while he's alone. I 'splained he'll be all right with Mr Harry, but he don't trust no one but me.'

'In that case, he had better come with you on the days you're working in the barber's.'

'Cor, do you fink he could? Would Mr and Mrs let him do that?'

'I'll have a word with them, but I'm sure it would be all right. They are very understanding.'

'That would be smashing, wouldn't it, Alfie?'

Alfie nodded, but his eyes were brimming with tears, so Vicki stooped down and wiped the moisture away with her clean handkerchief. 'We know you're frightened, Alfie, and it will take time for you to trust us, but we will not separate you from your brother. Do you believe me?'

'She'll keep her word,' his brother assured him. 'She's all right. I told you, Vicki knows what it's like to be bashed about and homeless. She won't tell us no lies. Do you know what she did?'

His brother shook his head.

'She dressed as a boy so she could get a job here. What do you think of that?' Dave grinned at his brother. 'She's clever, ain't she?'

'And it was a very good disguise,' Flo said, walking into the shop and stopping in front of Alfie. 'But she was starving and could hardly stand up. That won't happen to you, young man, because your brother has found you both a good home. Harry will see you are not harmed again. We all will. Now, why don't you both go and see if there is any of that pie left?'

'Cor, thanks.' Dave gave his brother a quick shove. 'Race you for the biggest piece.'

Alfie almost smiled as they raced out of the shop.

'We're making promises I hope we can keep, Vicki.' Flo looked concerned.

'We've got to! That boy is terribly damaged

121

and must never go back to those people. Has Harry said what he's going to do next?'

'Not exactly, but he's determined to keep them. Somehow he's got to make it legal so they can't be forced to return to an abusive home. We've told him we'll help and support him. The rest is up to him and his friends.'

Vicki sighed deeply and then fixed a bright smile on her face as the first customer arrived.

The next morning, Harry was in the barber's teaching Dave his duties, with Alfie shadowing his brother all the time.

'Go and see how they're getting on next door,' Flo told Vicki. 'If Alfie is getting in their way, see if he will come in here with us.'

'All right.' Vicki went through the connecting door to the barber's and stood where she could see but not be seen. After a while, a smile of satisfaction crossed her face. Harry was showing Dave how to collect any used towels and put them in the basket, then make sure that Bob and Sid were kept supplied with clean towels. Alfie was also listening intently, and she saw him pick up a towel Sid had dropped, grab a clean one and hand it to him. Everyone in the shop, including the customers, were talking to the boys and ignoring the fact that Alfie never said a word.

She quietly slipped back to Flo and told her what she had seen. 'I think they are all enjoying themselves.'

'Has Alfie said anything?'

Vicki shook her head. 'I don't think so, but he

doesn't look quite so frightened. When is your next customer due?'

'Eleven. Then no more until two. This is a quiet day, my dear, so you don't need to stay here.'

'I know, but what else can I do?'

'Come and meet my friends and help me get everyone settled in the house,' Harry said, walking into the salon with the boys right behind him. 'That will be all right, won't it, Flo?'

'Yes, take her away, Harry. Our girl works too hard and we have a difficult time trying to make her take time off.' Flo looked at the two youngsters and sighed. 'Go on, Vicki. Harry needs your help today.'

Knowing it was useless to protest, she nodded and then held out her hand to Alfie, who hesitantly took it, still holding on to his brother with the other hand.

Dave chatted happily as they walked to Harry's house, telling her what he had been doing that morning. 'And Alfie helped as well. He learns quick. Always has done. He's real bright, aren't you?'

Not a word from the child in response.

'You don't have to stay quiet no more, Alfie. I told you that.'

'Don't push him, Dave,' Harry warned. 'Your brother will speak when he's ready.'

'I 'spect so.' Dave frowned up at the tall man walking beside him. 'But it ain't right, and it worries me something rotten.'

'That is obvious. I will start your lessons today, and in time Alfie might join in, but he will only do that when he is feeling more secure.'

123

Dave was still frowning. 'Can you help him, Mr Harry?'

'I think I can. I've dealt with troubled children before.'

'You hear that, Alfie? Mr Harry's gonna help both of us.'

Vicki could feel tightness at the back of her throat as she listened. Whatever it took, these boys must be kept safe. Dave might talk and joke with his little brother, but it was obvious he thought the world of him and was worried sick. So worried, in fact, that it had driven him out on his own in a desperate search to find a way to get him away from where they were living.

Harry's friends were waiting for them as they reached the house, and when the little boy saw them, he would have bolted if Dave hadn't caught hold of him in time.

'It's all right, Alfie! They're friends of Mr Harry. I told you about them, remember?'

'That's right.' Harry smiled reassuringly at the child. 'This is Edward and Pearl. They are going to live with us and look after the house. Pearl is an excellent cook, so we'll be well fed.' Harry turned to his friends. 'Meet Vicki, Dave and Alfie.'

'Hello. We have heard a lot about you.'

Vicki shook hands with both of them and liked them on sight. Pearl was ample and homely, and Edward was tall and strong-looking, with a glint in his eye that suggested he smiled a lot. They were just the kind of people to help with two troubled boys.

'We've already unpacked, Harry, and lunch is

124

on its way.' Pearl delved into a capacious handbag and came out with a parcel which she handed to Alfie. 'I thought you might like a colouring book and crayons, young man.'

'Cor, thanks!' Dave exclaimed. 'Alfie likes drawing, don't you?'

There was no response from his brother, but he did accept the present from Pearl. She rummaged in the bag again and brought out a box containing a truck. 'And this is for you, Dave.'

'Wow!' He looked as if he couldn't believe his eyes. 'We ain't never had presents before, have we, Alfie?'

'Why don't you put them in your room and wash your hands ready for lunch?' Harry suggested. 'Whatever Pearl is cooking smells good.'

Dave grinned happily. 'We'll do that.'

As the boys tore up the stairs, Edward shook his head. 'Poor little buggers. Pardon my language, Vicki, but what has happened to those boys is criminal. What the hell are you going to do, Harry? If the people they were with come for them, you'll have to let them go.'

'Oh no!' Vicki said in alarm. 'That mustn't happen. Couldn't you report them to the police for cruelty?'

'I don't want to bring the police into this if I can avoid it. It could make things even more difficult. I'm going to try something else first. Dave gave a couple of clues when he was chatting to me early in the morning, and I have a good idea where they were living. After we've

125

eaten, I'm going to see them, and Edward is coming with me.'

'I'll come as well.'

'No. I want you to stay here with the boys. It's a rough area, Vicki.'

She looked at Harry in disbelief. 'Have you forgotten where I came from? I grew up in such a place, and I know the kind of people who live there. Many are good, honest people, but there are also some who are thieves and drunks, and violent. I might be able to help.'

Harry sighed. 'I can't imagine you living like that, but I'm asking you to leave this to me and Edward.'

'That's right, Vicki. We might look like a couple of gentlemen,' Edward told her, 'but it wouldn't be the first time we've dealt with this kind of thing. We were working at a school filled with difficult children – and some of their parents were worse.'

'You never told me that, Harry. I assumed you had been at some posh school.'

He laughed and slapped his friend on the back. 'Far from it, Vicki. It will be like old times, Edward.'

'You can safely leave it to them,' Pearl said. 'Lunch will be ready in five minutes.'

'Good, I'm starving. What have we got?'

'I haven't had much time today, so it's a quick meal of sausages and mash, Harry.'

'Lovely. The boys will enjoy that. I'll pop upstairs and get them.'

As he strode from the room, Vicki gave a knowing smile. 'I do believe he's enjoying himself.'

'Of course he is,' Pearl agreed. 'That man should never have retired. He revels in a challenge, and he's certainly taken one on with these boys.'

'I know, but how is he going to be able to keep them? It was different with me because I was older, but they are so young.'

'That's why we're here,' Edward explained. 'We are a married couple with a good reputation as parents. We've brought up three children, one of whom we adopted, and they are all doing well. If the authorities get difficult, we can apply to look after them.'

'Oh, that sounds hopeful.' Vicki nodded in relief.

'Don't think this is going to be easy, Vicki,' Pearl told her seriously. 'Setting up the school for abused children will be a long, hard struggle, but if we can succeed, then we will be able to help a few youngsters. You survived by your own efforts, and I suspect so would Dave, but Alfie is too young and vulnerable. He must have help.'

'Ah, here come the boys.' Edward listened to the clumping feet on the stairs. 'Let's eat.'

The sausage and mash was greatly enjoyed by everyone, especially the boys, who both wiped their plates clean and had seconds.

'At least there's nothing wrong with their appetites,' Pearl remarked quietly as she began to dish up a creamy rice pudding. 'And that's a hopeful sign. I'd be very concerned if the little one wasn't eating properly.'

'Right.' Harry stood up. 'That was lovely, but Alfie looks rather tired now, and so do you, Dave. Why don't you both go and have a nap?'

'Didn't you want to start our lessons today?' Dave stifled a yawn.

'We will begin tomorrow. I have to go out this afternoon.'

'Ah, right.' Dave helped his brother off the chair. 'In that case we will have a sleep. Alfie is tired out, ain't you, kid? You needn't worry 'cause I'll stay with you all the time. Thank Mrs Pearl for her smashing dinner.'

The boy gave his usual nod.

'I'm pleased you enjoyed it. You have a nice rest now.'

Vicki helped with the washing-up, and then crept up the stairs and peeped into the boys' room. They were both fast asleep.

When she came down, Harry and Edward were ready to leave, and Vicki tried again. 'Let me come with you.'

Harry shook his head firmly. 'I need you here. The youngsters don't know Pearl very well yet and might be frightened when they wake up if they don't see a familiar face.'

That was sensible, and she reluctantly agreed to stay behind. 'Be careful and good luck.'

Thirteen

The men hadn't returned after two hours and the wait was agony. What if those people wanted the boys back? What would they do? The thought of such a thing was making Vicki feel sick. With help, young Alfie might become a normal child again, but if he had to return to that abusive home, then he would only sink further down. Perhaps too far to rescue. It was awful to contemplate. How she wished Harry hadn't decided to do this. It might have been better to keep the boys hidden from everyone. She gave a ragged sigh. That was foolish thinking, of course, and would be quite impossible.

'Stop pacing, my dear.'

'Why are they taking so long? I should have gone with them. What can Harry possibly achieve by going to see those people? I'm worried, Pearl. We've got to keep the children safe!'

'Calm down, Vicki. Harry and Edward know what they are doing. Here, I've made a fresh pot of tea. Sit down and tell me about the two men who helped you.' Pearl guided her to a chair, made her sit and then placed a steaming cup of hot tea in front of her. 'Harry told us you want to find them if you can.'

'I don't have much chance of doing that.' Vicki sipped her tea. 'With Harry's help, though, I'm going to try.'

For the next half an hour she told Pearl all about her experiences after her father had thrown her out of the house.

'I understand now why you are so keen to find them.' Pearl poured her another cup of tea. 'And, you never know, something may happen to point you in the right direction. Things like that do happen. If you are meant to find them, then I am sure you will.'

'Are you an optimist, Pearl?' Vicki laughed,

realizing that the talking had calmed her nerves.

'Always, my dear. Always. If something is meant to be, then nothing can stop it.'

'Are those two children meant to be with you, your husband and Harry?'

'Well, you found Dave begging in the same place you had used, and that's where someone reached out to help you. Do you believe that to be a coincidence, or was it meant to be?'

'I agree that it was strange, and it shook me to see him standing there. The memories flooded in and I knew I had to help him.' At the sound of the front door opening, Vicki was immediately on her feet. 'They're back!'

'How did you get on?' she asked the moment they walked in. 'Did you find them?'

'We did, and they won't be taking the boys back. That's the first hurdle out of the way, but they are a greedy pair and only wanted the money I offered them.'

'You gave them money to give up the boys?'

Harry nodded. 'From their attitude, I gathered that they had never wanted to take the youngsters in, but their mother and her new boyfriend gave them money, and I'd say they are a couple who will do anything for money.'

'But they could keep coming back for more.' Vicki was even more worried now. She couldn't see how paying someone off in a case like this was going to work.

'We've thought of that,' Edward told her. 'We told them they had been reported to the authorities for cruelty and neglect, and if they came so much as within a mile of the children, then the law would be after them. They are a couple of shady characters, and the last thing they want is for the police to show an interest in them. They'll stay away.'

'And have you filed a complaint against them?'

'Not yet, Vicki, but it is an option we are keeping open.'

'You lied.' She shook her head, perplexed. 'And did they believe you?'

Edward glanced at Harry and raised his eyebrows. 'I'd say we did a good job of convincing them, didn't we, Harry?'

'Undoubtedly.' The men grinned at each other.

'You two!' Pearl smirked. 'You might be past your prime, but I wouldn't like to tangle with you when you are in this kind of mood. So, let's assume the boys are safe for the moment – what's next?'

'That was the easy part. Now I want to set up the school, and I need it to be a legally recognized establishment where the authorities can send abused children. It could take some time.'

'And I'd say we will have a fight on our hands.' Edward didn't look at all troubled by the prospect. 'And the biggest one could be this house. It isn't really suitable for what we want, Harry.'

'I know that, but it's all we've got, and somehow we've got to convince the authorities that we can make this work.' Harry smiled. 'But we've had a small victory today, and tomorrow is another day. Are the boys still asleep?'

'Yes, there hasn't been a sound from them. Are you going to tell them, Harry?' Vicki asked.

'I want them to feel safe as quickly as possible,

131

especially Alfie. That's most important if we are going to help him to talk again.'

'We are going to have our hands full, Harry,' Pearl agreed, 'but I've been talking to Vicki, and you must somehow find time to help her as well.'

'Oh, that can wait,' Vicki protested.

'No, my dear. We are here to take some of the burden from Harry's shoulders, so I'm sure he can make time for your search.'

'Of course I can. I promised and I'll keep my word. There will be spare time while we're trying to get the school up and running.'

'Thank you, Harry, but I really don't know what else we can do.'

'I'll start trying to track down the family who owned that book. It might give us a lead.'

'That's a good idea,' Pearl agreed. 'And you never know, Vicki, that stationmaster might see the other man again. I'm sure something will turn up.'

Edward grinned. 'My Pearl is always the optimist, but she's often right. It's most uncanny sometimes.'

'Then I must expect a good outcome,' Vicki laughed. 'I'll start to get tea ready. I expect the boys will be stirring soon, hungry and thirsty.'

The words were hardly out of her mouth when they heard footsteps on the stairs.

'Did we miss tea?' Dave wanted to know. 'We didn't mean to sleep so long, but we was worn out, and then Alfie wanted to colour in his book. Show them what you've done, Alfie. It's ever so good.'

Pearl smiled at the little boy who was clutching the book to his chest. 'What picture did you do?'

After a hesitant glance at his brother, he held out the book for them to see. They all gathered round.

'My goodness, that is excellent. Don't you think, Harry?'

'Very good indeed. You have chosen all the right colours for the animals, as well as the field they are in. Have you ever seen a real cow, young man?'

Alfie shook his head.

'Then you have a good eye for colour,' Harry praised. 'That is really excellent work. We shall have to put it on the wall by your bed.'

The child looked at the picture, up at Harry and then back to the picture again. And he almost smiled. Vicki held her breath in anticipation, but the hoped-for response never appeared.

Dave was delighted with the praise for his brother and beamed at them. 'He's clever, ain't he?'

'It would appear so.' Edward winked at his wife. 'How about some tea, Pearl? We can't have future artists going hungry.'

'We certainly can't. Give me a hand, Vicki, and we'll have it ready in no time.'

'And while we wait, Alfie, let's have a look at your crayons to see if they need sharpening,' Edward suggested. 'You might need more colours; I can get them for you tomorrow.'

The young boy's eyes opened wide at the thought of more crayons, and he pointed upstairs.

'Right. Lead the way.'

Vicki watched as Alfie walked with Edward towards the stairs. That was the first time she had seen him go anywhere without his brother.

When Dave started to follow, Harry caught his arm and said softly, 'Let him go. This is the first sign he's given that he's beginning to trust us.'

'That's good, then, isn't it?'

'Yes, it is, but don't expect miracles, Dave. His complete recovery is going to take time, so we must be patient. And you needn't worry about the people you were with because I've taken care of them.'

'You've seen them?' Alarm showed on Dave's face. 'How did you find them? Do they know we're here? How do you know they won't come for us? What did you do to them? Them's nasty people! They could've hurt you! My Alfie will never get over it if they take him back. I won't let them do that . . . never . . . never . . .'

'Don't get upset,' Harry told him firmly. 'I tracked them down and took Edward with me. They don't know where we live, so they won't come here. By the time we had finished with them, they were very frightened.'

Dave took a deep breath. 'Good, but you shouldn't have gone there, Mr Harry. Best they'd thought we'd just disappeared.'

'We had to do this,' Harry explained, 'or we would have been worrying about them all the time. I want to set up a school for children like you and Alfie, and it has to be done legally. Our first task had to be dealing with those people. Now that's done, we can start our plans to help more like you. Do you understand?'

134

Dave pursed his lips. 'I guess so. Were they really frightened?'

'Very frightened indeed. We told them that if they came anywhere near you and Alfie, then the law would be after them.'

'Gosh! Bet that did scare them. They were always up to no good. So I can tell Alfie we don't have to worry about them no more?'

'That's right, and either Edward or I will be with you all the time. They won't risk coming anywhere near us again.'

Dave gave Harry a thoughtful look. 'Don't 'spect they will. You might be old, but you're a couple of big blokes.'

Vicki stifled a laugh at Harry's expression.

He moved so quickly, taking Dave by surprise as he swept him off the floor and making the boy squeal with laughter. 'Not so much of the old, young man. I'm still strong enough to take anyone on.'

Dave's feet had just touched the floor when Alfie erupted into the room, but when he saw everyone was laughing, the panic left his face.

'It's all right, Alfie,' Dave told him, still laughing. 'We was just fooling around. Mr Harry was showing me how strong he is.'

Vicki guessed that laughter was as unusual in Alfie's life as it had once been in hers. She had been blessed to find affection, laughter and security, and, hopefully, these two boys had as well. She sent up a silent prayer that Harry, Edward and Pearl would be successful in their plans to help more children.

They all had tea together, and, seeing there

wasn't anything else she could do, Vicki decided to leave. Before she reached the front door, though, Harry stopped her. 'Come into the front room. We want to talk to you.'

Edward and Pearl were already there, and Harry made her sit down. 'We've been having a serious discussion about you, Vicki. We know you want to help as much as you can, but you are still learning your trade as a hairdresser, and you must put that first. It is your future, and I'm sure Bob and Flo would never have opened the ladies' salon if you hadn't been with them. They've done it to provide you with a secure future.'

Edward continued. 'I've talked to them and they love you like a daughter. It worries them that you haven't made friends with people of your own age. You should be going dancing and enjoying yourself like all the other bright young people.'

'That's right,' Pearl agreed. 'From what I've heard, you work far too hard, and if you start spending your spare time with us, you won't have a moment to yourself.'

Vicki stared at them in shock. 'Are you saying you don't want me here?'

'No, that isn't it at all.' Edward smiled gently. 'Don't look so hurt, young lady. What we are trying to make you understand is that the three of us can cope with whatever we have to do. Bob and Flo need you, and we mustn't take you away from them.'

'And we won't,' Harry said firmly. 'Don't worry about the boys. You will see them in the shop for a while, because Alfie won't be separated from his brother at the moment. You will be welcome to pop in and see us any time you can, but it must just be a visit. You have had enough to cope with in your life, my dear, and it's time to think of yourself for a change. Do you understand?'

'I do.' She gave a ragged sigh. 'And, of course, my loyalty to Bob and Flo will always be my first priority. My gratitude for what they have done for me is enormous, and I love them dearly. But if it hadn't been for me, you would never have been embarking on this ambitious scheme.'

'And we are very grateful to you for that,' Pearl told her. 'We've been on to Harry for ages to do something like this, but we weren't sure what form the school would take until Dave and Alfie arrived. Then it all fell into place.'

'That's true enough. I needed a push, and you gave me that, Vicki. Now, wipe that worried frown from your face. We promise to give you reports every week on our progress, and if there is anything you can help us with, we will ask.'

'All right, but you make sure you do,' she told them sternly. 'I will do as you say, except for one thing.' She pulled a face.

'And what is that?' they asked in unison.

'I can't promise on the dancing bit.'

Fourteen

The next two weeks at the shop was so busy that Vicki hardly had a moment to herself. The young

137

girls were going for the latest hairstyles, and she was becoming quite confident with waving and cutting hair in the styles they wanted. The clothes were shorter, more flamboyant, and new dances were all the rage. It seemed as if everyone was intent on enjoying themselves, and Vicki did wonder if it was in an effort to put memories of that dreadful war out of their minds.

'There you are,' Vicki said, holding the mirror for her customer to see the back of her hair. 'Is that to your liking?'

'Oh, you really are very good. I'm telling all my friends to come here. We're going dancing tonight – why don't you come with us?'

This wasn't the first invitation she had received, and the answer was always the same. 'No, thank you. I can't make it tonight.'

'Another time, then.' The customer paid and left the shop.

'You ought to go, Vicki,' Flo told her. 'It's time you mixed with people your own age. You are never going to meet any nice young men if you are always working.'

'There aren't enough men now, anyway, because so many were killed in the war. It looks as if quite a few girls will have to remain single. And, as I've said before, I don't want any young men. I'm never going to be tied to a man who thinks he can do what he likes with me.'

'And I've told you, not all men are brutes. In fact, very few are. I know your past was harsh, my dear, but your life is different now. Surely you can see that?'

'I know I'm surrounded by good people now,

138

but it's hard to forget how I lived for most of my life.' She smiled at Flo. 'Anyway, I'm not interested, and I can't dance.'

'Sid will teach you. He knows all the latest dances and says they are fun. I understand he's considered hot stuff at the Charleston.'

Vicki laughed at Flo's teasing. 'I don't doubt it, but I'm still not interested.'

'All right.' Flo lifted her hands in surrender. 'You've made your feelings known, and I won't bring up the subject again.'

'Oh, good,' Vicki joked. 'Will you tell Harry to do the same? He won't let the subject drop, either.'

'You can come in, Alfie,' Flo said when she saw his little face peering through the doorway. 'Do you want to help us?'

He nodded, edged into the shop and began collecting up the used towels.

There had been a slight improvement over the last couple of weeks. He still hadn't spoken, or even smiled, but he wasn't clinging quite so firmly to his brother. At first he wouldn't have left the barber's, but he was now beginning to come into the ladies' shop on his own. The Howards had bought the boys some good clothes and they now looked smart. With Harry's help, Dave's speech was a touch better, though still a bit rough, especially if he got excited or angry. Harry was including Alfie in the lessons, and he listened intently without making a sound. The customers in both shops appeared to be quite happy to see the boys, greeting them when they walked in.

✓ Flo's next customer only wanted a trim, and when she was preparing to leave she dropped her gloves. Alfie pounced on them and handed them back to her.

'Thank you, young man. I didn't know I had dropped them.' She opened her purse and gave him a coin, smiling at the serious little boy. 'That's for being so helpful.'

Alfie watched her leave, examined the tip he had been given and then held it out to Flo.

'No, you keep it, sweetheart. The lady gave it to you because she might have lost her gloves if you hadn't returned them to her. That was her way of thanking you.'

He thought about it for a few moments and then slipped the penny into his trouser pocket. Then he began collecting up the towels and putting them in the basket used for that purpose. He had clearly watched his brother working in the barber's very carefully and knew what to do. He was a thoughtful little boy, and there was no doubt that he was intelligent.

'Do you know, Vicki, young Alfie is so good in the shops that I think he ought to be paid, just like his brother.'

'I agree.' They were speaking quite clearly so Alfie could hear.

'Do you think a nice shiny threepenny piece would be a fair wage?'

'That would be very fair.'

Alfie had stopped what he was doing and stared at them. He watched Flo go to the till, open it and then walk over to him.

'This is for being such a help to us in the shop,

Alfie. You deserve to be paid just like everyone else.'

He took the coin from her and turned it over and over as he studied it. Then he pursed his lips, sighed deeply and slipped the money into his pocket with the other coin. Without any indication of what he was feeling, he picked up a small broom Vicki had bought for him to use, and began sweeping the floor.

The next customer arrived and they were busy once again. Alfie stayed in the shop and gave them clean towels whenever they needed them. He seemed quite happy and didn't keep disappearing to check that his brother was still nearby. It was progress, and they noted every sign with hope for the little boy's complete recovery from the abuse he had suffered.

In the middle of the afternoon, Vicki was just finishing the comb-out of her customer when a man came into the shop.

'I have been told someone here wants to see me.'

Vicki spun round at the sound of his voice, her heart thudding as she looked at him. 'Oh, sir, that's me. Thank you for coming.'

Flo took the brush out of her shaking hands. 'Take him out the back, and I'll see to your customer.'

He was frowning as she walked towards him. 'The stationmaster said Vicki was looking for me.'

'That's right, sir. I'm Vicki. Would you spare me a moment of your time, please?'

Her mind was racing as she led him through

the shop, trying to picture him that day at the station, but she had been in such a state the details about him were blurred. It was him, though, because he was still carrying the silver-topped cane. For some reason, that was what she remembered most clearly.

'Would you like a cup of tea, sir?' she asked.

'No, thank you, young lady. When I was told who wanted to see me, I assumed it was the homeless girl I found begging at the station.'

'I am that girl, sir.'

'My God!' he exclaimed. 'I would never have recognized you.'

'I don't suppose you would. Please sit down for a moment. You told me that you hoped you had saved a life that day. Well, you did, and I've wanted so much to be able to thank you. You bought me food and gave me money so that I would have a chance of getting a job.'

He leant back in the chair, studying her intently. 'Tell me about it.'

Vicki went through what had happened to her, and by the time she had finished her detailed story he was smiling. 'You, young lady, have just given me the best news I could ever hope to hear. Ever since that day I have thought about you and wished I had done more at the time. I feared you would not have survived for much longer.'

'I wouldn't have, sir.' She pulled a ten-shilling note out of the pocket of her apron, one she had been saving in the hope of being able to return it to the man who had helped her so much. 'What you did for me that day was beyond price, and

I would like to repay you the money you so generously gave me.'

'I don't want your money,' he told her sternly. 'You have pulled yourself out of that terrible situation by your own efforts. It is reward enough for me to see you here today, fit and well. May I ask why it has taken you so long to find me?'

'My recovery was slow, and I wanted to wait until I had made a decent life for myself.'

'You have certainly done that. Will you introduce me to the people who have been so kind to you?'

'I'd love to, sir, and they want to meet you.' She stood up and then paused. 'I don't even know your name.'

'Charles Denton.'

She shook his hand, at ease with him now. 'I am delighted to meet you again, Mr Denton.'

He gave an amused laugh. 'And I you, Vicki. More delighted than you could ever know.'

The shop was empty of customers when she introduced him to Flo. 'This is a wonderful day, Mr Denton. Thank you very much for what you did for Vicki. She is a remarkable girl, and a constant joy to us.'

He began asking questions, and Vicki noticed that Alfie hadn't scuttled away. He appeared to be fascinated by the silver-topped cane and was edging closer so he could see it better.

'And who is this?' Mr Denton asked when he caught sight of the boy.

'This is Alfie, and he seems to be interested in your cane,' Vicki told him.

'Ah, you want to have a closer look, do you?

143

It's the head of a dog. Do you know what breed it is?'

Alfie reached out tentatively and touched the emerald eyes.

When the boy didn't say anything, he said, 'It's a bulldog, and I don't suppose you've ever seen one before. They are not pretty animals, but they are strong and brave.'

Running a finger over the head, the little boy sighed and then shot into the other shop.

'Did I say something to upset him?'

'No.' Vicki shook her head and gave him a brief outline of the boys' plight.

'My word, Vicki, this is very interesting. You must introduce me to everyone. I need to hear more about this.'

'We would be honoured if you would join us for dinner, Mr Denton. That's if you can spare the time, of course?'

'Thank you, Mrs Howard. I accept your kind offer.'

The moment the shops were closed, Flo and Vicki rushed upstairs to begin preparing the meal for everyone. Dave and Alfie also helped by peeling potatoes and scraping carrots. The men were all enjoying a glass of something, and, to make sure Mr Denton met everyone, Sid called on Pearl and Edward on his way home. They soon arrived and joined the men in the front room.

The discussion they were having was so absorbing that they had to be practically dragged to the dining table. It was only during the meal that Vicki began to learn a little about one of her

144

strangers. Mr Denton was a lawyer of high standing who lived in Richmond, Surrey. He had served in the army during the war and was doing what he could to help ex-soldiers who needed legal help.

'Many of these men are being treated badly,' he explained, 'and need someone to fight for them. Many are still roaming the streets, lost and confused.'

Vicki nodded. 'I believe there were quite a few in the old warehouse I used.'

'Really? Would you show me where that is the next time I come to London? I might be able to get them proper accommodation.'

'I'd be pleased to.'

'Good, good. Now—' he turned his attention back to Harry – 'write down everyone you have contacted so far and I'll see if I can speed things up for you.'

'We would appreciate that very much, but you must tell us what your fees are first.'

Mr Denton waved his hand dismissively. 'I have seen too much suffering, Harry, and if I can help even a few, that is all the payment I need.' He glanced quickly at the boys and then back to Harry. 'And don't forget the other details we spoke about. I'll sort that matter out once and for all.'

'Give me a few minutes after dinner and you'll have all the information you need.'

Their guest then smiled at Bob and Flo. 'I thank you for your kind hospitality and the excellent meal. It has been an enlightening evening, and one it has been a pleasure to share with you all.'

'It has been a joy to meet the man who gave our girl the help she so desperately needed,' Bob told him. 'If you had just walked past her that day, she would never have been able to come to us. And for that we will be eternally grateful.'

'I couldn't ignore her. There was something that told me she was worth saving. And it heartens me to see I was right.'

Fifteen

A week had passed since Charles Denton had walked into the shop, and Vicki could still hardly believe it. Against all the odds, she had found one of her strangers, and she was so happy.

The men had been closeted together for a long time that evening, and she longed to know what they had been discussing, but Harry hadn't said a word. There was, however, more of a spring in his step, indicating that whatever had been said was good news for him. From the little said during dinner that evening, it seemed that Mr Denton was willing to help with any legal matters that arose from trying to set up the school. Not only had she found the man who had helped her at the railway station, but he was a lawyer with a desire to help those in need. It was nothing short of a miracle.

Vicki sang softly to herself as she checked that everything was ready before opening the shop.

She had found a home with people who cared for her and friends she could trust, she was learning the skill of hairdressing that would serve her well in the future, and she had even had the good fortune to find one of her strangers. If she could only find Bill now, then her happiness would be complete. Harry had asked to borrow the book again so she would take it to him this evening. She hadn't pressed to know if he had discovered anything because he had his hands full at the moment and would tell her if he found any new clues.

She unlocked the door as Flo arrived. Saturday was their busiest day of the week and two customers had already arrived, so they set to work immediately.

Dave was now working in the barber's without Harry, and his little brother was still coming with him. Although Alfie seemed happier, he still wouldn't let Dave go anywhere without him.

'Hello, Alfie,' Flo said as he walked into the shop. 'Come to help us, have you?'

He nodded.

'Good boy. We are busy today so we will need you. Get me a clean towel, please, sweetheart.' Flo winked at Vicki.

They always made sure he felt welcome and needed when he appeared. The customers liked seeing him as well, often slipping him a coin as they left. He also received his threepenny piece for his work in the shop at the end of the day.

They took a break for lunch at twelve o'clock, and Vicki was delighted when Mr Denton arrived.

'Please join us for lunch,' Flo said as soon as

he walked in. 'It's only a beef stew with home-made bread, but there's plenty for everyone.'

'Thank you; it smells delicious.'

With some shuffling round, there was just room for one more at the table, and they all enjoyed a tasty, nourishing meal.

When the plates were empty, Mr Denton sat back and sighed. 'That was delicious, Mrs Howard. How do you get the dumplings so light?'

'Years of practice. And, please, call me Flo.'

He inclined his head in agreement and then turned his attention to the boys. 'How are you getting on in the barber's, Dave?'

'All right, sir. I like it, and I try to do a good job.' He glanced hopefully at his boss.

'You are doing well, Dave, and the customers like you. Keep that up and you will be able to do a full week when you're a little older.'

'Cor, thanks, sir.'

'And what about you, young man? Do you enjoy being here?'

Alfie nodded.

'Good. Now let me see, where did I put that little present I have for you?'

Alfie watched intently as Mr Denton delved into a leather briefcase he had brought with him.

'Ah, here it is. I thought you might like this. It's identical to mine but only a foot in length, so more your size.'

The little boy's eyes opened wide when he saw the small replica of the cane, complete with a silver bulldog's head. He reached out and ran a finger over the silver head. Then little hands grasped the cane. 'Ow!'

Silence descended on the room and they watched, holding their breath as Alfie spun round to his brother. 'Look! Green eyes, too!'

Tears welled up in Dave's eyes, but he managed to smile. 'It's smashing. Thank the kind gentleman for this special gift, Alfie.'

Alfie spun back. 'T'ank you, sir.'

'My pleasure, young man. I'm pleased you like it.'

'Like it!' Alfie gave a proper smile, nodding vigorously.

'I'll make a fresh pot of tea.' Flo's voice was husky with emotion. She was struggling as much as everyone else to act normally.

Dave had quickly wiped away the moisture from his eyes, not wanting his brother to see him so emotional, and Vicki suspected that they were all doing the same – she certainly was. They had longed so much to hear the little boy begin to speak again, and, perhaps, this was the start of his recovery.

While his brother was intent on examining the replica cane, Dave was making signs to everyone in the room. He spoke in a whisper. 'Don't say nothing. Mr Harry said we was just to treat him like we always do.'

'The other reason for my visit,' Mr Denton said, ignoring the tension vibrating through the room, 'is to ask Vicki if she will take me to the warehouse she slept in?'

'Yes, of course. When would you like to go?'

'This evening, if you don't mind? After you close the salon. I'll be at Harry's.'

She smiled and nodded. 'I'll come there just after six.'

'Perfect. Thank you, Vicki.'

'Time for our next customers.' Flo stood up. 'We'll clear up later, Vicki.'

They hurried down to the shop in time to open as the ladies began to arrive.

The afternoon passed quickly, as it always did when they were busy. They had just said goodbye to their last customers when Dave tumbled into the shop, a broad grin on his face.

'We're closing now, Mrs Howard. You ain't washed up yet, so I can stay and help if you want? Then I can walk back to Mr Harry's with Vicki.'

'Thank you, Dave, we'll be glad of your help. Where's Alfie? We haven't seen him this afternoon.'

Dave was almost dancing with excitement. 'He went with sir after lunch.'

'What?' Vicki and Flo spoke at the same time.

'That's right. Ain't it good? He spoke for the first time, and when sir said he was going to Mr Harry's, Alfie went with him, happy as you like. It's bloody marvellous!' Dave clapped a hand over his mouth. 'Oops, sorry.'

'We'll forgive you this time,' Flo told him, trying not to smile. 'We are all thrilled that Alfie is making progress at last.'

'Terrific, ain't it?' The boy laughed out loud. 'I'll nip upstairs and start clearing up for you.'

An hour later, Vicki and Dave arrived at Harry's. 'Sorry I'm a bit late, Mr Denton, but we helped Flo first.' Vicki handed her book to Harry. 'You asked to see this again.'

'Ah, thank you.' He put it on his desk. 'I'll do a bit more investigating in my spare time.'

'I don't think you are going to get much of that,' she laughed.

'Where's Alfie?' Dave asked.

'In the kitchen, helping Pearl with the dinner. He's only said a couple of words, but that is hugely encouraging. He has been silent for so long it will take him time to start stringing a sentence together, so don't push him, Dave.'

'I won't. I knows what you told me.'

'You *know*,' Harry corrected.

'Sorry.' Dave pulled a face. 'I got so excited today and forgot my lessons.'

As the boy headed for the kitchen, Vicki smiled at the men in the room. 'It was wonderful to see the change in Alfie today.'

'Yes, and it was that beautiful gift Charles gave him. It appears to have helped by unlocking something inside him.'

'It did. That was very thoughtful of you, Mr Denton.' But he wasn't listening to Vicki. He was standing by the desk and turning the book over and over in his hands, studying it intently.

'Is this the book you brought with you?' he asked Vicki.

'Yes, that's the one I was given by the man we are trying to trace. I told you about him.'

'If I'm not mistaken, this is the crest of the Ashington family.'

'That's correct, Charles,' Harry said eagerly. 'Do you know anything about them?'

'Only that they had an estate not far from mine, but I've only ever met one of the family, and that was during the war. He had a small Bible in this colour leather with the same embossed crest on it.'

'Oh, what was his name? Was it Bill or William?'

'No, it was James, Vicki.' He looked at her face, full of hope, and shook his head. 'He was killed, I'm sorry to say. We only met briefly, but he was a good officer. I remember the Bible because it was among his belongings. I wrote to his family and sent everything to them.'

'Where to?' Harry asked.

'To their family estate. However, when I returned home, I discovered that they had moved. I don't know where, Harry, but I'll give you the address of the people who own it now. They might know where they went.' Mr Denton gave Vicki a sympathetic smile. 'I don't think your man is anything to do with that family.'

'Maybe not,' she agreed, 'but every clue must be looked into, however unlikely. We don't have anything else.'

'That's true, but don't dismiss this information. When the new owners moved to the estate, they may have inherited the library, and Bill might have something to do with that family. You never know, he might have worked on the estate.'

'I never thought of that.' Vicki pursed her lips as she considered that, and then shook her head. 'That doesn't fit him somehow.'

'It's a long shot, I know, but, as you said, it's all we've got.'

When the men began discussing some legal issues they were dealing with, Vicki left them and went to the kitchen to see if Pearl needed any help. Her hope of finding Bill had risen for a while, only to be dashed again. The one thing they had to go on was the book, and that might be leading them in the wrong direction. Their only hope was that they would stumble across some clue to set them on the right path.

Sixteen

Harry and Edward were spending most of their time with Charles. They were in the throes of a legal battle about the school and, she suspected, guardianship of the boys, as Harry was insistent that everything must be done legally.

On Sunday she went to Harry's to spend some time with Pearl and the boys, hoping to hear some news about how things were going. Alfie was making good progress now, and although he never said a great deal, he did answer when spoken to. Dave's speech was improving slowly, so Harry was obviously finding time to fit in regular lessons.

'Hello, Vicki,' Pearl greeted her with a teasing smile. 'You're just in time to help me change the beds.'

'I think you save that job for my visits,' she laughed. 'Where are the boys?'

'They're in the garden. Edward dug over a plot for them, and Alfie wants to grow pretty flowers so he can draw them. They're busy planting seeds and bulbs now.'

'That will keep them busy. Alfie doesn't come to the shop quite so much now. How has he been this week?'

'Doing quite well. I've heard him talking to Dave a lot more, but he's still frightened of anyone he doesn't know. I think there's still a lingering fear that those people will come for him again.'

'Do you think he will ever make a full recovery, or will he always be damaged by his experiences?'

'Hard to tell at this point, but he has a brother who loves him, and that is a great blessing. Also, he's young, and we hope that time will gradually heal the mental wounds. He's getting help now.'

'Yes, thank goodness. Do you know how the men are getting on?' Vicki asked, changing the subject.

'They've got a real fight on their hands.' Pearl shook her head. 'I don't know the details, but I gather from Edward that having Charles with them is helping. He did say that they wouldn't stand much of a chance without him.'

'What does that mean? Chance to set up the school, or keep the boys?'

'Both.'

'Oh dear.' Vicki chewed her bottom lip anxiously.

'Don't look so worried, my dear. Charles is quite confident they will win in the end, and solutions will be found. Ah, here they come,' Pearl announced when she heard the front door close.

'Isn't Mr Denton with you?' Vicki asked as soon as Harry and Edward arrived.

'He's had to go back early today.' Harry sat down and smiled at Pearl. 'He said to tell you he's sorry to miss one of your excellent meals.'

'It must be something important to make him leave. He's become quite a regular visitor for Sunday lunch.'

'It is important,' Edward told his wife. 'We've hit a brick wall regarding the school, but Charles has found a way around the objections.'

'Are you going to tell us?' Pearl eyed the men suspiciously. 'You are both looking in a better mood. Or is that just the beer you've been enjoying in the pub?'

'Please tell us what is happening,' Vicki pleaded. 'I'm so worried about the boys. Are they safe?'

'The boys were our first priority, and Charles has made a good case for us. The terrible way they have been treated is being looked into. In the meantime, it has been agreed that they can stay with us, with the prospect of making us the legal guardians.' Edward kissed his wife's cheek. 'Looks as if we might have acquired two more children.'

'Good. That's a relief, but what about the school?'

'Sit down, both of you,' Harry ordered, 'and I'll tell you what Charles has suggested.'

Pearl and Vicki sat down and waited anxiously for the news.

'The authorities have declared that this house is unsuitable for what we have planned, and no amount of arguing and even pleading has made them change their mind. Charles has a large house on his estate which is empty, and he has offered it to us. There is plenty of land around it and

155

even a stable block. He'll give us some ponies so the children can learn to ride.'

Vicki was so astonished she was unable to speak, but Pearl managed to stutter. 'Harry . . . Harry! We'll never be able to afford to pay the rent on a place like that!'

'It's all free.'

'What?'

Edward was smiling and nodding. 'That's right. There are ten bedrooms and a separate wing for us. From the sound of it, we should be able to have a football pitch and room for many other activities, but we will have to wait to see exactly what the situation is.'

'How can Mr Denton afford to be so generous?' Vicki gasped. 'And how large is this estate?'

'Enormous, by the sound of it.' Harry laughed at Vicki's expression. 'Oh, and, by the way, his title is Sir Charles Denton, but he has insisted that we all call him Charles, and that includes you, Vicki.'

'Sir? Oh, why didn't he tell me when I addressed him as Mr Denton?'

'He said he only uses his title for his work as a lawyer. Anyway,' Harry continued, 'we've all got to go to his estate to inspect the premises. It's in the New Forest area.'

'I thought he lived in Richmond.'

'He does most of the time. He has a house there because it's close to London.'

Pearl stood up. 'I don't know about you, but I need a strong cup of tea. This is all hard to take in.'

'Good idea,' Harry said, turning to Vicki. 'Can

you get tomorrow off? While we're down there, we can go and see the family who bought the Ashington estate. Charles said he will let them know we will be calling.'

'I'm sure I can. Bob and Flo are as keen as us to try to find Bill. I'll bring the book with me just in case they want to see it.'

'All right, but don't get your hopes up too much. It will most likely be another dead end.'

'I know, Harry, but I can't help being a little hopeful. Finding one of my strangers has turned out to be wonderful for all of us, and to be able to trace Bill would make me so happy. There was something about him – I don't know what it was, but I feel he's special.' She gave a self-conscious laugh. 'Such silly thoughts when I only met him once.'

'Not at all silly,' Edward told her. 'You must have been very frightened after you were thrown out of your home, and suddenly here was this well-spoken man treating you calmly and with understanding. That must have been like a healing balm to you.'

'Yes, it was. You used the word "calmly" – and that is exactly the thing I remember the most about him.'

'Let's hope we can find him, then, because I'd really like to meet this man.'

'I'd like you to as well,' she said wistfully.

The Howards were as delighted as everyone else about the news, and, at Harry's suggestion, they closed the shops for the day so they could come as well.

The next morning, they set out for the station in high spirits. The boys were especially excited about going on a train to the country, and Vicki had a job controlling them at first. However, one stern word from Harry and they quietened down a little, but the broad smiles remained firmly in place. No one minded them being boisterous, though, because it was a joy to see Alfie so animated.

The travel arrangements had been left to Harry as he knew where they were going. Vicki paid little attention to the journey as she was occupied with the boys and thoughts of what the day might bring. It was hard to control her feelings, but she knew Harry was right and she mustn't hope for too much. She opened her bag and looked at the book, just to make sure she hadn't left it behind. This was the best clue they'd had so far, and it was wonderful to feel they were doing something that might lead somewhere.

Eventually, Harry said, 'This is as far as we go by train. Everyone out, and watch your step.'

'Are we there?' Dave wanted to know when they were standing on the platform.

'Not yet. Charles said he would have cars waiting outside to take us the rest of the way.'

'Cor!' Alfie's eyes opened wide. 'We riding in a car now?'

'Yes, young man. It's an exciting day, isn't it?' Harry teased. 'Why don't you and Dave run outside and see if they are there?'

And run they did, making everyone laugh when they heard shouts of glee.

'I guess that means the cars are waiting for us,' Bob remarked.

'My goodness!' Flo gasped, staring at the two large vehicles and smartly dressed chauffeurs.

One of the chauffeurs stepped forward. 'We have instructions to take you to the estate of Sir Charles Denton. The journey will take about an hour.'

The chauffeur held the door open for them. Bob, Flo and Pearl went in one car, and Harry, Vicki and the boys in the other. Only ever used to London, Vicki was enthralled by the beauty of the countryside they were driving through.

'Look!' Dave squealed. 'Horses, and they're just walking anywhere. Why isn't anyone with them, Mr Harry? Are they lost?'

'This is the New Forest and they are allowed to roam free.'

'Cor, what do you think of that, Alfie? Don't see nothing like that in London, do we?'

Alfie smiled. 'Nice.'

Harry winked at Vicki, and she knew exactly what he meant. Although Alfie was beginning to talk a little, a genuine smile was still a rare thing to see.

'Nervous?' Harry asked her quietly.

Taking a deep breath, she nodded.

'So am I. I can't believe this is happening. When Charles stopped that day to help you, I bet you never thought it would turn out to be a blessing for so many of us. I do believe two special men came into your life at that terrible time. We must, somehow, find the other one.'

'Yes, I want to so much. I've never forgotten

159

the kindness of both of them. They could have just ignored me, but they didn't. They stopped to talk and encourage a young girl in desperate straits. I very quickly discovered that that was very rare.'

The rest of the journey was silent as they enjoyed the lovely scenery and the novelty of riding in a motor car. Even the boys were quiet, with their noses glued to the windows, not wanting to miss a thing.

When they drove through large iron gates, Vicki gasped in wonder. In front of them was a mansion, and the long drive leading to it was lined with mature oak trees.

'We going there?' Dave whispered, making urgent signs towards the impressive building.

'Yes, that's where Sir Charles lives,' Harry told them. 'Now, I'm sure I don't have to tell you because you are both very well-behaved children, but don't touch anything unless given permission to do so. There will probably be a lot of valuable items in there.'

Dave shook his head vigorously. 'We'll be ever so good, won't we, Alfie?'

'Always good.'

Harry smiled at the little boy. 'Yes, you are, Alfie. And you know Charles, so there's no need to be frightened. We will also be going to see another house we might be living in soon. Do you think you would like that?'

'Lots of green grass. Nice.'

'What about you, Dave? Would you like to live in the country?'

'Cor, not 'arf! It's smashing here.'

160

They pulled up outside the front doors, and as soon as they came to a stop Charles walked out to greet them.

'Welcome,' he said as they scrambled out of the cars, shaking hands with everyone. 'You must be hungry and thirsty after your journey. Cook has prepared a snack for you. Follow me.'

The entrance hall was enormous. Vicki had only ever seen pictures of places like this. Both boys were also just as stunned and wide-eyed as they spun round and round in wonder.

'Bloody hell!' Dave exclaimed, and immediately began apologizing. 'Sorry, sir, sorry, Mr Harry, but I ain't seen nothing like this before.'

The corners of Charles mouth twitched as he controlled a laugh. Turning it into a gentle smile, he looked at Alfie. 'I see you've brought your cane with you, young man.'

'He don't go nowhere without it,' Dave told him. 'He even sleeps with it in his bed at night so no one can pinch it.'

Alfie ran his fingers over the dog's head and smiled up at Charles. 'I like it.'

'That pleases me.' Charles took hold of the little boy's hand. 'Come into the library and see what cook has prepared for you to eat. You must be hungry after that exciting journey on the train.'

Alfie nodded, trotting along with the man he now believed wouldn't hurt him. 'And car.'

The library was huge, with books lining the walls almost to the ceiling. The carpet was like walking on springy grass, and the dark green colour in the pattern matched the sumptuous leather chairs. Beside the marble fireplace was a long table laden with food, and Vicki smiled to herself. Charles's idea of a snack was more like a feast, and the boys obviously thought so as well because they ran over to the table and just stared in wonder at the array of delicacies.

'This is beautiful,' Vicki sighed as she gazed around, taking in every detail of the room.

'It's my favourite room. Now, help yourselves to the food. Cook will be upset if you don't eat it all up.' Charles began explaining what everything was to the boys so they could make a choice.

Once they had all decided what to have and were comfortably sitting down, Charles said, 'We have a busy day ahead of us, and I suggest we inspect the house you can have as a school first. Then back here for lunch, and then the boys can explore the house if they want to. I have made arrangements for Harry and Vicki to visit Mr and Mrs Harmond. I have taken the liberty of explaining why you want to talk to them, and it seems they knew the Ashington family well. Their children used to play together. As they knew the estate so well, when it came up for sale they bought it for themselves and gave their own property to their son. They are looking forward to meeting you.'

'That's good news, Charles,' Harry said, looking at Vicki. 'That means they could well have some useful information for us. A glimmer of hope, Vicki.'

Seventeen

'Oh,' Harry gasped when he stood in front of the large house. 'This would be perfect for the school.'

'You haven't seen inside yet. It has been neglected and will take work to make it suitable. You tell me what you need and I'll instruct the workmen to start straight away. I'll be pleased to see the place in good repair again and being put to such splendid use.'

'Could we have a bit of land for a sports field?' Edward asked.

'How about down to that tree line? Would that be enough?'

'That's far too much,' Harry protested, gazing into the distance at the wooded area. 'We can't take the house and so much of your land.'

'Of course you can. The estate has a hundred acres. Some of it is parkland, and the rest put over to crops and cattle. This section here is not being used for anything.'

Vicki couldn't believe what she was hearing and began to study the surroundings. The house in front of them was nowhere near as large as the mansion, but it was substantial, and she could see that it would make a perfect school. The land around it was clear and would need very little work to make it into a sports field, with ample room for anything else they wanted to do. The wooded area was in the distance, and over to the right of that she could just see the movement of animals grazing. She was finding it difficult to grasp that one man could own so much space.

There was a muffled sound of a horse approaching, and a man rode up, dismounted and came over to them.

'This is my estate manager, Jim Baker,' Charles introduced.

He smiled and shook their hands. 'Sir Charles has told me what you are planning; it will be good to see the place come to life again.'

'Can we fence off the area up to the tree line, Jim, and make the stables habitable for ponies?'

'Yes, sir. I've already got men working on the stables. They haven't been used for a long time and are in a bit of a mess. Do I have your permission to employ men from the village to erect the fence, sir?'

'Go ahead, but ex-soldiers only, if you can. We must give them employment. Any with injuries can be given whatever tasks they can manage.'

'Understood, sir.'

'And see if you can find two men who know about horses. Tell them the jobs will be permanent.'

'I have just the men in mind. They are both finding it hard to get jobs because of war injuries, but they will be quite capable of the work at the stables. I'll go and see them at once.'

'Perfect. I'll leave everything to you then, Jim. Consult with Harry to see if he needs anything we haven't thought of so far.'

'My pleasure, sir.'

As the estate manager walked back to his horse, Vicki noticed that he had a pronounced limp, and her respect for Charles rose even higher. He was clearly wealthy, but there was no doubt he cared about others less fortunate, like the men who had fought in the war and who were still having a bad time. And a starving girl begging at a railway station. His generosity didn't end there. He was now helping to set up a school for abused children – how they would love it here with all this space! It would give them a chance to grow and develop – a chance they would never have in the slums of London.

'Now that's settled, let's go inside and decide what work needs to be done.'

Harry looked agitated as Charles ushered them into the house. 'You've instructed Jim to employ two men for the stables, Charles. How much will that cost?'

'Don't worry about that. I have been making plans for the school to be financed by private donations. The staff won't cost the school anything.'

'How on earth as you going to manage that?' Harry was now stunned.

'I have many wealthy friends.' Charles slapped Harry on the back, smiling broadly. 'And, contrary to general belief, many of us do care about the plight of the poor, and especially the children.'

'You are doing so much for us, and we don't know yet if we will get permission to set up a school here.'

'No problem. I've already seen to that.'

'Do you mean it has been agreed already?' Now Edward was astounded by this news.

'Of course, and I have it in writing. As soon as the house is ready, you can move down here. And I don't believe it will be long before the children start to arrive. They will be coming mostly from London, but there could be some from this area as well.'

'My goodness, Charles!' Pearl exclaimed. 'You have been busy. How have you managed all of this so quickly?'

'Can't waste time when the need is great. I do use my status and influence when it is necessary.' He smiled at Vicki and the two boys. 'Mustn't delay.'

The next hour was spent making a thorough inspection of the house and deciding on necessary alterations. From past experience, Harry and Edward knew exactly what was needed, and when they were satisfied that every detail had been covered, they returned to the mansion for lunch.

'What a smashing place,' Dave said to Vicki on the way back. 'We really gonna live there?'

'Yes, once all the work is done. Do you think you'll like it?'

'Not 'arf! All those fields to run around in, and Mr Harry said we'll have ponies to ride. Alfie's excited about that.'

'Did he tell you he was?'

'Nope, but I know because I heard him ask Sir what colour they would be.'

'Did he?'

Dave nodded. 'He likes Sir. He told me. See,

166

he's walking with him, quite happy. Never thought he'd do that after the way those brutes treated him.'

'He's making good progress now, and I'm sure living in this lovely place will really help him.'

'Bound to, 'cause it's miles away from those buggers in London. He'll feel safe then.'

'Language, Dave.'

'Sorry, but when I think of them, I needs to swear. Do you feel like that about the way you was treated?'

'I did at first, but not any more. I think people who act like that are very unhappy.'

'Why do they do it, then?'

'I wish I knew, Dave. It's a complete mystery to me why some people need to hurt others weaker than themselves.'

'You're right.' Dave was nodding. 'It's a mystery, all right. But do you know, there are an awful lot of nice people around as well. Like all of you. I was damned lucky you came by that day and found me.'

'And we feel lucky to have found you and Alfie.'

'Cor.' His smile couldn't have been any brighter. 'No one's ever wanted us before, 'cept Dad. He was smashing – used to play with us and everything – but Mum never cared. When Dad was killed in the war, she couldn't wait to get rid of us. Did your mum want you?'

'No, Dave. My parents wanted a son, not a daughter.'

'Ah, that ain't right, is it?'

'No, it isn't. But that's in the past for all of us

167

now, so we can forget it and look forward to a happy future.'

'You bet. I like talking to you, Vicki, because you know what things are like. Ah, we're back. Must keep my eye on Alfie now and see he don't get frightened about being in such a huge place with strange people walking around in there. Sir's got lots of servants, ain't he?'

Vicki watched him rush to his young brother's side and couldn't help thinking that he was very mature for his age. He was also a sensible boy and thought deeply about things. An enquiring mind was surprising in a child with so little education. Harry was going to have a responsive pupil there, and it would be interesting to see him in a few years' time.

The dining room was decorated in a beautiful pale peach colour, and the long table shone so much you could see your face in it. When they were all seated, Vicki noticed that Dave was studying the array of cutlery with a puzzled expression. And she had to admit that she didn't know what some of the items were for.

Alfie was on her right and Dave next to his brother, so she leant across and spoke quietly. 'Dave, just watch Sir Charles and copy what he uses each time.'

'Do you know what it's all for?' he whispered.

She shook her head, making him grin.

Charles stood up. 'There will be a varied selection of food, and I want you to choose whatever you like. And, boys, if you don't fancy anything you are offered, then tell my butler what you would like and he will get it for you.'

Dave smiled and nodded.

During the meal Vicki tried things she's never had before, such as smoked salmon, which she found very pleasant, and something called beef Wellington. She thought it was strange to put a lovely joint of beef in pastry, but she was enjoying the experience of tasting quite different food.

Flo was sitting next to Dave and she helped him, while Vicki looked after Alfie. They both struggled with some of the cutlery, but, with a little help, they did quite well. They also seemed to be enjoying the food and tried everything that was put in front of them. And they both behaved so well that she was proud of them.

'Well done,' she praised them as they retired to the sitting room where tea, coffee and soft drinks were waiting for them.

'Harry, my driver will be outside when you and Vicki are ready, and he'll take you to the Harmonds'.'

'Thank you.' Knowing Vicki was anxious about this visit, Harry stood up. 'Shall we go now, Vicki?'

She finished the last of her coffee, trying to appear calm, but she was bracing herself for disappointment, knowing full well that this could be another dead end.

'Good luck,' Edward said, as they prepared to leave.

'Luck has nothing to do with it,' Pearl said. 'If it is meant to be, then Vicki will find Bill.'

'And if it isn't meant to be?' Bob queried.

'Then no amount of searching will find him.' Pearl smiled at Vicki. 'But that won't happen

169

– you'll see. As I've already told you, something will happen to set you on the right path.'

'Pearl,' Harry admonished, 'we are just going to talk to the people who bought the house the book originally came from.'

'I know. Enjoy your visit.'

Harry laughed. 'You never change, Pearl. Always the optimist. Come on, Vicki, let's go and see another beautiful house. Have you got the book with you?'

She patted her handbag. 'In here.'

It was only a short drive to the Harmonds', and Vicki thought they could have walked it. She couldn't help being nervous and, as the butler escorted them to the library, she said to Harry, 'I'm going to leave the talking to you.'

He smiled down at her but said nothing.

Mr and Mrs Harmond greeted them warmly, and the lady of the house offered them refreshments.

'Thank you, Mrs Harmond, but we have just had a rather large meal.'

'Please sit down,' Mr Harmond told them. 'Sir Charles has told us a little about your desire to see us, and we would be interested to hear more.'

Vicki chose a chair close to a beautiful grand piano, and Harry sat next to her.

'It is very kind of you to see us,' Harry began. 'We are trying to trace a man who helped Vicki when she was homeless.'

'That much we know, but what makes you think we can help you?'

Harry explained about the book, took it from Vicki and handed it to them. 'Yes, that's the

Ashington crest, but we don't have any of the books here. They took them when they moved.' Mrs Harmond gave the book back to Vicki.

'Can you tell us if they had a son called William?'

'They only had one son, James, and sadly he was killed in the war.'

'He was their only child.' Mr Harmond shook his head. 'Terrible loss. Our son was devastated by his death. They grew up together, and James attended Harrow at the same time. We were lucky – our son came home, but so many didn't. Peter lost his best friends.'

When Mr Harmond began talking about the boys, Vicki's attention wandered, and she began to look at the array of photographs on top of the piano. They were obviously family photographs, many of them of children laughing happily at the camera, and she wondered how many of them were alive now after that awful conflict.

Suddenly, one caught her attention and she stood up to take a closer look. It was of a group of youngsters around twelve years old, she guessed. Waiting until Mr Harmond had finished what he was saying, she then asked, 'Mrs Harmond, may I pick up this photograph?'

'Of course.' She came over and stood beside Vicki. 'The boy in the middle is our son Peter; James is next to him.'

'Who is this boy?' She pointed to one of the group.

'That's another friend, Henry Manton, but we all called him Will, because he liked that more than Henry.'

Harry had now joined them to study the picture. 'What is it, Vicki? Does he look familiar?'

'Yes, he does,' she said, staring at the image.

'Oh, he can't be the one you are looking for,' Mr Harmond told her. 'He was also killed in the war. It was so upsetting for Peter to lose both of his friends, and he still misses them very much. Will was at Harrow as well, and had a fine mind. He had just started his teaching career and could have gone far in life. That war was such a waste of young lives. From what we heard, Will was serving with James, and they died in the same week.'

Vicki was shaking her head. This boy was Bill; she was sure of it. There was something about the way he was leaning against the fence, feet crossed at the ankles. Exactly the same way he had been when she came out of that warehouse washroom.

'He didn't die,' she said softly. 'That's Bill.'

'How can you be sure?' Harry wanted to know. 'That's only a young boy in the photograph. He was a grown man when you met him.'

'It's the way he's leaning on the fence and the amused expression on his face. That's exactly the way I remember him, and he's taller than the other boys. It's him, Harry! The reports of his death must be wrong.'

'I admit there was a lot of confusion at the time.' Harry didn't look convinced, though.

'Could you tell us where we can find the Manton family, Mr Harmond?'

'I'm sorry, young lady, but we lost track of them when they moved out of the area. Our son told us that James and Will had been killed, and he wouldn't have said that if there had been any doubt.' Mr Harmond turned to his wife. 'We should have a picture of the boys when they went into the army for Vicki to see.'

'There's bound to be one in the albums.' She removed two large books from the shelf, handing one to her husband and opening the other herself.

As they turned the pages, Vicki waited in anticipation. She was fairly certain that the young Will was indeed Bill, but a picture of him when he was older would help to confirm his identity.

After what seemed an age, Mr Harmond exclaimed, 'Ah, here he is! Have a look at this, Vicki.'

When she saw the photograph of the young officer, her eyes misted with tears and she wiped them away quickly. 'That's Bill. You have been given the wrong information. He survived the war.'

'You have no doubt that this is the man who gave you the book?'

'No doubt at all, Mr Harmond.'

'We must tell Peter!'

'Hold on, my dear. From what we've just been told, it was some time ago and he was living rough. Peter was shattered by the reports of their deaths, so it wouldn't be wise to raise his hopes yet.'

Mrs Harmond sighed. 'No, you are right, of course, my dear.'

'What are you going to do now?' Mr Harmond asked Harry.

'Try to find out the truth about this. You are

wise not to say anything to your son at this point. All Vicki knows is that he was moving on, and he could be anywhere. Tracking him down could take time.'

'Providing he is still alive, of course.' Mr Harmond gave Vicki a sympathetic smile. 'I'm sorry if I sound as if I doubt you, but we only have your word that he is still alive.'

'I understand that, but I know it's him and I will do everything I can to find him.'

'With no guarantee that you will be successful,' Mr Harmond declared. 'I would ask a favour. If you do find him, we would be grateful to be told where he is – and what condition he is in. He might need help. So many of the poor devils still do.'

'We promise to contact you the moment we have any news.'

'Thank you.' Mr Harmond's lips firmed in a grim line. 'He grew into a fine man, and it makes me angry to think that he could be out there somewhere struggling to overcome lingering problems.'

Mrs Harmond removed the photograph from the album and handed it to Vicki. 'You take this. Will obviously means a lot to you.'

'He does, and thank you. I will return it to you when I've been able to give the book back to Bill.'

'Let's pray that you are right and that day will come soon.'

Eighteen

'How did you get on?' everyone wanted to know when they arrived back from the Harmonds'.

'It was an interesting and fruitful visit, wasn't it, Vicki? Show them the photograph.'

'That's Bill,' she told them, without the slightest hint of doubt.

The photograph was passed round. When it reached Charles, he studied it carefully. 'That's Manton! You must be mistaken, Vicki. He was killed. I was there and he couldn't possibly have survived. The barrage was so fierce we couldn't get to them for hours, and I was told that they were all dead.'

'Did they recover all the bodies?' Harry asked.

'As far as I know. They were all listed as killed, so they must have done.'

'Then they made a mistake.' Vicki was adamant. 'I'm absolutely certain that's the man I met at the old warehouse. Do you know where his family live?'

Charles shook his head. 'Sorry. I didn't deal with the paperwork for Manton.'

'Did you know him well?'

'We only met a couple of times, Harry, but I liked him. He was a damned fine officer. I could make some enquiries with the military. They should be able to give us more information.'

'An address, if possible. Even if his family are no longer there, it would be a starting point.'

'Leave it with me. I'll see what I can do.'

Vicki slipped the photograph carefully in the book and put it safely in her handbag. Now they must wait and see if the army could provide something to help. She was content. It had been a good day. She now knew his name and had learnt more about him, and she even had a picture of him. They had taken a step forward, and she was hopeful that the chance of finding him had increased.

'Where are the boys?' Harry asked.

Charles gave a quiet rumbling laugh. 'Upstairs, sleeping in a four-poster bed. By the time they'd had a tour of the stables and house, they were tired. When they saw the large bed, they were fascinated, so I said they could have an afternoon nap in it. They are still up there. One of the maids is keeping an eye on them in case they wake and don't know where they are.'

That amused Vicki. 'I bet they couldn't wait to get in it.'

'They couldn't,' Pearl told her. 'They both had the biggest smiles on their faces I have ever seen. But the bed is so huge I hope we can find them in it.'

'Oh, this I've got to see. Come on, Vicki.' Harry stood up. 'We won't wake them up. Which room, Charles?'

'Top of the stairs, turn left and it's the third door along on the right.'

Harry and Vicki found the room. The maid was sitting outside, with the door open just a crack. 'Are they still asleep?' Vicki whispered.

'Not a peep from them.'

Opening the door cautiously, Vicki and Harry doubled over with laughter at the sight. The boys were awake and propped up against lace pillows. They grinned at them as they walked into the room.

'You look comfortable,' Harry said.

'Have you ever seen such a bed?' Dave wiggled around. 'It's ever so soft – it's like sleeping on air. Come and try it, Vicki.'

She ran over and jumped on the bed, making the boys squeal in delight. They both began to hit her with the pillows until the three of them were rolling around shouting with delight.

'I like this place,' Alfie giggled. 'Can we stay here, Mr Harry?'

'We will be moving into the house we saw this morning when it's all fixed up,' Harry told them, sitting on the edge of the bed. 'Did you like that?'

He nodded enthusiastically. 'We saw horses, so can we have horses as well?'

'Yes, and you can learn to ride them.'

'Cor . . .' His eyes opened wide. 'When can we move there?'

'In about three weeks.' Charles walked into the room. 'Pearl and Edward will need to be here to oversee the work, so would you like to stay as well? You can sleep in that bed. Unless you want to go back to London, of course.'

'No, no! Never want to go back there!' Alfie declared. 'Nice here. Nice people here.'

'Then that's decided. Is that all right with you, Harry?'

'That will be fine, and thank you, Charles.'

'The invitation to stay includes you as well.

177

You will also need to be on site a lot of the time. I know you will have to go back to London and sort things out there. I will send a van to collect your belongings, and you can return with it.'

'That would be a great help. I can then close up the house until I decide what to do with it.'

'Good, good. It will be nice to have the house spring into life again, and the staff will enjoy that. It has been quiet for too long. Now, who wants tea and cakes?'

'We do!'

Charles lifted Alfie off the bed. 'I thought you might. Come on, young man, let's beat your brother to the food.'

Harry looked at Vicki and nodded as Dave raced down the stairs, trying to beat Charles and Alfie. 'Our young lad is making more progress than I dared hope when we first saw him, and I'd say we can thank Charles for that.'

'Having that replica stick made for him was the turning point, wasn't it?'

'Yes, Charles is a good man, and we are so pleased you met him.'

'He appears to have a talent for turning lives around,' she said.

'There's no doubt about that, and perhaps we are helping him. His wife died after only two years of marriage and he doesn't have any close family.'

'Oh, that's sad.'

The journey back to London that evening seemed strange with only four out of the eight sitting in the carriage.

'We are going to miss you and the boys, Harry,' Bob said. 'We've got used to having you around.'

'You'll have to come and visit often.' Harry ran a hand through his still-abundant hair. 'Everything has happened so fast I can hardly believe it. To be offered such a fantastic place to start the school is beyond my wildest dreams. I keep thinking I'll wake up and none of this will be true.'

Flo laughed. 'You'll soon come back to reality when the children start arriving. Charles is very enthusiastic about having a school on his property, and it wouldn't surprise me if he's already demanding that the authorities send you youngsters straight away. He's clearly a man who likes things done, and done quickly.'

Harry nodded in agreement.

'You're going to need more teachers, Harry. Three of you can't run a place of that size on your own. Your original plans were more modest, but once Charles stepped in things changed.'

'You're right.' He grinned at Flo. 'It will be too much for the three of us, especially at our age, eh?'

'I didn't say that!' she protested.

'Of course you didn't. You're far too well brought up.'

She punched his arm, laughing, and then slipped into the London accent. 'The way I was brought up ain't got nuffin' to do with it, mate. I'd 'ave told you straight you're too old for this lark.'

'Ouch!' Harry raised his eyes to the roof of the carriage and grimaced. 'Have you been taking lessons from Dave?'

'Vicki, mostly. She can slip back into her old accent when she wants to tease us.'

'Thank heavens for Bill,' Harry muttered with feeling, watching a broad smile of mischief cross Vicki's face. 'I've got to shake that man's hand one day.'

The atmosphere in the carriage turned serious, and Flo asked, 'Are you absolutely certain the man in that photograph is the one you met, Vicki? That was a traumatic time for you, and you might be mistaken.'

Vicki pursed her lips. 'I know what you are saying, but when I saw that picture the recognition was instant. I didn't have to look and wonder; I knew it was him. I did tell myself I could be making a mistake when everyone kept telling me he had died in the war, but that didn't last long.'

'Well, there's only one way to find out for sure, isn't there?'

Vicki nodded. 'I'm hoping Charles and his army connections can help. All we can do is wait and see if they turn up anything useful. So, what are you going to do about more teachers, Harry?' she asked, changing the subject.

'I know one who might be persuaded to join us. His name is John Steadman, and he's an excellent teacher with experience of working in some of the most difficult schools in London. He's just the kind we need, and you'll be pleased to know that he's only in his early thirties. I'll see him as soon as we get back to London.'

'You'll also need help packing the things you want to take with you,' Flo pointed out. 'We'll

180

all pitch in with that. When did Charles say he was sending the van?'

'The day after tomorrow. It will be mostly clothes; anything else can wait until we know what is needed.'

'Even so,' Bob exclaimed, 'we'll have to get a move on. Charles isn't wasting any time again.'

'Now, why doesn't that surprise us?' Flo remarked drily.

By the time the van arrived, they had all the essentials ready. It was loaded and Harry locked up the house, leaving a key with Bob so he and Flo could keep an eye on the place for him.

'It's going to be quieter without Harry and the boys around,' Bob said as the van drove away. 'I will miss them around the shop. However, it was too good an offer for Harry to turn down, and the boys will be happy down there.'

'Especially Alfie,' Vicki said as they walked back home. 'He'll feel safe away from London, and once the school is ready we can visit. I've asked Harry to write and let us know how things are going. I hope he does.'

'I expect Charles will let us know. His work brings him to London regularly.'

Vicki had been spending every spare moment at Harry's since Dave and Alfie had moved in, and she missed them. It was now nearly two weeks, and, apart from a brief note from Harry saying that they were all well, they had no idea how the work was progressing.

'I know they will be very busy and probably

don't want visitors yet, but I'm tempted to go down there tomorrow,' Vicki told Flo as they shut the shop.

'Give it another week and then we'll all go,' Bob told them. 'They should be nearly finished by then.'

She nodded agreement just as Sid strolled into the salon with a huge smile on his face.

'Get your glad rags on, Vicki. You're coming dancing with me tonight. And it's no good you protesting. I am not taking no for an answer.'

'Sid! I've told you time and time again that I can't dance.'

'Then it's time you learnt. Come on, Vicki, there's a big dance at the town hall tonight. You'll enjoy it.'

She gave him a suspicious look. 'What about the crowd you usually go with? What's happened to them?'

'They are still going. You'll like them, too.'

'I can't come. I haven't got the right kind of frock.'

'Yes, you have,' Flo told her. 'Do you remember that lovely frock you wouldn't let me buy for you? Well, I went back the next day and bought it anyway. It's been in my wardrobe just waiting for an occasion like this.'

'Aha!' Sid grinned. 'You can't possibly refuse now. Can she, Flo?'

'I can't think of one reason.'

Vicki sighed, knowing she was trapped. The three people smiling at her cared, and she knew that her isolation from any kind of social life troubled them. She owed them so much, and if going to a dance with Sid would make them happy, then it would have to be endured.

'All right, but just this once.'

'Get the frock out, Flo.' Sid spun Vicki round and round. 'I'll go home and get changed, then come back for you at seven o'clock.'

The dance hall was crowded and so noisy that Vicki wanted to turn around and go back to her lovely peaceful room. She couldn't do that after all the trouble they had gone to. Her hair had been washed and styled, the frock pressed while she'd had a bath, and Bob and Flo had been so pleased.

'It's all right, Vicki.' Sid took her arm as she hesitated. 'I know you've never been to anything like this before, so I'll stay with you all the time. You look beautiful – I'll have to fight off the men trying to get to you.'

That thought horrified her. 'I do hope you're joking, Sid!'

He glanced at her shocked expression. 'Ah, sorry, that was the wrong thing to say. Most girls would take that as a compliment.'

'I'm not like most girls.'

'I know that what you have been through has made you cautious, but you can trust me.' He smiled and patted her hand. 'I won't let anything unpleasant happen to you. Bob and Flo would never have allowed me to bring you if they had any doubts, would they?'

She shook her head.

'Right, then, put a smile on your face and let's enjoy the evening. They are playing a waltz, and that's an easy dance for you to start with.'

Sid was very patient as he taught her the steps, and she concentrated very hard, not wanting to make a fool of herself in front of this huge crowd. They all seemed so good, and so was Sid. He led her quite expertly into the steps.

She began to relax as much as she could, although it made her nervous to be surrounded by so many people. Once or twice during the dance, a sense of panic tried to overwhelm her, but she fought it off. From a young age, she had been left to look after herself and, not making friends easily, she had led a rather solitary life. The isolation and loneliness had been even worse when her dad had thrown her out of the house. The time spent in that awful warehouse had been purgatory. Her life had changed dramatically when the Howards had given her a home and their love, but the scars remained. Perhaps she was like Alfie in some ways. He had stopped talking; she had shut herself off from people, except the few she had come to love and trust. Why had she never realized that before?

The dance came to an end, and she managed to smile at Sid. 'I didn't step on your toes too much, did I?'

'Not once! You're as light as a feather on your feet. Come and meet my friends.'

There were eight of them, and the names were just a blur to her, but two of the girls were customers at the shop, so she did know them.

During the evening, although she was asked to dance by quite a few young men, she would only dance with Sid, and for most of the evening she

184

was content to sit and watch the antics of the dancers in bemusement. They all appeared to be having fun, but all that jumping around was not for her. She did, however, quite enjoy the slow ballroom dances with Sid, and by the end of the evening was fairly competent at them.

Bob and Flo were waiting up when Sid returned her home, wanting to hear all about the evening.

'Vicki will become a good dancer when she's had more practice,' Sid told them. 'She has a lovely sense of rhythm and timing. Next time, I'll get her doing the Charleston.'

Oh no, you won't, she thought while keeping a smile on her face. There wouldn't be a next time if she could avoid it.

Nineteen

Much to Vicki's relief, there was no question about going dancing again because Harry arrived on Saturday afternoon.

'How are things going?' she asked, eager for news.

'Very well.' His grin was infectious. 'The school is ready and we moved in there two days ago. The boys are happy and thriving in the country air. And they've got some company now because we've been sent two more youngsters. Charles has certainly moved quickly.'

'That's wonderful!' Bob told him. 'When can

we see it? We're having a job to keep Vicki from jumping on a train to visit you, and I must admit we are all missing you and the boys.'

'You can come back with me tomorrow if you like. I've definitely got another teacher – John Steadman – and he's coming at the end of next week. Once I've collected a few things from the house, we can catch an early train. If you closed the shop on Monday, you could stay the night.'

'Don't see why not – Monday is always a slow day. What about you, Flo?'

'We've only got two bookings for a trim, and they are regular customers. We'll pop round and ask if they mind changing their appointments. I don't see any problem there.'

'I don't think they will mind,' Vicki said, checking the appointment book. 'It would be lovely to stay overnight. How is Alfie now he's away from London?'

'There is a huge improvement in him. He knows he's miles away from the people who treated him so cruelly, and he feels safe at last. Dave asked me to bring you back with me. They both want to see you.'

'I do miss them as well, but I'm relieved to hear they are happy.'

'We all are.' He grinned again. 'This is a dream come true. Now I must see John and tell him he can come as early as he likes because everything is ready with the staff accommodation. We are going to need him because it looks as if Charles is determined to scour the countryside for children needing our help.'

* * *

The sound of children shouting and laughing could be heard as they approached the house, and the cause of the noise was a boisterous game of football going on. Edward was having a rough time in goal as the youngsters were determined to get the ball in the back of the net by fair means or foul.

'That's cheating!' Bob laughed as two of the boys jumped on Edward and held him down while another boy kicked the ball in the net. 'Don't they know the rules, Harry?'

'Where they come from, it's every man for himself, and we encourage them to let off steam out here. It helps to get rid of a bit of aggression, which is something many of them suffer from at the moment.' Harry put a whistle to his lips and blew hard.

The assault on Edward stopped and the boys spun round and stared for a moment, then there was a shriek as Dave and Alfie hurtled towards them. The other boys, laughing, helped Edward to his feet.

Vicki was nearly knocked over in the excited rush.

'You've come!' Dave was spinning from one person to the next in an effort to greet them all at once. 'We've got such a lot to show you!'

'Introduce everyone to your friends first,' Harry told them, 'and then we can all have a cup of tea together. Vicki and Mr and Mrs Howard are staying overnight, so there will be plenty of time to show them around.'

'Oh, goody.' Alfie beamed with pleasure and chased after his brother who was already pulling the other three boys towards them.

'I thought you only had two more pupils so far, Harry.'

'The tallest one arrived yesterday, Vicki. He isn't too sure of us at the moment. We need him to open up and start talking to us because he has problems locked up inside him.'

Edward had dusted himself off and now greeted them, slightly out of breath, his usual good humour shining in his eyes.

'This is Jack.' Dave pulled the new boy forward, and then the other two. 'This is Ron, and Sam is the same age as Alfie.'

'We are pleased to meet you.' Flo smiled. 'That was a good game you were playing, but you didn't give the goalie much of a chance.'

'He don't play fair, neither.' Ron smirked as he looked up at Edward.

Alfie was holding on to Vicki's arm, and she was thrilled to see the difference in him. The haunted look had left his eyes, and he was much more relaxed.

Jack was eyeing her with curiosity. 'You that girl Dave told us about? The one who's old man chucked her out?'

'That's right, Jack. I'm Vicki.'

'Blimey! You look and sound proper posh.'

'I was lucky and found people who cared about me. I took the chance they gave me to make a better life for myself. Now the same thing has happened to you, you will be able to do the same.'

'Hmm. Perhaps.'

'You will, but it will be up to you.'

Jack pursed his lips and smirked, as if it was

a huge joke. 'What you fink, Ron? Reckon we can get posh too?'

'Well,' Ron pointed towards the house, 'we're living in a posh place, ain't we? Guess that's a start.'

Pearl came out to meet them, all smiles. 'Welcome to our school. Tea and biscuits are waiting for you in the school dining room. That includes all of you,' she told the boys.

During this tea break they were able to get to know the other boys a little better, and then they ran out to play again, eager to be away from the older people. Dave and Alfie stayed with them as Pearl proudly showed them the rooms. Alfie followed Vicki everywhere, and once she had seen where she would be sleeping, he tugged her arm.

'Show you Gypsy.'

'And who is Gypsy?

'My friend.' The little boy caught her hand impatiently. 'You'll like her.'

'Well, lead the way, then.'

He was so eager to get to his friend that Vicki had to practically run to keep up with him. He made straight for the kitchen, and jumped up and down in front of Pearl.

'I bet I know what you want, young man.' Pearl winked at Vicki and then opened the door leading to a large cupboard.

'One for Vicki, too, please!'

'Of course.' Pearl handed them both a carrot.

It was only then that it dawned on Vicki what the boy was talking about. 'Have you got the ponies already?'

'They arrived two days ago,' Pearl told her. 'Alfie fell in love with Gypsy the moment he saw her.'

'I'm gonna ride her! She'll let me because she likes me.' He spun on his heels and shot through the back door.

'My goodness, that's the most I've ever heard him say.' Vicki ran after him.

When she arrived at the stables, she saw that Alfie was talking to a young man in his twenties, she guessed. When he moved, it was noticeable that he favoured his left leg and was obviously one of the ex-soldiers Charles was helping. There was also a scar down his cheek, but it didn't detract from his good looks as he smiled down at Alfie.

The little boy spun round when he heard her coming. 'This is Fred, and he looks after the ponies.'

'I'm pleased to meet you, Fred. I'm Vicki.'

'And it's nice to meet you, miss. I've heard a lot about you from young Alfie.'

'Have you still got the carrot, Vicki?'

She held it up and Alfie beamed at Fred. 'Can we see Gypsy now, please?'

Fred laid a hand gently on top of Alfie's head to stop him jumping about in excitement. 'Quietly now. You remember what I told you?'

The boy nodded, then turned to Vicki and put his fingers to his lips. 'Mustn't frighten her.'

'I understand,' she said softly.

Fred led them to a stall and began speaking quietly to the animal until she put her head over the partition and eyed them.

'Ah, she's beautiful, Alfie.'

He nodded, gazing at the pony in rapture.

'She said that carrot looks tasty,' Fred told him, scooping the boy up so he was level with Gypsy's face.

Vicki could hardly believe her eyes as Alfie gave the pony his gift and then let her push her face against his. His little hands rubbed her nose, showing no sign of fear.

Fred put Alfie down again and then told Vicki to give the animal the other carrot.

The pony took it quickly and watched them as they walked away. 'Thank you, Fred.'

'My pleasure, miss.'

'When are you going to start the riding lessons?' she asked.

'In a couple of days when the animals have settled in and all the tack has arrived, miss.'

Alfie was looking up at them, puzzled. 'Why'd you call her that? Her name's Vicki.'

'He's being polite,' Vicki explained to the boy, and then smiled at Fred. 'I would rather you addressed me as Vicki.'

He responded with a slight bow of his head. 'As you wish, Vicki.'

Satisfied with that, Alfie took off at speed for the house, and she had to run to catch up.

Later that evening when the children were in bed, Vicki asked Harry if Charles had said anything about his army search for information about Bill.

'We've hardly seen him. He's been working in London on a difficult case, so I don't suppose he's had much time, Vicki.'

'Oh.' Vicki sighed, disappointed. 'When we saw the photograph and were told his name, my hopes did rise, but now I'm not so sure we will ever find him.'

✓ 'I did warn you in the beginning that we might not succeed,' Harry reminded her gently. 'You've found Charles, though – isn't that enough?'

'No, it isn't.' Her eyes were troubled when she looked at him. 'I don't know why, but for some reason he haunts me.' She shook her head. 'That isn't the right word . . . I'm worried about him, and I need to know he's all right.'

'Can you explain why you feel like that?'

'I don't know why.' She gave a slightly embarrassed smile. 'This all sounds silly, doesn't it? I only met him for a couple of hours, and then he walked away, but the feeling that I must find him again some day has never left me. Somehow it's important. I have more in life now than I could ever have dreamed of, and there is only this one thing nagging at me – this need to find Bill. It won't leave me.'

Harry studied her thoughtfully. 'Did you fall in love with him?'

'Of course not! I was fourteen years old, and he was old enough to be my father. It wasn't anything like that.' She raised her hands in exasperation. 'I can't explain why I can't let this go.'

'All right, Vicki. Don't get upset. I'm just trying to understand, that's all. Charles might be back now, so why don't you go and talk to him in the morning? You say Manton is the man you are looking for, so everything now rests on whether

192

Charles has been able to trace him or not. At the moment, I've done all I can.'

She smiled at hm. 'You've been very kind to spend time on this when you are so busy, and I'm very grateful. I'll see Charles, as you suggest.'

Harry stood up. 'Now, my dear, you must get some sleep. You are going to need plenty of energy tomorrow because the boys will run you ragged. They haven't shown you everything yet.'

'There's more?'

Harry chuckled. 'Lots.'

'Ah, in that case, I will go to bed. Goodnight, Harry.'

'Goodnight, Vicki.'

It was a clear and bright spring morning when Vicki wandered outside. It was early, and the only one up was Pearl, already working in the kitchen preparing breakfast. When Vicki had offered to help, Pearl had waved her away, so she had left the house to drink in the tranquillity of the countryside. It was a beautiful sight. Vast open space was not something she was used to. She had visited the London parks, of course, but they could not compare with this. As far as the eyes could see were various shades of green. She let the quiet and peace wash over her.

'Peaceful, isn't it?'

Startled, she spun round. 'Oh, I didn't hear you coming, Charles.'

'I arrived about an hour ago and have been talking to Fred. There will be two more ponies arriving tomorrow.'

'That will please the boys. Alfie has already chosen one for himself.'

'So I have been told.' Charles slipped Vicki's hand through his arm. 'Walk with me. We need to talk.'

As they strolled slowly along, Vicki took a deep breath and then asked, 'Have you some news about Bill?'

'I have, but it isn't good, I'm afraid. According to army records, Manton died in France.'

'No!'

He patted her hand. 'I know you are adamant that he is the man you met, but I'm sorry, Vicki, you must be mistaken. Everyone we've met has said the same thing, and now the army has confirmed it. Manton can't be your man.'

She stopped walking and turned to face him. 'I am not the one who is mistaken, Charles. The army records must be wrong.'

'I know that it was hard to keep accurate records in the confusion of battle, and mistakes could have been made, but in this case I doubt it.'

'Well, I am not ready to accept that, and I will continue to follow this lead. Did you manage to get his home address?'

'I thought you'd ask for that.' He handed her a sheet of paper. 'The information you want is there.'

'Thank you very much for taking the time to contact the army. You are a busy man and I'm grateful for your help.' She slipped the paper into her pocket.

'It wasn't any trouble. I only wish it had been better news. What are you going to do now?'

'Visit the address you have given me and try to discover, once and for all, why everyone thinks he died in the war.'

Twenty

They arrived back home late on the Monday evening having spent a lovely time in the country. The new school was impressive, and Harry, Pearl and Edward were looking forward to receiving more pupils. But this was going to be more than a school; its other purpose would be to give the troubled children the chance of a better life. Dave and Alfie would always stay with Pearl and Edward as family, but the others would be helped to move on when they were old enough to support themselves. Harry was determined that not one of the pupils would be abandoned. This meant that more staff would have to be found who were young enough to carry on the work in the future.

Vicki hadn't even glanced at the paper Charles had given her, but now she was alone in her room she took it out of her pocket. There was more information than she had expected.

Record found dated July 1916
Henry William Manton – Captain.
Age: 24. Height: 6 feet 2 inches.
Hair: Light brown. Eyes: Green
Home address: The Dale House, Harrogate,
Yorkshire.

The description definitely fitted Bill, but his home would cause her a problem. Yorkshire was a long way to go, and the address was somewhat vague. She was used to houses being numbered and with street names.

Knowing Bob and Flo were still up, Vicki went upstairs. They might be able to help her with this.

'Hello, my dear. Would you like a cup of cocoa?'

'Yes, please,' she said as she sat down. 'Charles told me that the army records show that a Captain Manton was killed in France. He gave me this.'

Bob took the paper from her, and his wife looked over his shoulder.

'The description fits Bill perfectly, and I would like to visit his home, but the address doesn't have a street name or house number. How would it be possible to find it?'

'Hmm.' Bob frowned as he studied the information. 'I don't think this is an ordinary house, Vicki. It could be an estate. Charles's place is just called High Meadows.'

'Of course! I never thought of that. Everyone knows where High Meadows is, so I'll just need to ask for directions to The Dale House.'

'You're not thinking of going there, are you?' Flo looked concerned.

'I must. It's the only way to clear this up. If there's the slightest chance Captain Manton isn't the man I met at the warehouse, then I've got to find out. Having said that, I am still positive this man is Bill. I've got enough money saved up for the fare.'

'You can't go on your own, Vicki. You will

need at least three days – two for travelling, and one to visit The Dale House. Neither of us can close the shops for that long.'

'Bob's right, my dear. I would gladly come with you, but it just isn't possible.' Flo sat down, frowning. 'I thought you said he was old enough to be your father.'

'I suppose he seemed older to a fourteen-year-old. When I met him, he must have been around twenty-eight.'

'His experiences could have made him look older.' Flo studied the paper again. 'I can see you are determined to do this, and we understand your reasons, but who can we find to go with you?'

'I'll be all right on my own.'

'I'm sure you would, but we would be happier to know you had someone with you. I wish Harry was here.' Bob smiled at Vicki. 'But we know nothing will stop you, so when do you intend to go?'

Vicki shrugged. 'There are a couple of things to consider first. I'll have to choose a time when we are not booked solid in the shop. Then I'll want to find out which train to catch, and I don't know how to do that. If it's a large estate like High Meadows, then Harrogate might not be the nearest station. I do miss not being able to run to Harry with problems like this.'

'Why not write to him and explain? I'm sure he'll be able to get you the information you need.'

'Yes, that's the best thing to do.' Vicki finished her cocoa and stood up. 'Thank you for listening to me, and not telling me I'm being silly.'

'My dear, you are never silly.' Flo kissed her cheek. 'Don't stay up too late writing letters.'

'I won't. Goodnight, sleep well.'

They listened to Vicki going down the stairs, and when they heard the click of her door, Bob turned to his wife. 'We must also write to Harry. I don't want her to have to face this alone. Not because I think she isn't capable of doing this on her own – there's no problem there – but she could be in for a terrible disappointment, and it would be better if she had someone with her. Also, another worrying point is that the Mantons believe their son is dead, and if she goes in there telling them he is alive, they will be distressed and perhaps even angry. After all, it is only her word; she has no proof.'

'I agree. Despite all the reports that Manton was killed, she is still convinced that he is her Bill. Harry might be able to find the time to go with her if we tell him what she is planning.' Flo took a deep breath. 'I had hoped that in time our girl would forget about her past, but that hasn't happened, has it?'

'I think that was too much to hope for, my dear. When she came to us, she was obviously in desperate trouble. However, we can have no idea what she went through mentally and physically from day to day. She has told us the facts, but all that private suffering is still locked inside her. Two strangers who reached out to her with kindness during that traumatic time dominate her thoughts. One of them she has found, but I honestly don't think she will rest until the other one is found, too.'

Flo nodded. 'Bill – the one who seems to be most important to her. That part of her past needs to be dealt with, don't you think?'

'It looks that way, and if she can do that, then she might, finally, be able to move on with her life. I tell you one thing, though; I hope she does find him because I'd love to meet him. There must be something about him to make her so obsessed about this search. I guess that whatever happened in that brief meeting sustained her with a determination to stay alive.'

'I agree, and that is why we must give her all the help and support she needs, Bob. Let's write that letter to Harry and see if we can persuade him to go with Vicki to Yorkshire. If he can't, then perhaps Edward or Pearl could spare the time.'

'I'd be happier if Harry went. He has been with this search from the start, and I believe he understands what's driving her more than the others.' He reached for the notepaper and pen. 'Now, just how persuasive can we get?'

It was a week before a letter arrived from Harry telling them he had heard from Vicki and would be coming to see them. Bob and Flo were heartened when Harry wrote at the end of his letter that they were right and Vicki must not go to Yorkshire on her own.

'That's a relief.' Bob nodded. 'He could be coming to take her himself.'

'Let's hope so. Vicki's restless, Bob, and if she has to wait much longer, I think she will just go and try to find this place by herself. When does Harry say he will be here?'

Bob looked at the date on the letter. 'He hopes to arrive some time tomorrow. Where's Vicki now?'

'Downstairs, doing the accounts.'

'Right. I'll pop down and tell her Harry's coming. That will please her.'

Much to Bob's surprise when he walked into the shop, Harry was already there talking to Vicki. 'When did you arrive, Harry? We only received your letter a couple of hours ago.'

He smiled as he shook hands with Bob. 'I could have brought it with me, then. I've only been here for about ten minutes. I saw Vicki in the shop so I came to see her first.'

'Harry says everything is going well at the school so he can take a couple of days off.' Vicki smiled happily. 'He's going to help me find this house in Yorkshire and wants to leave tomorrow. Will it be all right for me to take the time off?'

'Of course it will, Vicki. You take all the time you need, and we hope it will be a successful visit. But you must promise me one thing. If you are fortunate enough to find Bill, then we want to meet him.'

'That's a promise.'

Harry gave a slight shake of his head as if to say there wasn't much hope of that happening. They changed the subject and talked about the boys and the school for a while, and then Vicki went to her room to get ready for the journey the next day.

'You think this trip will end in disappointment, Harry?' Bob asked as they walked up to see Flo.

'I'm afraid so, but I hope for her sake that I'm

wrong. Vicki's going to be more than disappointed, and that's why I'm going with her. She really believes Manton is her stranger, and if it leads nowhere – as I believe it will – then she is going to need someone with her who understands how much this means to her.'

They explained all this to Flo, and she sighed, clearly worried. 'Perhaps after this she will give up and accept that he cannot be found.'

'I wish I could believe that, but that's unlikely to happen. Isn't it, Harry?'

'I don't believe she will ever stop searching, Bob. Kindness was something she had seen very little of in her life, and she has been driven to find two men who took the trouble to help her. And her quest won't be complete until she finds both of them. But it's more than that. I have the feeling she's worried about Bill. I don't know why; when she talks about him, he comes across as a very calm and composed man quite able to look after himself. He wasn't short of money either and was obviously capable of working to support himself.'

'That's also our impression, but there must be something she isn't telling us.'

'I'm certain there is a great deal she hasn't told us about that time.'

'Take good care of her, Harry.'

'I'll do that, Flo. I'm as fond of that girl as you are.' Harry stood up. 'Don't worry. Vicki has had a lot of grief to deal with in her life, and she knows how to handle it. If this isn't Bill, she will be dreadfully upset, but she's a sensible girl and will cope.'

'And come back even more determined,' Bob said wryly.

'Absolutely.' Harry headed for the door. 'I'll be here tomorrow at seven o'clock so we can catch the eight o'clock train.'

'Ah, that will give you time to join us for breakfast.'

'That's very kind of you, Flo.' Harry grinned at them before disappearing down the stairs.

They were at the station in good time, and Vicki went straight up to the ticket office. When Harry tried to pay, she waved him away. 'I'm paying for our train fare. I've got enough saved up for this trip, and I insist. You are leaving the school to come with me, and I know it is time you can ill afford to lose. I won't have you using your money for this.'

Seeing the determined tilt of her head, he decided not to argue.

With the tickets safely in her handbag, they walked on to the platform. 'I'm really grateful you can come with me. Especially as you believe I am wrong and this will only be a waste of time.'

'Yes, I do think you are wrong, but I also know this is something you have to get out of the way.'

'Exactly! If Captain Manton isn't Bill, then I've got to get off this path and on to the right one.'

Harry studied her intently. 'Are you beginning to have doubts?'

'I admit that many things point to the fact that I could be mistaken.' She pursed her lips and then shook her head. 'But, deep down, something is telling me I'm right. This is the man I'm looking for.'

'Here's our train. Let's go and clear up this mystery, once and for all, Vicki.'

Twenty-One

Harrogate was a busy place and Vicki gazed around, enjoying the sights and sounds. She had never been so far away from London before and it was exciting. Smiling up at Harry as they walked along, she asked, 'Where do we start?'

'First, we find somewhere to stay for the night, and then have something to eat. After that, a good night's sleep is required so we can start fresh in the morning.'

She nodded, knowing that was sensible, but she would have liked to find The Dale House straight away. However, impatience must be controlled because the weather was warm now and it had been a long journey. Harry probably needed a rest.

'Don't look so disappointed,' he laughed softly. 'You have a very expressive face and it isn't hard to guess what you are thinking. There isn't a lot of daylight left, so we can't go running around the countryside in the dark.'

'No, of course not, but we could make some enquiries this evening, couldn't we? Unless you already know where the house is.'

'I have a rough idea, but we will need someone

to give us directions. And yes, we can start asking, but not until we've had something to eat. I'm hungry.'

'Me too. Where are we going to stay? It will have to be something quite cheap, Harry, because I've got to make my money last.'

'I let you pay for the train tickets, but that is all. Bob gave me enough money for our lodgings and food.' He opened the door of a gentleman's outfitters and ushered her inside.

An assistant approached them immediately. 'Can I help you, sir?'

'We have just arrived in town and need a place to stay. I wondered if you could recommend a nice bed and breakfast.'

'Indeed I can, sir. If you turn left out of the shop, then take the first right, you will find number twenty-eight about half way along the road. Mrs Benson will make you and your daughter very comfortable. Tell her we sent you.'

'Thank you very much.' Harry shook hands with the assistant and had to practically push Vicki out of the shop.

'Why didn't you ask him if he knew where The Dale House is?'

'Because Mrs Benson will know. She's a land-lady and will know the area well.'

'Ah, I never thought of that.' Vicki sighed as they walked along. It was a blessing Harry was with her; otherwise, she would be running around in circles and getting nowhere. 'I'm so glad you came, Harry. If I'd been on my own, I wouldn't have known the right way to go about this.'

'That's what fathers are for, isn't it?' he joked.

Vicki laughed, remembering what the man in the shop had said. Harry might have thought it was funny, but she had taken it as a compliment.

'Ah, this looks like it.'

They stopped outside a large house with pristine net curtains at the windows and a brass knocker on the door that had been polished until you could see your face in it.

'Looks nice, Harry, but can we afford it?' Vicki was nervous; she had never done anything like this before.

'Only one way to find out.'

The door opened even before they had knocked, and a woman of around forty greeted them with a broad smile. Harry told her they would like two rooms for one night, possibly two.

'You're in luck, sir. I have just two rooms remaining for tonight. Come in.'

The rooms they were shown to were clean and comfortable, but Vicki doubted she would be able to sleep much that night. Her feelings were in a jumble. There was excitement to be actually doing something positive to find Bill, but she was also acutely aware that there could be disappointment at the end of this journey. Everything pointed to that possibility, but her stubborn mind refused to accept that Captain Manton was not her Bill, no matter what everyone said.

She unpacked her few belongings and sat on the bed with the photograph in her hands. She stared at it hard and long, and sighed deeply. If this wasn't the man she had met, then it was his double.

There was a rap on her open door and Harry

was standing there. 'Come on, Vicki; let's eat before we turn in. Mrs Benson has told me where to find a place that serves good food.'

Slipping the photograph back in the book and putting this safely in her handbag, she joined Harry for the short walk to the cafe. As they enjoyed a plate of excellent fish and chips, Harry told her he had the information they needed to find The Dale House.

'Oh, good. Is it far?'

'Quite a way. We will need to get two buses and then there will be a walk of about a mile, Mrs Benson said. We will leave immediately after breakfast.'

'Did you ask if she knows anything about the family?'

Harry nodded. 'She was a mine of information, but you're not going to like it, Vicki. They are a wealthy family with two children, a son and a daughter. The daughter is now married and lives in Scotland. The son, Henry, went to Harrow school and was evidently a brilliant student. He was an academic who intended one day to become a professor, but the war came and put a stop to that.' Harry paused.

Vicki braced herself. 'Go on.'

'He was killed in the war.'

Vicki let out an exasperated sound. 'Do you know, Harry, I'm getting tired of hearing that! Did he come back without telling anyone? Is he still wandering and never told his family he'd survived? I don't understand! What are you doing, Bill? Whatever it is, we've got to find him. He obviously needs help.'

'Perhaps we'll get some answers tomorrow, and if everything we've heard is confirmed by his family, then you will have to accept it, Vicki.'

'I'm not wrong,' she told him stubbornly.

There was a clear blue sky and birds were singing happily as they walked the last part of the journey, but Vicki didn't take any notice. Her mind was completely fixed on wondering what they were going to find on reaching their destination.

'Ah, this is it.' Harry pointed to a sign on a large gate.

The gate was open and they made their way along a drive lined with trees. The large house in front of them was lovely, built in the Yorkshire stone of the area.

'Be careful what you say, Vicki,' Harry warned. 'We must try not to distress Mr and Mrs Manton if we can help it.'

'I know it's unlikely we will be very welcome with this story, Harry, so I'm going to leave most of the talking to you.'

As they reached the end of the driveway, the front door opened and a middle-aged man greeted them. Vicki stifled a gasp of surprise, for standing there was an older version of Bill – or was she just seeing what she wanted to see? Harry would tell her that the mind can play strange tricks when we desire something very much.

'Hello, are you lost?'

'No, sir.' Harry introduced himself and Vicki. 'Would it be possible to see Mr and Mrs Manton?'

'May I ask the reason?'

'We are trying to trace a man who helped Vicki

when she was in a desperate situation, and our enquiries have led us here.'

'How intriguing. I'm Manton. Please come in.'

He led them into a comfortable sitting room. Mr Manton introduced them to his wife and told her why they were calling. She was an elegant woman and quite tall when she stood up, but her husband was more than six inches taller still. Vicki studied them carefully, almost afraid to breathe. There were characteristics in both of them she had seen before – she was sure of it.

'Please sit down and I'll order refreshments. You must be thirsty after your journey.'

They waited until Mrs Manton had arranged the refreshments, and it didn't take long for tea and sandwiches to arrive.

Once they had been served, Mr Manton said, 'Now, how do you think we can help you?'

'I'll let Vicki tell you. It's her story.'

She was taken aback, expecting Harry to do all the talking, but he had placed it straight on to her. 'Two years ago my father threw me out of the house and told me never to come back. I was only fourteen then. I found an abandoned warehouse to sleep in that night. I was very frightened and barricaded myself into a small room to keep safe. In the morning I found an old outhouse outside, but it was locked, and I wanted to wash. A man helped me to get it open, and then he bought me breakfast. My London accent was strong, and he gave me this to study.' Taking the book out of her handbag, she handed it to Mr Manton. 'Does it mean anything to you?'

Frowning, Mr Manton studied the cover of the

book and then flicked through a few pages. 'This is from the Ashington library, and the only one I can think of who would have this would have been a member of the family, such as the son, James. But I'm afraid he was killed in the war, and anyway James wouldn't have been carrying a book on English Grammar.'

Mrs Manton had gone very pale. 'No, dear, but Henry would. It was his subject.'

'That's impossible, Alice. I know you have never believed our son was dead, but it's been too long.'

Alarmed by the obvious distress, Vicki was on her feet instantly. 'I'm so sorry. I didn't mean to upset you, but we are following any clues, and what we've found out so far has led us here. Please forgive me. We shouldn't have come, but I want so much to find this man who helped me, and I don't know where else to look. I'm afraid I'm too stubborn to give up the search.'

'That's all right.' Mrs Manton gave a strained smile, still holding the book. 'I understand. I am also too stubborn to accept that my son died in that terrible war.'

Harry stepped in. 'During Vicki's ordeal, two men took the trouble to help her. She calls them her two strangers. One we have been successful in finding. She has always considered the book a loan and wants to be able to return it with her thanks for the kindness shown to her. The advice he gave her has been a tremendous help, as you can hear from her speech now.'

'We understand that.' Mr Manton looked grim. 'Tell us what this man looked like.'

'Tall, over six feet.' Vicki gazed into space trying to picture Bill clearly. 'His hair was light brown, and he had the most beautiful green eyes I had ever seen. When he spoke, his voice was soft – I could have listened to him talking for hours. I was wary of him at first, but there was an air of gentleness about him, and I trusted him.'

There was silence when she stopped her description. Mr and Mrs Manton were just staring at her, making her shift uncomfortably in her chair. 'I'm sorry – that wasn't very helpful, I know, but it is the way I remember him.'

'You have just described our son,' Mrs Manton whispered, a catch in her voice.

Mr Manton surged to his feet. 'Come with me, young lady!'

She gave Harry a startled glance and followed, relieved to see Harry and Mrs Manton coming as well.

The room he took them to was a study, and over the fireplace hung a large portrait. 'Is that him?'

Vicki gasped, speechless when she saw the man in the painting.

'Well?' Mr Manton demanded. 'And be very careful. Don't you dare make a mistake.'

She took a deep shuddering breath as her eyes misted over, and, wiping her hand quickly across her face, she turned to the Mantons. 'That is the man I met. That is Bill.'

'You must be sure.' Mr Manton's voice was raw with emotion.

'I'm positive.'

A cry came from his wife. 'I knew he was still alive. But where is he? Why hasn't he come home?'

When Mr Manton went to comfort his wife, Harry spoke to Vicki urgently. 'I hope you haven't made a mistake.'

'I haven't, Harry. Their son survived, and he's the man who gave me the book. I'd stake my life on it!'

He nodded. 'Then I believe you.'

'I think we all need a stiff drink, so let's go back to the sitting room. We have a lot to discuss.'

Mr Manton poured them all a generous tot of brandy and sat down, giving a ragged sigh. 'I don't know whether you have brought us good news or bad. If you really did meet our son, then where the devil is he? Or was it just a ghost you saw?'

'He was very real, I can assure you, sir. I am not prone to having hallucinations.'

'Then how can you explain this?'

'I can only tell you that I did meet the man in that portrait, and I have the book to prove it, but I'm afraid we don't know where he is. We were hoping to find him here. Did you actually receive a letter saying he had been killed in France?'

Mrs Manton wiped tears from her eyes. 'The letter said he was missing, presumed dead. If he came back from France, then why haven't we seen or heard from him?'

'It doesn't make sense.' Mr Manton paced the room, sat down again and took a large swig of the fiery liquid. 'It's too early in the day to be drinking this stuff, but, by God, I need it! I'm not calling you a liar, young lady, but I still think you are mistaken.'

'She isn't, dear,' his wife said. 'She described him perfectly, and he gave her an English grammar book to help her to improve her speech. That was the teacher in him, and he never did like the name Henry. His friends all called him Will.'

After draining his glass, Mr Manton closed his eyes for a moment, and then opened them again and looked straight at Harry. 'If our son really is alive, do you have any idea why he would be wandering around the country and sleeping rough, instead of coming home?'

'I can think of only one. I have spent my adult life teaching difficult children with a wide variety of problems, and we have in our care at the moment a young boy. He had been so cruelly treated that he stopped speaking and didn't utter a word for a long time. When someone is traumatized, it can cause many different symptoms. One is loss of memory.'

Vicki gasped at that suggestion, and so did the Mantons. She took a sip of the drink she hadn't touched before. 'He didn't seem like a man who didn't know who he was.'

'I'm only surmising, Vicki. Can you think of another reason why he hasn't even contacted his parents?'

She shook her head. 'He never spoke about himself to anyone, so I suppose it could be possible, but he appeared to be very self-confident. Not at all confused or lost.'

'Nevertheless, it is the only answer that makes sense,' Mr Manton said.

'Oh, we must find him!' Mrs Manton was having trouble keeping the tears of distress at bay. 'What can we do?'

'We will keep looking,' Harry replied, 'but it would be helpful if you contacted family and anyone who was close to him. If he is suffering from loss of memory, he might gravitate to a familiar place, even if he doesn't know why.'

'Is that possible if he doesn't remember his past?'

'I wouldn't rule anything out, Mr Manton. The mind is a strange thing, and we really don't know enough about it. He is using the name Bill, which is almost the same as the Will used by his friends, so there is obviously still something there. That's if this is the reason he hasn't contacted you,' Harry warned. 'I could be wrong.'

'I think we'll just have to work on the assumption that this is what has happened to him.' Mr Manton held out a pad and pencil to Harry. 'We will need a contact address. If we discover anything, we'll let you know, and you will do the same, please.'

'Of course.' Harry wrote on the pad. 'I'll give you Vicki's address as well as mine.'

'Thank you.' He took the pad from Harry and handed it to his wife. 'Keep that safe, my dear.'

Mrs Manton was more composed when she turned to Vicki. 'I'm so pleased to hear that our son was kind to you, and that you are taking the trouble to find him again. If you hadn't, then we would never have known that he is alive, and although it is distressing to think he is wandering around, perhaps not knowing who he is, we are grateful you came to us. What will you do now?'

'I honestly don't know, Mrs Manton. We had hoped our search would end here.'

'That's right,' Harry agreed. 'This hasn't given us the result we were hoping for, but it has answered a few questions. Everyone we've spoken to so far has told us that Vicki has made a mistake in insisting that your son is the man she met, but she has never wavered in her conviction. We won't give up. The answer is out there somewhere and we will find him. We must find him.'

Twenty-Two

They stayed one more night in Harrogate and travelled to London early the next day. Harry was anxious to get back to the school, so he continued on, not even stopping for a cup of tea. It was a subdued and worried girl who arrived home.

Bob and Flo wanted to hear all about the trip, and Vicki spent some time telling them what had happened.

'Do you think Harry is right?' Bob asked when she had finished the account of their meeting with the Mantons.

'I find it hard to believe. He didn't strike me as a man who was troubled or confused. My impression was that he was a man who knew who he was and where he was going. The Mantons were very upset, so perhaps Harry came up with that suggestion to comfort them – to give a reason why he hadn't come home.' Vicki shrugged. 'I really don't know what to think.'

'Where are you going to look now?'

Vicki raised her hands in a helpless gesture. 'I haven't any idea, and neither has Harry. We are hoping Bill's parents can unearth some clue.'

'Hmm.' Bob looked thoughtful. 'You seem to have a very clear memory of him, so go over your meeting and try to recall every detail, no matter how small. There might be something you've forgotten that could point you in the right direction.'

'I'll do that, and there is one good thing to come out of our search so far. I know a lot more about him.' Vicki stood up and yawned. 'I'll turn in now. It has been a tiring few days.'

'Good night, my dear, sleep well. And try not to worry. It will all turn out right in the end.'

Vicki laughed and kissed Flo's cheek. 'You sound just like Pearl. Goodnight.'

The next day, Vicki was back in the shop, talking and laughing with customers. She loved being a hairdresser and blessed the day she had walked into the barber's looking for work. The Howards had taken her into their home and their hearts, giving her the kind of life she could only have dreamed of. They were her family now and she loved them dearly, making sure she showed them the affection and devotion they deserved. Her circle of friends was also expanding with Harry,

215

Edward, Pearl and Charles. How she longed to add Bill to that list, but that was looking more and more unlikely. At last she knew who he was, but there was such a mystery surrounding him that he could be impossible to find. Especially if he didn't want to be found.

They were just closing up for the day when Sid wandered in. 'Hey, Vicki, want to come dancing tonight?'

'But it isn't Saturday.'

'They have dances in the week as well. They're very popular.'

'Who wants to go dancing when they have to get up for work the next day?'

Sid raised his eyebrows. 'Flo, do you keep this girl in a cage when she isn't working? She doesn't know she should be enjoying herself, and we can't let that go on. You've got to come, Vicki. I'll be back at seven for you. And I won't listen to any excuses!'

He began to walk away and then stopped, looking over his shoulder and winking. 'Pete asked me to bring you. I think he's sweet on you.'

'Then I'm definitely not coming, Sid.' She practically growled in frustration.

'Yes, you are. See you at seven.' He disappeared before she could say anything else.

'I swear I'll clout him one day! He's determined to find me a boyfriend.' When she saw Bob standing in the doorway and laughing, she said, 'Did you put him up to this?'

'Me?'

'Yes, and don't look so innocent,' she teased.

'Nothing to do with me, Vicki. It's all Sid's idea.' The broad grin was still on his face. 'If I was younger, I'd come myself. It should be fun.'

'Fun!' She grimaced. 'The place will be packed and the noise deafening.'

He laughed even more. 'Don't you let Sid hear you refer to his favourite music as noise?'

'I wouldn't dare!' A smile of defeat touched her face, and she asked Flo, 'What shall I wear for this evening of fun?'

'Ah, good, you're going.'

'Of course I am. I wouldn't want to disappoint Sid,' she told them drily. 'He's determined to teach me how to enjoy myself.'

Bob and Flo roared with laughter at her expression of disgust.

It was as Vicki had feared. Although they were early, the place was already packed, and the noise level was so high they had to shout to make themselves heard. However, it didn't worry her quite so much this time because she had known what it would be like and was prepared. In fact, she was much more relaxed, and after the upsetting trip to Harrogate this was just what was needed – music, noise and crowds of happy people. It amazed her to realize she was thinking that way.

'Come on, Vicki.' Sid pulled her on to the dance floor. 'It's a nice gentle waltz, and I thought I'd better grab the chance while Pete's trying to pluck up the courage to ask you to dance.'

She thumped him on the arm. 'Will you stop that?'

Laughing, he spun her into the dance, and after a while said, 'You've remembered the steps. I knew you would be a good dancer. You have good timing, rhythm and a natural grace in the way you move. I still can't believe you fooled us all into believing you were a boy.'

'My life depended on it, Sid.'

He nodded and gently kissed her on the top of her head. 'I know, and I'm proud to have you as my friend.'

The dance ended and he led her back to the rest of their group. Vicki remembered most of them from last time.

During the evening she danced with several of the boys, including Pete, who asked her if she would go to the pictures with him one evening. He was a nice boy and she didn't want to hurt him, so she refused as gently as she could. She was glad at that moment that Sid claimed her for a dance – a quickstep this time.

'Are you enjoying yourself?' he asked as they spun around the dance floor.

'I do believe I am.'

'That's good, and you've been doing the dances as if it's something you have been used to for a long time.'

'You're a good teacher. I haven't had to concentrate on the steps so much, and that makes it more enjoyable.'

'That's right. The music takes over and you don't have to think about it. When something is familiar, you just follow automatically.'

Vicki felt as if she had been struck by a solid object and all the breath left her body. 'Sid!'

'What?' He stopped dancing. 'Are you all right?'

Taking a deep breath, she nodded. 'You know we've been looking for Bill without success. Well, you've just given me an idea. I think I might know where he is!'

'Where?'

'I'm not saying until I've spoken to Harry. He'll know if it's possible, or if I'm completely wrong. I've got to see Harry!'

'You can't go tonight. It's too late to catch a train.'

'And we're too busy at the salon for me to take time off. I'll go on Sunday.' She smiled up at him. 'I've been going round and round in my mind, trying to imagine what he would have done, and you suddenly gave me an idea. Thanks, Sid.'

He shrugged. 'I don't know what I said, but if it has helped to make you smile like this, then I'm pleased. Come on, there isn't anything you can do tonight, so let's have another dance.'

Vicki glanced across at the group they were with and saw the pretty blonde watching them. 'You'll make Amy jealous if you spend too much time with me. Is she your girlfriend?'

'I take her out now and again, but she knows our relationship will never come to anything permanent. I've made that quite clear.'

'Are you still looking for the right girl, then?'

'No, I'm like you. I don't want to be tied down.'

She looked up in surprise. 'I really don't know much about you, apart from working together in the shop.'

'Well, let me see. I went to work for Bob when

219

I was fourteen. When the war started, I was too young, but I had to join up a year before it ended. I was shipped out to France, and that's a part of my life I try to forget. When I came back, Bob had kept the job open for me and I picked up where I'd left off at the barber's.'

'I had no idea you had been in the army.' His mouth was set in a grim line when she looked at him. Something she had never seen before. He was always laughing and joking, and she had assumed he didn't have a care in the world. Was he so protective towards her because he had also experienced suffering?

The dance ended. They were walking back to the others when she stopped. 'Why do you insist on bringing me dancing, Sid?'

'When you came to the barber's I watched your daily struggle to hide the fact that you were so weak you could hardly stand up. I was in awe of the courage and determination you showed. Now I can see that the horror you experienced has coloured your outlook on life, Vicki. You've come a long way since Flo and Bob took you in, but that time still haunts you. We can't live in the past. The only moment we have is now, and we should make the most of it. You deserve to be happy.'

'I am happy.'

'To a degree, you are, but I don't think you will be able to walk away from your past until you find your other stranger. I wish you would give up this search and move on with your life. We all do.'

She shook her head. 'I can't do that.'

'I know you can't, so hurry up and find him.' He grinned at her then. 'And I think that's enough serious talk for tonight, don't you?'

'Definitely. There's a good deal more to you than appears on the surface. You're a good man, Sid.'

'Oh, Lord,' he laughed. 'Don't tell the others that or my reputation as a carefree joker will be ruined!'

Sunday arrived and Vicki couldn't wait to talk to Harry. He might dismiss her idea as nonsense. If he did, she would be guided by him, but she couldn't help feeling that this was a possibility. The more she had thought about it, the stronger that feeling became.

She had told Bob and Flo what Sid had said to spark this idea; although they hadn't appeared convinced, they had agreed that it was worth investigating. They were coming with her so they could see the boys, and she was glad of the company during the journey.

When they reached their station, they were lucky enough to find a farmer with a large truck who was going past the estate, and he was happy to give them a lift. It was a bit of a squeeze, but they didn't mind.

There were shouts of delight when the boys saw them, and they were almost knocked off their feet by the enthusiastic greeting. Vicki could hardly believe the change in them. They now had more flesh on their bones, colour in their cheeks, and eyes shining with happiness. And she was sure they had both grown a couple of inches.

Alfie had lost that frightened look and was chattering away, just like his brother. The little boy still carried the replica stick Charles had given him, and it was stuck proudly through his belt.

Hearing the commotion, Harry appeared and strode towards them, smiling. 'What a lovely surprise. Boys, run and tell Pearl to put the kettle on as we have visitors.'

They shot off, still laughing. Flo watched them. 'What a difference in them, Harry. The country suits them. I can see quite a few children playing. How many have you got now?'

'Eight, and two more coming next week. Dave and Alfie are a treasure, helping the new arrivals to settle in. Come and have a cup of tea and I'll tell you all about it.'

Pearl and Edward were waiting for them, and the boys were busy putting out a plate of biscuits to have with their tea.

'Can we stay, Mr Harry, please?' Dave asked. 'It's ages since we've all been together. The others are playing with Mr John.'

'Of course you can stay. It's good to have the family all together again, isn't it?'

Both boys grinned happily.

'John Steadman is settling in quite well, then?' Bob asked.

'Yes, he's enjoying the challenge, but if we keep expanding at this rate, I will have to get more help. We've got room for twelve boys, and I don't believe it will be long before we reach that total. We've already been able to employ two women from the village to help in the kitchen. Pearl can't possibly do it all on her own now.'

'How on earth are you going to pay for all this?' Flo asked.

'Ah, well, we've had some luck. Charles has been championing our cause and we are receiving a grant from the council for every child we take, because they would otherwise have to be put in care. He's also persuaded some of his wealthy friends to support us financially, and most of our food comes from his farms, free of charge. He's very enthusiastic about the school and what we are trying to do here.'

'My goodness,' Vicki gasped. 'I'm glad we found him.'

Everyone laughed. 'So are we!'

'That's wonderful to hear, and we might have a bit more good news,' Bob told Harry. 'Vicki could have an idea where Bill might be found.'

'Really?' Harry turned his full attention to Vicki.

'It could be a silly idea, but I'd like your opinion.'

'Tell me.'

It took a few moments to compose her thoughts. 'I'm going on the assumption that he is suffering from loss of memory. When I met him, he said his name was Bill, and we now know that is close to the name his friends called him. Also, he told me straight away to improve my speech and gave me the book on English Grammar. He was instinctively being a teacher. When I was dancing with Sid, he complimented me on remembering the steps and said that when something is familiar we do it without thinking about it.'

'True,' Harry remarked when she paused. 'Carry on.'

'That gave me the idea. Bill had spent much of his childhood in this area, so something deep in his memory could have brought him back to a place he was familiar with.'

'You think he's here?' Edward exclaimed.

She nodded. 'Somewhere on the estate that he knew as a child and now belongs to the Harmonds.'

'But, Vicki, if he turned up at the Harmonds', they would have told us.' Pearl was clearly doubtful. 'He was also a close friend of their son, Peter.'

'It's a large estate and there could be unoccupied buildings or barns he could stay in without going near the house. He roamed that place as a child and would probably know every inch of it.'

Harry hadn't said anything; he was staring out of the window, deep in thought.

'What do you think?' she asked hesitantly. 'Is what I've just told you plausible, or is my imagination running away with me?'

He stood up quickly. 'It's a sound idea, Vicki. Come on, let's go and see the Harmonds.'

Twenty-Three

They were in luck. Not only were the Harmonds at home, but their son was also there.

After introductions, Mr Harmond asked, 'Do you have any news?'

Harry explained about the trip to Harrogate to

see the Mantons, and by the time he had finished the account, their son, Peter, was on his feet. 'You are absolutely certain that Will is alive?'

'Yes, I'm sure,' Vicki told him. 'There was no mistaking the portrait as the man I had met.'

'Oh, dear Lord!' Peter paced up and down, overcome with emotion. 'Why hasn't he been home? He loves his family, and they love him. I don't understand.'

'That is the reaction of everyone, and the only answer I can come up with is that he might be suffering from loss of memory.'

The son sat down with a thump and stared at Harry. 'That does make sense, but if that is the case, how are we going to find him? He could be anywhere!'

'You might be able to help us with that. We think he might be somewhere on this estate.' Vicki spoke urgently. 'Do you have empty buildings he could be staying in?'

'Quite a few. This is a large rambling place. But what makes you think he might be here?'

'Instinct is the only reason we can think of. It isn't much to go on, I agree, but we have to follow every avenue.'

'Vicki is right,' Mrs Harmond told her son. 'What about those two farm workers' cottages, Peter. You all used to ride your horses to that part of the estate to fish in the stream.'

'It's a possibility, and there are a couple of old barns as well.' Peter was on his feet again. 'We must go and check at once. I'll get my car because it's quite a walk.'

The barns were the nearest, but, apart from the

birds nesting in the beams, there wasn't any sign of life there. They drove next to the two cottages.

They were on a neglected part of the estate which had been allowed to grow wild, but the cottages were sturdy, built of stone, and there was a fast-running stream at the back of the properties. Vicki felt her heart rate quicken as she gazed at the location. If she had found something like this when she had been homeless, it would have seemed like paradise to her.

The first one they went in was completely empty, but the next one gave them all a shock. It was clean and sparsely furnished, with crockery and pans in the kitchen, along with a small camping stove for cooking.

'Well done, Vicki,' Harry told her as he began to examine some papers he'd found. 'This is interesting.'

'What is it?' Peter asked, coming over to have a look.

'School work being marked for young pupils. Is there a school nearby, Peter?'

'There's a school for six- to eight-year-olds in the next village, but it's at least a four-mile walk from here.'

'Well, if it is Bill and he is working there, then he could have bought himself a bicycle.'

Peter walked to the door and scanned the surrounding area. 'There's no sign of anyone, but whoever is living here could come back at any minute. We'll wait.'

'No, we should leave now,' Harry told him firmly. 'And put everything back exactly as we found it.'

'Why?' Peter demanded. 'If it's Will living here, then I want to see him!'

'I know you do, and so does Vicki, but if this man is still suffering from memory loss, as we believe, then our being here could make him run again. He is, after all, trespassing.' Harry looked at the two anxious faces staring at him. 'Whoever is here has made the place habitable and has a job. He has made a life for himself. If we barge in and start telling him who he really is, we could do a lot of harm. I'm asking you both to leave this to me.'

'I suppose you're right.' Peter sighed in frustration. 'What do you think, Vicki?'

'I'm desperate to find Bill, but Harry knows what he's doing. Hard as it is, I'm prepared to leave it to him.'

'Are you both agreed?' Harry asked. They nodded and he ushered them out of the cottage. 'Let's get out of here before we are seen.' They left the area quickly.

While driving back, Peter wanted to know, 'What are you going to do, Harry?'

'I'll go and pay the school a visit tomorrow. I know what Bill looks like, but he's never seen me before. If it is him, I'll talk to him, teacher to teacher, and that will seem quite natural to him. I'll decide what to do after I've found out if he really doesn't know who he is, or if, for some reason, he has cut himself off from everyone by choice.'

'No.' Peter was shaking his head. 'He would never do that! We grew up together and I know him. He would never hurt his family like this.'

'That terrible war has changed many men. Have you considered that the boy you've known all your life doesn't exist any more?'

'I won't accept that. What was he like when you met him, Vicki?'

'Calm, understanding, caring, but also strong. Apart from telling me his first name, he didn't say a word about himself. Not to me or the people he met regularly in the cafe.'

'You are right about him being strong, but that strength was never used in a cruel way. And it's interesting you said he was calm. Nothing ever seemed to disturb him. Whatever problems faced him, he met them head on and dealt with them without fuss or anger.'

'That's good to know, because if this is your friend, then it could be easier to help him. Providing he wants our help, of course.'

'Even if he doesn't, and it turns out he has his own reasons for staying away from his home, I still want to see him, Harry.'

'So do I,' Peter said.

'I'll do what I can, but he has a right to live his life as he pleases and we must respect that. Now, I want a solemn promise from both of you that you will not go anywhere near him until I've had a chance to talk with him.'

Peter and Vicki glanced at each other, and then nodded in agreement.

'I know this is hard for you, but be patient. I'll let you know as soon as I have any news.'

That evening, after Harry had taken Vicki and the Howards to the station in the small bus he had bought for the school, he sat at the kitchen table with Pearl and Edward.

'Do you think they will keep their promise not to approach Bill?' Pearl asked.

'Vicki has gone home, and I believe I've managed to convince Peter that it would be better for Bill if he leaves this to me.'

'You are being very cautious, Harry. What are you worried about?'

'It's just a feeling I have. Something is telling me we mustn't suddenly barge into this man's life. The war has been over for a long time now and yet he's still living rough. Is he hiding from something, Edward?'

'Maybe he's just hiding from himself.'

'If that is the case, then we must be careful. Vicki has never once said he had any injuries. When she talks about him, the impression I get is that he was fit, healthy and strong.'

'That's true,' Pearl agreed. 'So, what's your plan?'

'First, I've got to make sure it is Vicki's stranger, and to do that I will go to the junior school we think he might be working at. If it isn't him, I will walk away, tell Peter and leave him to decide what to do about someone making use of the cottage on his parents' estate. If it is him, then I'll see if I can talk to him. I am, after all, looking for another teacher.'

'Ah, that's a good idea,' Edward nodded in approval. 'It will appear quite natural for you to ask personal questions.'

Harry stood up. 'I'll do the rounds and make sure the boys are all asleep, and then turn in myself. You are on duty tonight, Edward?'

'I am. And while you're thinking of more staff, Harry, we need a matron, or someone with nursing skills to look after the boys' medical needs. We have two more youngsters arriving at the end of next week.'

'I've already thought of that, so while I'm in the village tomorrow I'll have a word with the local doctor. He might be able to recommend someone. And what do you think about a permanent night manager?'

'Now that is a good idea!' Edward grinned. 'An ex-soldier would please Charles, and John and I will get a bit more sleep.'

'Leave it with me. Looks as if I will have a busy day tomorrow.'

The children were just arriving at the village school when Harry got there. He had parked the bus on the outskirts of the village and walked the rest of the way. He mingled with the parents standing outside and waving to their children as they scampered into the playground to meet their friends. There was only one teacher outside and that was a woman. Harry was just debating whether to go and have a word with her when a tall man came out of the door and blew a whistle. As the children rushed into the school, he watched the man give a slow smile of amusement, then follow them inside.

There was no mistaking him. It was definitely Bill!

Harry stood there, unable to believe they had finally found him. Oh, everything had pointed to the possibility that this would be him; even so,

Harry had doubted Vicki's memory of someone she had met so briefly. But she had never wavered in her conviction that the man everyone said had died in the war was alive.

He took a deep breath. He had really thought he would come here today, see someone and then walk away to tell Vicki and Peter that it wasn't the man they were looking for. Or had he just hoped that would be the case? He was very fond of Vicki, and he didn't want her to be hurt. She'd had enough to deal with in her life, and he felt protective towards her. He had hoped that another disappointment would persuade her to stop searching. But her persistence had paid off, and Bill had looked healthy, without a sign of anything wrong with him.

Deep in thought, he walked towards the few shops he'd passed on his way here. He couldn't go and talk to Bill in the middle of classes, so he would have to wait until the lunch break. Meanwhile, they needed a matron, and he would see if he could find a doctor for advice.

The assistant at the greengrocer's shop pointed him in the right direction. The doctor was seeing patients, and Harry waited until the last one had left.

Dr Saunders was happy to talk to him, showing a great interest in the school. 'I've heard about this and I'm very pleased to meet you. How can I help?'

'I'm looking for someone with nursing skills to look after the children. It will be a permanent position, and they would have to live in. We have good accommodation for staff. Do you know anyone who would be interested?'

'There is someone I know would like the job. Elsie Adams was a ward sister. Since her retirement, she has been living with her daughter's family. The arrangement isn't working out, and I know she would like to move, but she doesn't know where to go. Although retired, she is a fit and sturdy woman.'

'She sounds ideal. I'd like to talk to her today, if possible. Could you give me her home address?'

'I'll do better than that.' He stood up and opened the surgery door. 'Betty, would you pop round and ask Mrs Adams if she would come and see me, please?'

While they waited, the doctor asked a lot of questions about the school and the pupils they were taking, and Harry told him how it had all come about.

'This is something badly needed. I come across cases of abuse from time to time, and it is distressing not to be able to do more. I would very much like to visit your school, if I may?'

'We would be pleased to show you around and let you meet the children.'

'Thank you. Would this evening be convenient?' he asked eagerly.

'Any time that suits you.' Harry studied the man in front of him. He was around fifty, of average height and with hair just greying at the temples. He was friendly, with a ready smile. Harry liked him. 'I'm sure you have a very busy practice, but would it be possible to engage you as our doctor so we could call on you if needed?'

'I would be delighted and honoured to help. I

will give you my home address as well as the surgery. Please call me at any time, day or night.'

They were shaking hands, both well pleased with the agreement, when the door opened and Mrs Adams looked in.

'You wanted me, Dr Saunders?'

'Yes, come in, Elsie. This gentleman wants to talk to you. I have a call to make so I'll leave you to it.' He smiled at Harry. 'I'll see you this evening, then.'

Elsie Adams was just as the doctor had described and looked very suitable for the job. He told her what he was looking for and asked her if she would be interested in the position.

'Oh, sir, I would love to look after the boys. It would be the answer to my problems at home. Living with my daughter isn't a good idea. I'm used to working, and, to be honest, I miss it dreadfully.'

'Then the job is yours. When can you move in?'

'At once, sir.'

Harry smiled at her enthusiasm. 'Dr Saunders is coming to see us this evening, so why don't you come with him? You should see what you're letting yourself in for before making a final decision.'

'I'll certainly come this evening, sir, but I can tell you now that I'll accept the position.'

'Well, if you are sure, then we will move you in tomorrow. Will that suit you?'

'Absolutely, sir.'

'Good, and my name is Harry. We only use Christian names at the school.'

'Then I'm Elsie.'

'We will be delighted and relieved to have you with us, Elsie.' Harry stood up. 'I have one more task to do today, so please excuse me. We will look forward to seeing you this evening.'

Harry walked towards the school, pleased that it had been so easy to find someone suitable – and not only that, but a doctor willing to be on call when needed. That was a good morning's work, he acknowledged, as he strode along.

Now he had to talk to Bill.

Twenty-Four

When Harry reached the junior school, the children were just streaming out of the door for their break. A teacher was in charge of the youngsters, but it wasn't Bill, so Harry went in and found the headmaster's room. The door was open and a middle-aged man was sitting behind a large desk covered in papers.

Harry rapped on the door and waited for the man to look up. 'My apologies for disturbing you, sir, but could you spare me a moment of your time?'

The man nodded. 'Come in and sit down. It's time I took a break. Are you by any chance the man who is setting up a school for abused children?'

Harry was taken aback. 'I am, but how did you know?'

234

'There has been a lot of talk amongst those of us in education, and you have been described to me in great detail. How can I help you?'

'As you have probably already heard,' Harry said drily, 'our school is growing quickly, and so is our need for qualified teachers. When I passed this morning, I saw a tall man ushering the children into the school. He seemed just the age and type I am looking for, but I expect he is a valuable member of your staff and I wouldn't approach him without your permission.'

'I would expect no less from a man of your excellent reputation. You must be talking about Bill. He's a fine man, a first-class teacher, and the children like him. I wish I could keep him, but that isn't possible. He is standing in for our permanent teacher who has had a long illness. He is fit again and we are expecting him back next week.'

'Ah, so he could be looking for work. What is his full name?'

'William Dale.'

Harry started. Dale! He was using the name of his parents' house. Now, why would he do that?

The headmaster stood up. 'If you'd like to have a word with him, he'll be in the staff room. I'll show you the way.'

'Thank you. I would indeed like to meet him.' Harry smiled. 'Looks as if I might have come just at the right time. If I can add another teacher to my staff, then I'll have done very well today.'

The man Harry and Vicki had searched for was alone in the room and stood up as soon as they entered.

'Bill, this gentleman would like to have a word with you. Take your time. I'll look after your class if necessary.' The headmaster shook hands with Harry. 'A great pleasure to have met you, and I wish you every success with your school.'

'Thank you.' As soon as he had left, Harry turned his attention to the tall man standing in front of him, and found himself looking into a pair of stunning green eyes. They were so much brighter than the portrait they had seen of him, and he could understand why Vicki remembered him so clearly. It was then he noticed the scar just showing an inch or so from his hairline. A head injury!

'Would you like a cup of tea? I've just made a fresh pot.'

'That would be welcome.' Harry sat down, watching every move Bill made to see if there were any other injuries evident. 'I've had a busy morning.'

'Why do you want to see me?' Bill handed Harry a cup of tea and then sat opposite him.

'The headmaster told me you might be looking for a job soon. I have opened a school for children who have suffered neglect or abuse, and we need another teacher. The children who come to us are troubled and need a great deal of care and understanding. The work is very rewarding, but not always easy. Would you be interested in taking on such a challenge?'

Bill sat slightly forward, his expressive eyes alive with interest. 'I would welcome the chance to do something so necessary.'

'That's good. The headmaster has given me a

glowing report of your teaching abilities, but I would like to know where you studied, and any past experience you've had. Another reference would be helpful.'

Bill sat back, his expression closed. 'Then you have wasted your time, sir. I cannot supply you with the information you require.'

'And why is that?'

After a long pause, Bill clearly came to a decision. 'No one here knows what I am about to tell you, so I must ask that you keep this to yourself.'

'You can rest assured that whatever you tell me in confidence will go no further.'

'I cannot tell you about my past because I can't remember. I believe I was injured during the war.' His hand went up to the scar. 'This goes right across my head.'

'You've lost your memory. I understand.' There was no doubt in Harry's mind that this man was telling the truth. He'd seen the disappointment on Bill's face when he thought the chance of the job had slipped away.

'I have glimpses, but they never last long and I can't seem to retain them, and I'm never sure if they are real memories or my mind playing tricks.'

'Have you seen doctors?'

Bill lifted his hands in a frustrated gesture. 'I suppose I have.'

Harry had the urge to reach out with comfort, to tell this man who he was and give him back his life and the people who loved him. But he'd had enough experience with troubled children to know it was the last thing he must do. His respect for the man sitting opposite him grew and grew. He must have a strong character to have carried this burden for so long. It was evident that he had hidden his disability in order to have some kind of a normal life, and Harry was determined to help him.

'How soon will you be able to join us?'

Caution and then hope flooded his expression. 'You would still offer me the job without references, without details of my education?'

'I don't need them. From your accent it is clear you have had an excellent education. A private one, I would say. And although you carry the frustration of loss of memory, you are dealing with it calmly and sensibly. It shows a man of sound character, and that is enough for me.'

Bill surged to his feet and shook Harry's hand. 'Thank you for giving me the chance. I won't let you down, sir.'

'I know you won't, and the name is Harry. Do you know where we are?'

'Yes, I have heard you are at the old house on Sir Charles Denton's estate. I can find it.'

'We have had signs put up now, so you won't have any difficulty. Oh, and I forgot to mention. We need our staff to live at the school. We have good accommodation, and if that is all right with you, you can move in at once. We have an old bus if you need to move your things.'

'I have very little. I will move in tomorrow, if I may?'

'Of course.' Harry stood up. 'We will be delighted to welcome you to our special school.'

'Was it him?' Edward asked, pulling the door of the bus open the moment it stopped. 'You've been a long time.'

Harry climbed out. 'Bring Pearl out here. I don't want the children to hear any of this.'

Without saying another word, Edward walked smartly to the house, reappearing almost at once with his wife.

'Don't keep us in suspense,' Pearl demanded. 'What happened? Is it Vicki's Bill?'

'Yes, it is, and we guessed correctly. He suffered a nasty head injury and has lost his memory.'

'Oh, the poor man. Did you tell him who he was?'

'No, Pearl, that would have been the wrong thing to do at this point and you know that well enough. We can't rush in and overload him with what we know. This has got to be done slowly, gently, as we did with Alfie.'

'That might be difficult once Vicki hears that you've found him. She'll be down here at once, with Peter right behind her.'

'That's why I'm not going to tell them just yet, Edward.' Harry then explained about his meeting with Bill, and the promise he'd made him. 'I'm breaking that promise by telling you, but you have to know.'

Pearl nodded. 'Do you think he'll come tomorrow?'

'I'm sure he will. The temporary teaching job he has finishes at the end of the week, and I believe he wants this job very badly. And what is just as important is that we need him. I was impressed.'

'In what way?' Edward asked.

'It's hard to put it into words, so wait until you meet him; then you will understand. The enthusiastic teacher is still there, despite his loss of memory. I'm convinced he will be a great asset here.'

'Your judgement is usually sound, Harry. But have you spent all this time with him?'

A broad smile lit up his face as he told them about the new matron and the doctor.

'That's wonderful news!' Edward declared. 'And we also have some news for you. Jim Baker brought us a man who would like the job as night manager. He's an ex-soldier who has lost an arm, but he's eager, and we believe he will suit us very nicely.'

'Wonderful. Did you employ him?'

'We did, and he starts next week. We asked him if he would like to live in or stay at his parents' home in the village. He jumped at the chance to have a room here.' Pearl gave Harry an enquiring look, her mouth turning up slightly at the corners. 'With all the new boys and extra staff moving in, could we manage to employ a girl to help with the housekeeping? George has a young sister who's looking for work.'

'Who on earth is George?'

'The night manager.'

'Oh, you didn't mention his name. Go ahead, Pearl, and, while you're at it, you also need more kitchen staff.' Harry's eyes glinted with amusement. 'Has George by any chance got a brother who is good at accounts? I'm beginning to do more administration work than teaching.'

They laughed, and Edward said, 'I'm sure he would know someone. Are you serious?'

'No, that's enough for today, but if we continue to expand at this rate, it will be something to consider in the near future. Come on, Pearl, put the kettle on – I'm gasping. And remember, not a word to anyone about Bill's condition. Let's get him here; as we come to know him, we can decide how best to help.'

'After all this time it is unlikely he will ever regain his full memory,' Edward said as they walked back to the school. 'We can't keep his family away from him for long.'

'I know that is going to be a problem, but solving problems is what we do best, isn't it?'

'Right,' Edward agreed. 'And we are getting plenty now. One of the new boys is belligerent, and two more have just withdrawn into themselves. They all react differently to the troubled lives they've had.'

Harry nodded. 'Poor little devils. But that's why they are here, and thank heavens they are. We can give them a chance in life – if they are willing to take it, of course.'

That evening, Elsie and the doctor arrived. After she had given them a tour of the school, Pearl took the new matron to view her rooms. They had set aside a bedroom with an adjoining room she could use as a private sitting room.

'Will the rooms be all right for you?' Harry asked Elsie when they returned.

'They will be perfect.' She sat down, her expression serious. 'Would it be possible to have another room down here that I could use as a surgery? A small one would do. I could then encourage the boys to come and talk to me if they have any problems.'

'An excellent idea. When you move in, we will decide on the best place, and you can tell us what you need in there.'

'Thank you, Harry.' She relaxed then, smiling. 'I can't wait to move in and meet the children.'

'We intended to get here before the boys went to bed,' Dr Saunders told them, 'but I was delayed with an emergency. I would like to come during the day to see them. If they do need a doctor, it will be less stressful for them if they already know me.'

'Come any time you are free,' Harry told him. 'Walk around and talk to the children. The more they see you, the better.'

'I'll do that.' The doctor stood up. 'Thank you for showing me around. It has been an interesting visit.'

'Do you need help moving?' Edward asked Elsie. 'I could bring the bus for your belongings and any furniture you'd like for your rooms.'

'That is kind of you. I would appreciate the help. Would tomorrow afternoon be all right?'

'Two o'clock?'

'I'll be ready.'

When their visitors had driven away, Harry turned to his friends. 'What did you think?'

'Perfect.' Pearl put the kettle on to make a fresh pot of tea. 'All we've got to do is get the matron and night porter settled in, and that leaves Bill. I do hope he turns up tomorrow.'

242

Twenty-Five

The next day was very busy. First George arrived, and it was bedlam for a while as three of his family came to help him move in. They had just left when Edward arrived with Elsie and her belongings. She had brought quite a few pieces of furniture with her and needed help to get them up the stairs.

'Phew! What a day.' Pearl joined Harry and her husband as they watched the children playing football with John to work off excess energy after their lessons.

'Look!' Edward brought their attention to someone approaching on a bicycle. 'Is that Bill, Harry?'

'That's him.' He sighed in relief. 'Thank goodness he's come.'

'Good-looking man,' Pearl remarked.

'Eyes off, and remember you're a married woman,' her husband teased. 'Besides, he's too young for you.'

'I know, but I can still look.'

Harry stepped forward as soon as Bill got off the bicycle. He shook hands, smiling warmly. 'Good to see you again, Bill. Let me introduce you to my friends and partners in this school of ours, Edward and Pearl.'

When they had shaken hands, Harry said, 'I'll introduce you to other members of the staff, and then you can have a look round before you decide if this will be for you.'

'I'm sure it will be.' Bill gave a slow smile and pointed to the package tied on the back of the bicycle. 'I've brought my things ready to move in right now, if I may?'

'You weren't joking when you said you didn't have much. Your room is ready for you, so if you have no doubts about working here, we are delighted to welcome you to the school.'

'And I'm more than delighted to be here.' Bill studied the building and the children playing in the field, then nodded. 'Yes, I'm sure I will like it here. Would you mind if I go and talk to some of the children? Who is the man they are playing with?'

'That's John. Please go ahead, but remember they are disturbed children and very wary of strangers.'

'I won't upset them.'

As Bill strode across the field, Edward murmured, 'Do you think that's a good idea, Harry? Shouldn't one of us introduce him to them first?'

'We'll wait and see what happens and step in if necessary.'

They watched him approach the boys, talking to them and clearly getting answers that made him laugh out loud.

'Wonder what he's saying?' Pearl said.

'Whatever it is, they don't seem frightened of him, which is surprising because he's a big man.'

One of the boys kicked the ball towards Bill,

and suddenly he was running around the field with them, amidst howls of protest and laughter when he kept kicking the ball in the net.

'Well,' Harry chuckled, 'I don't think there's going to be a problem there, do you?'

Edward was doubled over with laughter. 'Those youngsters can get as rough as they like with him and it won't matter. He's already helping them to get rid of some of their aggression.'

The boisterous game came to an end and Bill stayed for a while talking to the boys. Then, with a wave, he began to walk back.

Dave was sprinting towards them, skidding to a halt in front of them, out of breath. 'Who is he? Is he staying?'

'He's going to be your new teacher,' Harry told him.

'Wow!'

Bill reached them, Alfie trotting beside him. 'Lively bunch you've got here, Harry.'

Dave was gazing at him in awe. 'You're a size. How tall are you?'

'About six feet three inches.' Bill turned his head slowly to look at the small boy lurking behind him. He turned and hunkered down. 'What's your name, young man?'

'Alfie,' he said after a pause, edging slightly away.

'I'm pleased to meet you, Alfie. 'That's a lovely cane you have stuck in your belt. May I have a look at it?'

This time there was an even longer pause as the little boy tried to decide.

Bill waited, not moving from his position, until

eventually Alfie slid the cane out of his belt and handed it over.

Taking it gently, Bill examined it. 'It's beautiful. Do you know what the dog is?'

'Bulldog.' Alfie edged closer. 'It's got green eyes like Sir's big cane. Made it for me.'

'That was very kind of him.'

Alfie nodded and, with a look of relief, took the cane when Bill handed it back to him.

Pearl was delighted by the way Bill had handled the little boy, and smiled with pleasure. 'Bill, this is Dave and his brother, Alfie. They came with us from London, and we are their guardians. Would you like to see your room now? Then you can join us and the rest of the staff for a meal.'

'Thank you.' Bill untied the parcel from the bicycle and smiled at Dave and Alfie. 'Want to come with us, and you can tell me all about the school?'

After a nod from Harry, the boys hurried off with Bill and Pearl. When they were out of hearing range, Edward whistled through his teeth. 'No wonder Vicki's been so insistent on finding him. He isn't someone you could easily forget – or that deep soft voice.'

'Vicki once told me that although he was a big man she found him non-threatening. I know what she means now.'

'What are you going to do about Vicki, Peter and the Mantons, Harry?'

'I want to give him time to settle in, but know I won't be able to leave it more than a week. I'll ask Vicki to meet him first, but she must only talk about the time at the warehouse and what has happened to her since. I'll try to persuade Peter and Bill's parents to let him have a little more time. They can come here and see him, but that is all. I don't want him faced with loads of information from people he doesn't remember. That could do him more harm than good.'

'I understand your concerns, Harry, but you are going to be asking a lot of them.'

'I know.' Harry started to walk back to the school with Edward. 'The important thing is we've got him here, but there's no telling how he is going to react when he's told who these people are. We could lose him, Edward, and that is the last thing I want to happen. The school needs him – *we* need him. We must have people around us who will be willing to take over the running of the school when we are no longer able to.'

Edward nodded in agreement. 'You're thinking John and Bill might be just the men to take over the reins.'

'Exactly. We've done all we can at the moment, so let's eat.'

When Dave and Alfie had been the only pupils, they had taken all their meals with Pearl and the men, but now they joined the other boys in the school dining room. Elsie had insisted that she oversee the mealtimes, starting immediately, so she left them after she had been introduced to Bill. Relieved of that task, John Steadman joined them for dinner that evening and told Bill tales of the pupils' exploits. There was a relaxed atmosphere, which pleased Harry.

George, the new night manager, also started

work that night, leaving Edward and Harry free for the first time since the arrival of new pupils.

It was nearly midnight and everyone was in bed, but Harry couldn't sleep, so he wandered down to the kitchen. With a steaming mug of cocoa in front of him, he stared at blank sheets of paper.

'Dinner went well tonight.' Edward joined him.

'Can't you sleep, either?' Harry asked him.

'My mind is reeling all over the place.' Edward looked at the paper in front of his friend. 'Trying to write letters?'

'I can't leave the Mantons in suspense, and I want to ask them to treat Bill like a stranger when they see him, but I can't do it. He's their son, for heaven's sake! The son they thought was dead.'

'I know you want to take this slowly, and I agree it would be the correct thing to do, but we can't dictate to his family and friends what they should do. The only one who will do as you ask is Vicki. She understands and wants only what is best for this man. You've got to stand back and let them all meet, and just hope all goes well. There's a good chance Bill will handle it calmly; you never know, he might be grateful to know who he really is.'

'You're right, of course, but I was so hoping we could give him a few weeks to settle in.'

'Not possible.' Edward shook his head. 'Get Vicki down here to meet him before anyone else. She isn't anything to do with the life he can't remember, and she's a sensible girl.'

Sighing deeply, Harry ran a hand through his

hair. 'I'll write a brief note asking her to come on Sunday. I'll also write to the Mantons and Peter, explaining the situation and asking them to wait until after Sunday.'

Harry picked up the pen. 'I'll get Vicki to talk to Peter before he sees Bill.'

Edward laughed softly. 'Coward.'

'Absolutely.' He began writing and then looked up at his friend. 'Are you thinking of making some more cocoa? This could take some time.'

'It will send you to sleep and you'll never get those letters written.'

'I've decided to ask Vicki to come the Sunday after next.'

By the time the letter was finished, there was another cup of cocoa in front of him. He pushed the note towards Edward. 'What do you think?'

'I think she'll give you a piece of her mind when she gets here.'

Harry grinned. 'I'll have to risk that. I'm not telling her any more until she arrives.'

'Can I come to the station with you to collect her?'

'No.'

'Spoilsport.'

Both men drank their cocoa with broad grins on their faces.

Bill finished his temporary job on the Friday and started work at the school on Monday. He was an excellent teacher, and, although he was softly spoken, the more difficult boys soon discovered that they couldn't misbehave with him. It only took a couple of days for him to gain their respect, and by the end of the week he had them studying willingly.

Harry and Edward were delighted and earnestly hoping they would be able to keep him. With what was about to happen, however, they were by no means certain of that. It all depended on how he reacted to the news he was soon to be given. He would either run or stay, and they hoped it would be the latter.

Vicki read the letter again for the hundredth time and fumed. 'Just wait until I see Harry! How can he send me a letter like this? It's no more than a paragraph asking me to come and bring the book with me, and to wait until this Sunday. He knows how anxious I am to know if the man at that junior school is Bill, and there isn't one piece of information in this. Has he found Bill?'

'Stop pacing.' Flo took the crumpled letter out of Vicki's hands and folded it carefully. 'Our train leaves in half an hour and we'll miss it if you don't get ready.'

'Sorry. I *am* ready.' She sighed. 'He should have at least told me if he'd found him or not.'

'You'll soon know why he's being so mysterious. You know Harry never does anything without a very good reason.' Bob ushered her out of the door.

'Whatever he's found out, he's frightened to tell me,' Vicki declared as they hurried to the station. 'It is bad news, I just know it; otherwise, he would have told me if it was Bill.'

Twenty-Six

The moment they reached their destination, Vicki hurried out of the station and up to Harry who was waiting by the old bus. 'I want to know what's going on, Harry! Why did you send that short note? Couldn't you have put some explanation in it? I've had a week of worry. Have you found Bill, or not?'

'If you'll just stop talking, I will explain.' Harry greeted Bob and Flo. 'I'm glad you came. The boys have been asking when you were coming to visit again. Please get in the bus; I want to talk to you before we go to the school.'

Once they were in, Harry took Vicki's hand. 'I didn't want to put the news in a letter. We have a delicate situation and I want it handled as sensitively as possible. He's a fine man and I don't want anyone barging in with news he can't handle.'

'Oh, you've found him.' Vicki's eyes misted with tears. 'But you're frightening me, Harry. What's wrong?'

'It was Bill living in that cottage, and he's at the school now, working as one of our teachers. He's only been with us for a week, but the children like him. He's perfect for the job, and I want to keep him if possible.'

'That's understandable, Harry,' Bob told him, 'but you haven't told us what's wrong with him.'

251

'During the war he suffered a head injury, and our guess was correct: he has lost his memory. He told me he has brief flashes, but they're gone almost at once. He's using the name of William Dale.'

Vicki gasped. 'That's the name of his parents' house, and he has come back to the place where he spent his childhood. There must be a glimmer of memory there, Harry.'

'That's more by instinct than actual memory, I think, because he doesn't appear to know anything about his life before or immediately after the injury. I asked him if he'd seen any doctors, and all he said was that he must have.'

'So he doesn't even remember what happened to him in France?'

'I'm afraid not, Flo.'

'But, Harry, I didn't notice any injury when I met him.'

'His hair has grown over the scar so only a little is showing.'

'Poor man.' Bob was shaking his head. 'It must be torment not knowing who you are.'

'I agree, but he's a strong man, mentally and physically, and appears to have come to terms with his condition. He's doing his best to make a normal life for himself, but my worry is that after all this time he might not want to know what happened to him. Now, apart from Edward and Pearl, we are the only ones who know about this.'

'You haven't told his parents or Peter yet?' Vicki was astonished. 'They have a right to know, Harry.'

'I have written to Peter's parents and they are on their way to stay with Charles, and I have managed to get Peter to wait a few days. I want you to meet him first, Vicki. You are the only one who isn't connected to his past life, so I am asking you to talk to him about that and nothing else. Please don't give any indication that you know anything about him.'

'I promise not to say a word.'

'Thank you, I knew you would understand. Then all I've got to do is persuade Peter to do the same. His parents are more difficult because I have no right to ask them to hide the fact that they are his family.'

'How does he look?' Vicki asked softly.

Harry smiled. 'Impressive. I could never understand how you could remember so clearly a man you had only met once. Now I know. I like him, Vicki, and I want to help him get his life back, if possible.'

'Let's hope it *is* possible.'

Harry stood up and patted Vicki's shoulder. 'And let's hope he hasn't decided to go for a ride on his bicycle.'

Vicki was tense all the way to the school. She had found both of her strangers – the two men who had reached out to help a scruffy, homeless girl. Without them, she wouldn't be the person she was now.

They pulled up outside the house, and immediately Dave and Alfie were there, jumping up and down, delighted to see them.

Once the excited greetings were over, the boys

dragged Bob away to join them in a game of football. Vicki turned to Harry. 'Is he here?'

He turned her to face away from the school. 'See that man sitting on the fence? That's Bill. I've seen him there a couple of times and he seems to like that spot. Go and talk to him, Vicki.'

She removed the book from her bag, gave Pearl her handbag to look after, and then she walked towards the man on the fence. Her heart was racing. Would he recognize her after all this time?

He hadn't heard her footsteps on the soft ground, and she was right beside him before he turned and looked at her. She smiled. 'Hello, Bill. It's good to see you again.'

Jumping off the fence, he looked down at her and frowned.

'I don't suppose you recognize me, but I'm Vicki, the girl you helped to get into that old wash-house.' She held out the book. 'You kindly lent this to me, and I'd like to return it now. It has helped me very much.'

He continued to stare at her for a few more heartbeats, and then he nodded. 'You are right, I wouldn't have recognized you. You have done well for yourself.'

She smiled again, but he wasn't making any attempt to take the book from her. He was still frowning.

'How did you know I was here?'

'Harry is a friend of the people who took me in, and we come down here often to see Dave and Alfie. I recognized you when we arrived.'

'You must have very good eyesight,' he remarked, not looking convinced.

'I would know you anywhere, Bill,' she said softly. Something wasn't right. This wasn't going the way she had always imagined it would. 'You are engraved on my memory. I had a terrible time, and if it hadn't been for two strangers, I don't think I would be alive now.'

'Tell me about it.'

She began from the moment she had met him, to her life now, only leaving out the search for him.

'You have had a rough time and deserve to be happy.'

'I am happy. Bob and Flo treat me like a daughter, and they love me. It was a lucky day when I walked into the barber's shop looking for work.'

'I would say you've had more luck than that.' Bill gazed thoughtfully into the distance. 'The school is on Sir Charles Denton's land, and now you've found me here. Rather a coincidence, isn't it?'

Alarm shot through her at the tone of his voice. He was suspicious. 'Coincidences do happen, and I have so longed to be able to thank both of you. Now, against all the odds, I am able to do that. Please allow me to return your book with my gratitude for your kindness to a girl who had experienced little of that in her life. I will always remember that.'

Tears filled her eyes as she turned away. He wasn't pleased about seeing her, only suspicious, and it tore her apart.

'Wait!'

She stopped but didn't turn round. 'Don't

worry, Bill, I won't come here again. You needn't leave. Harry needs you.'

'You can't expect me to believe this meeting is a coincidence. Don't take me for a fool!' He swore under his breath when she didn't turn to face him. 'Do you know who I am?'

On hearing that demand, she did turn. 'You are not the man I remember, so I do not know you.'

Tears were running silently down her face when she reached the others. 'I am going home now,' she told Bob and Flo.

'Oh, my dear.' Flo put her arm around her. 'What has happened?'

'I'll tell you later. Harry, it's up to you now. He wasn't happy to see me, and he's suspicious. If I stay, you might lose him, and I know you don't want that to happen.'

'You are not leaving! Pearl, make Vicki a nice strong cup of tea while I deal with Bill. No one upsets our girl like this. She has cherished his memory all this time and I will not let him get away with this!'

Alarmed, Vicki caught Harry's arm. 'Please leave it. He's got the chance to make a life for himself here. That mustn't be taken away from him.'

'I'm sorry. If he's suspicious, then I have no choice but to tell him the truth. If he's the man I think he is, then he'll cope with it. Now, dry your eyes, Vicki; here are the boys. Dave and Alfie won't understand if you leave without spending some time with them.'

'All right, I'll stay.' She quickly wiped her face clean of tears. 'Please be careful, Harry.'

Harry watched her walk away with Pearl and the boys, and then said to Edward, 'I thought it would be a joyous reunion, but it appears that Bill is more troubled than appears on the surface. I didn't want to do it this way, but it's unavoidable now.'

'Do you want me to come with you?'

'No, thanks, Edward. This is my mess and I must deal with it.'

When Harry reached Bill, he was again perched on the fence and staring at the book in his hands. 'That's a first edition and quite a valuable book.'

Bill turned his head, and Harry was shocked at the anguish showing in his green eyes. He continued talking. 'When Vicki walked into the barber's shop, she was so thin she could hardly stand. She was starving, and much later when she showed me that book I asked her why she hadn't sold it for food. She told me she couldn't do that because it belonged to you, and one day she would return it to you. Even her desperate need for food would not make her part with it, and she has kept it safe and cherished for this day. You threw her gratitude back in her face, Bill. That was cruel, and I don't think you are a cruel man. How can I help you?'

Bill ran a finger over the crest. 'Does this belong to my family?'

'No, but you can find out for yourself. All the reference books you need are in the library. I'm not going to make this easy for you. You have family and friends who have grieved for you, believing you were killed in the war. You need

257

to start jogging your memory, but you have to *want* to remember. Do you want to, Bill?'

'I don't know.'

'I thought that might be the case, but I can't keep the people who love you away for much longer. You can run again, of course, so no one can find you, and I promise we will not search for you again. But if your memory should return one day, we will help you through it, for I suspect it won't be easy. Whatever happened to you has been locked away, and only you can turn the key.'

Bill glared at Harry. 'At this moment I wish I had never met you. Did you employ me out of pity, like one of your damaged children?'

'This school is too important for me to do such a foolish thing. I employed you because you are an excellent teacher, and the kind of man we desperately need. This is where you belong. Don't turn your back on us, and we will stand by you whatever you face in the future.'

'I've done with running.'

'Good, I'm relieved to hear that. We are here for you, and that includes Vicki. She's distressed and told me she wouldn't come here again because she doesn't want to upset you. Her concern is that you have the chance to make a good life for yourself here, and she is afraid you will leave if she is around. This school is here because of her and the boys. Dave and Alfie love her, and so do we. If, for some reason, seeing her troubles you, then keep out of her way, because she will be here quite often.'

'She told me this meeting was a coincidence and she didn't know I was here. I found that hard to believe.'

'Vicki didn't know you were working for me until I told her at the station, but she knew I was going to see if you were a teacher at the junior school. It is my fault she wasn't more open with you. I told her not to say anything.'

'Then I owe her an apology for being so sharp with her.'

'That would be appreciated. She is very upset.' Harry started to walk away, but then stopped when Bill called him.

'Harry. Thank you for being frank with me. You are right. I have been drifting, part of me wanting my memory to return, and part of me hoping it never would.'

'And now?' Harry asked, turning.

'Now I want to know – *need* to know.'

'Good. Then start with the book. We did, and it eventually led us to you.'

Bill nodded. 'Will you at least tell me what my name is?'

'Captain Henry William Manton.'

When Harry reached Edward, he asked, 'What have you told him?'

'His name, and not much more. It's no good telling him everything because that probably won't bring his memory back. His family and friends will still be strangers to him. I've told him to start by researching the crest on the book, like we did, and there's a chance that might jog his memory.'

'There's also the possibility he will never

remember. We don't know how serious that head injury was.'

'Only time will tell how this is going to work out.'

'Ah, but have we got time, Harry? Is he going to stay with us?'

'I believe I've convinced him this is where he belongs, and we'll give him all the help and support he needs. He won't disappear.'

'I hope you're right!'

Twenty-Seven

The pony pushed Vicki gently, asking for another carrot, and she rubbed his nose. She found being with the animal soothing. If she hadn't made that promise to Harry and told Bill the truth, would he have been more pleased to see her? Putting her arms around the pony's neck, she told him, 'I looked for him for a long time, and he didn't want to see me again. I thought he would be pleased to know I had studied the book and it had helped me, not only with my speech, but also through those terrible months when I was starving and desperate. He didn't even notice my improved speech. I upset him, when all I've ever wanted to do was help him. It's hard when you care about someone to be turned away like that. I think I must be a very silly girl, little pony, to imagine he might have cared what had happened to me.'

'I'm sorry, Vicki. Harry has spoken to me and I'm ashamed to have been so rude to you. You don't deserve to be treated like that.'

She spun round at the sound of Bill's voice. 'Harry said it could distress you if we told you too much, too quickly, about your past.'

'He said I should try to discover details about my past for myself. I don't even know what kind of a person I am, or how I've lived my life.'

'You have been described to us as a fine man by the people who love you. You are greatly missed, Bill.'

'Then I must follow Harry's advice and show some of the courage you did when you faced a frightening situation. I'm feeling utterly lost at the moment.'

'I expect you are, but everyone here wants to help you, including me. You are not alone, Bill.'

'Thank you; that is comforting. Now, will you forgive? I apologize for being so suspicious. I really am very pleased to see you. The little girl I met is growing into a beautiful woman – and you are far from silly. The pony didn't believe that, and neither do I.'

Relief flooded through her. Now he sounded like the man she had met before. 'There is nothing to forgive. You had every reason to be suspicious. It was too much to ask that you believed our meeting was merely chance.'

A wry smile appeared. 'You frightened me.'

She stopped stroking the pony's nose, astonished. 'Me? I couldn't frighten anyone!'

'When you said you had found the two men who helped you, I knew our meeting wasn't

261

chance. You must have found out who I really was, and I was afraid you were going to blurt out everything you knew. I don't think I could have handled that.'

'I wouldn't have done that. Harry said it would probably shock you and it would be better if you found out gradually. I wouldn't do anything to cause you distress. I am happy and have a good life, due to you and Charles. I want the same for both of you as well.'

'I did very little for you. What you have now has come about by your own courage and determination.'

'I don't see it that way. I held on to your words during those dreadful months and studied the precious book you had given me. All the time, I remembered your voice, how you spoke, and tried to do the same. I believe it helped to keep me alive when I could so easily have given up.'

Sadness showed in his face. 'I should never have walked away from you.'

She shook her head. 'You did what you had to do, and so did I.'

'Ah, but the difference was you knew what you were doing, and why. I didn't.'

'Well, that's all over now. We have both found our right place.' She hesitated a moment. 'You didn't come to this area by chance, Bill. You belong here.'

He let out a slow breath. 'So somewhere in my mind I knew I had to come here.'

'And your choice of name wasn't random, either. If you start jogging your memory, as Harry suggested, there's a chance you will remember some, if not all, of your life before you were injured.'

When he looked as if he was going to ask more questions, she held up her hand to stop him. 'We can't give you your life back by telling you things you don't remember. Only you can fill in that blank page, Bill.'

'It's hard, but I know you are right, and it has given me hope for the future at last.'

'I'm glad.' She studied the tall man in front of her and saw there was still a troubled look in his eyes. 'When I finally told Bob and Flo that I was really a girl, I was terrified they would throw me out, but they didn't. Do you know what happened?'

Bill shook his head.

'Flo hugged me. No one had ever done that to me before and it was such a comfort. I am relieved to have found you again, so would you mind if I gave you a hug?'

He held out his arms and she stepped forward. He rested his chin on the top of her head, and they stood there, both giving and receiving comfort from each other. Just two people who had suffered, albeit in different ways, but they understood, and that made a bond between them.

'Get away from my Vicki!' A furious child's voice broke through the silence.

'Ouch!' Bill stepped away from Vicki and began fending off Alfie who was thumping him with the silver topped head of the cane.

'Get away! Get away! You won't hurt my Vicki!'

'Alfie,' she shouted. 'Bill wasn't hurting me.

We are friends and pleased to see each other again.'

Dave skidded into the stables. 'What's going on? What are you doing, Alfie? Stop that; you'll hurt Mr Bill.'

'He mustn't do that!'

'Do what?' Dave caught hold of his brother to stop him lashing out.

'He had hold of Vicki. Won't let him hurt her.'

'I wasn't hurting her, young man.' Bill was laughing now, and so was Vicki. 'It's very laudable of you to want to protect her, but it isn't necessary, Alfie. We were just giving each other a hug like old friends do.'

Alfie came over to Vicki and took hold of her hand. 'Are you his friend, then?'

'Yes. Do you remember I've talked about the two men who helped me when I was homeless? Well, Sir Charles was one of them, and Bill is the other. I was so pleased to have found him and I gave him a hug, like this.' She gently held the little boy. 'There, that didn't hurt, did it?'

'It's nice,' he sighed. Then he went back to Bill, head down. 'Sorry, I thought you was hurting her.'

'I'd never do that, Alfie.'

'Gosh!' Dave was staring at Bill. 'Are you that stranger who met Vicki at the old warehouse and gave her food and that book?'

'That's right, Dave.' Bill looked down at Alfie who was examining the place he had been hitting on Bill's leg. 'What are you doing, Alfie?'

The little boy tipped his head back to look up. 'Er . . . have I bruised you?'

Bill reached down and swept Alfie up. 'Probably, but I've had worse. Don't worry about it. You were very brave to defend Vicki like that.'

'She's kind.' He smiled at Bill then. 'You were kind to her, so I won't hit you again.'

'I'm relieved to hear that, young man. Now we are all friends, how about us taking the ponies out for a ride. I expect they would like that.'

'Yes, yes!' Alfie was wriggling with excitement as Bill put him down. As soon as his feet touched the ground, he was running around in search of Fred. 'We're gonna ride the ponies, Fred!' he shouted. 'Fred!'

'I'm coming. What's all this racket for?'

Alfie grabbed his sleeve and dragged him towards the others. 'Mr Bill's gonna take us riding!'

'Ah, I see.' The young man in charge of the stables grinned. 'How many of you going?'

'All of us!' Alfie was jumping up and down. 'I'll help get the ponies ready.'

'We can't all go,' Dave told his brother. 'Mr Bill can't ride a pony. His feet will touch the ground.'

'Course not.' Alfie gave his brother a disgusted look. 'Fred's got a big horse, haven't you?'

Fred eyed the little boy with suspicion. 'He only arrived yesterday, and he has a bit of a temper. I hope you haven't been near him, Alfie?'

'I only looked. I didn't touch him.'

Dave groaned. 'I don't know what's happened to him since we came here. I can't take my eyes off him for a moment and he's off. He's crazy about the animals.'

Completely ignoring his brother's remarks, Alfie tugged at Fred again. 'I'll go and tell Mr Harry we're going out.' Then he was gone.

'Oh blast!' Dave muttered as he took off after his brother.

By now, Vicki and the two men were almost doubled over with laughter.

'Oh, I haven't laughed like this for a long time,' Bill told them. 'And it feels good. That little rascal deserves a treat.'

'Will you walk beside them, sir?' Fred managed to ask once he had controlled his amusement.

'No, I'll take the new horse. Have you got anything suitable for Vicki?'

'I've never been on a horse,' she said in alarm. 'I'll stay with Alfie and see he doesn't fall off.'

'He won't do that. Dave is the one liable to topple off. His little imp of a brother is as steady as a rock in the saddle. Are you sure you want to ride the stallion, sir? He could be difficult.'

'Let me have a look at him.'

'He's in the very end stall.'

Vicki followed the two men. As they approached the stall, a large black face peered over the door and glared at them. She didn't like the look of him and held back.

'Hello, old fellow,' Bill said softly as he walked slowly up to the animal. 'Fed up with everything, are you?'

The horse snorted and kicked the door. Bill then reached out and took hold of his head and began to talk quietly. That seemed to calm the horse down, and after a while Bill stepped back.

'I'll saddle him up, Fred. It will do him good to get out.'

'Very well, sir.' Fred was eyeing the tall man with respect. 'You obviously know what you're doing. If anyone can handle him, it will be you. I'll get the tack for you. I've got a suitable mount for the young lady.'

Vicki opened her mouth to refuse, but, before she could speak, Bill said, 'Excellent.'

'I told you I can't ride,' she protested after Fred left them. 'And how do you know you can handle that stallion?'

He grinned. 'I don't, but I'm about to find out.'

Within a short time, the ponies and horses were ready and waiting in the yard. Bill swung Alfie into the saddle and then gave Dave a boost up. Fred put a mounting block for Vicki to use and steadied her as she settled in the saddle.

'Don't worry,' he told her. 'I'm coming as well and will stay beside you all the time. You'll be quite safe; she's a gentle mare.'

'Relieved to hear that, Vicki watched as Bill talked to the fractious horse and then swung himself into the saddle with fluid grace.

Fred nodded in approval and they set off at a slow walk. Everyone looked comfortable on the animals except Vicki and Dave. He pulled a face at her as they made their way out of the yard, and she knew how he felt.

The stallion was protesting at the slow pace, and, once in open country, Fred said, 'Why don't you let the animal have a good gallop, sir? I will look after everyone.'

'I think I will have to. He's losing his temper.'

'Off you go then, sir.'

Vicki held her breath as the big horse took off at speed, hooves flying over the grass.

'Wow!' Dave cried. 'Look at him go!'

'He's jumped that hedge!' Alfie was so excited. 'Fred! I want to learn to ride like that.'

'Very few become that expert, Alfie, but if you keep riding and listen to what I say, then I think you could be good when you are older. You already sit the pony well.'

Alfie grinned, happy with the compliment, but not taking his eyes of the horizon where Bill had disappeared.

'Mr Dale is one of the best horsemen I've seen. Notice how he rides, Alfie. He is at one with the animal. Quite remarkable.'

Vicki watched as Bill thundered back to them, her hopes rising. Some deep memory must have told him he was capable of controlling a difficult animal.

'Superb riding, sir,' Fred told him when Bill pulled up in front of them. 'I would appreciate it if you could find the time to ride him. He needs exercise like that, and we don't have anyone capable of controlling him. I was going to ask Sir Charles to find him another home, but I won't do that now.'

'I would love to ride him, Fred.' Bill slapped the animal's neck and bent down to speak in his ear. 'But you remember I'm the boss.'

'Mr Bill, can I ride him?' Alfie edged his pony next to the stallion.

Bill plucked Alfie from the saddle and sat the little boy in front of him, making him squeal with

268

delight. 'You can ride him only with me, young man. If I am not around, you are not to go near him. Do you understand?'

'Yes, Mr Bill.' Alfie craned his neck to look up. 'Can we gallop?'

'No, but we'll trot.' Holding the youngster firmly with one hand, Bill urged the horse into motion.

'Crikey!' Dave exclaimed. 'We're never gonna hear the last of this. He didn't talk for ages; now he won't stop. Marvellous, ain't it?'

'It certainly is. It's wonderful to see him so happy.' Vicki looked across at Dave. 'And what about you? Are you happy as well?'

'I couldn't be happier, Vicki. This is like heaven after the rotten life we had before. You understand how we feel, don't you?'

'Yes, I understand,' she said softly.

'We had better get back now.' Fred guided Vicki's horse. 'Don't grip the reins so tightly. Hold them loosely . . . and you, Dave.'

When they reached the stables, Alfie was waiting for them. 'We beat you back. Mr Bill's seeing to his horse, and he's gonna take me riding with him again. We went ever so fast!'

'Yes, we saw you,' Vicki told the excited boy.

'Ah, there you are.' John Steadman came into the stables. 'Lunch is ready, boys.'

'What we got, Mr John?' Alfie wanted to know. 'I'm starving. I've been riding the big horse!'

'Told you. We'll never hear the last of this.' Still grinning, Dave took off after John and his brother.

Fred was seeing to the ponies, so Vicki waited

for Bill. When he came out of the stall, his expression was serious. She had expected him to be happy after the ride. 'What's the matter?'

'While I was galloping along, I had a brief flash of doing the same thing before, only I was younger then, and had others with me as well. I tried to see the faces, but I couldn't hold the picture long enough. It's like trying to grasp at mist, and it is so frustrating.'

'Don't let it upset you too much. You have discovered today that you are an excellent horseman, and you used to ride with friends when you were young. That's something, Bill. I'm sure it will all come back eventually.'

'I hope you're right. I haven't really tried to regain my memory, not wanting to see the horrors I'm sure are there, but things have changed. Now I want to know.'

Twenty-Eight

'Did you enjoy your ride?' Bob asked when Vicki joined them for lunch.

'Not as much as Alfie.'

'Or Bill?' Harry studied Vicki intently. 'I was pleased to see you talking to him. Can I take it that he did apologize for the way he treated you?'

'Yes, he did, and it was good to see him laughing.'

Edward nodded. 'That was an encouraging

sight. And my goodness, he can certainly ride a horse.'

'Alfie has declared he is going to ride just like him.' Vicki smiled at the memory of the little boy's excitement.

'I think the whole school knows that by now,' Pearl said drily. 'I'm sure his shouts even reached the village.'

'Without a doubt.' Vicki got up to help Pearl serve the meal. 'Bill is his hero now.'

'And is he still yours?' Flo asked gently.

'Yes, and always will be. He's going to need help, Harry. I fear we have thrown his life into turmoil, and he now wants his memory back.'

'I'm relieved to hear that he wants to regain his memory. He's been drifting for far too long. Don't worry, Vicki; I've told him we are here for him if he needs help, or just to talk.'

'You'll write and let me know how he is, won't you, Harry?'

'I will. Now, eat your lunch. Charles is coming this afternoon. He says we should have a tennis court and must decide where to put it.'

'A tennis court?' Vicki was astonished. 'You are going to end up with the best school in the county. Parents will soon be paying you to educate their children.'

Edward's mouth twitched. 'Perhaps we should ask Charles for a swimming pool as well.'

That sent them all into peals of laughter, releasing the tension of the morning.

'I've brought you a present,' Charles declared, indicating the horsebox attached to the van he

271

had arrived in. 'Thought you might need a couple more horses. Your new students are too big for the ponies.'

'New students?'

'Yes, Harry. They will be arriving tomorrow from Andover. Sad story. Father died in the war, and the mother has been sick all the time. The two youngsters have been trying to survive without any help. Mother died last month. I've met them, and they need your help.'

'They will have to share a room. We can't take many more, Charles.'

'I've thought of that. The builders will be starting next week on an extension to the main house. Will another five bedrooms be sufficient?'

'Oh, plenty.' Harry ran a hand over his eyes. 'Charles, will you please ask us before you find more children who need our help! We have our hands full already.'

He laughed at Harry's pained expression. 'All right, but there are so many poor little scraps who need this place, just like the ex-soldiers needing a helping hand who are having a job to cope with life in one way and another.'

'We can't save the whole world,' Harry reminded him.

'I know, but we can have a damned good try. Don't worry, funds are pouring in, and you've just employed a new teacher. Where is Manton? Couldn't get here before, but I'd like to meet him.'

'He's around somewhere, but remember what I told you about him,' Harry warned. 'He knows his real name now, but not much more.'

'I understand the situation.'

'I'll go and find him.' Edward headed for the stables and in only a few minutes was coming back with Bill beside him.

'That's him,' Charles declared. 'Even at a distance I can recognize him. My dear mother used to say that some people are like that – once seen never forgotten. I must admit I believed you were mistaken, Vicki.'

'I never forgot either of my strangers,' she told him, smiling affectionately at him.

As soon as Bill reached them Charles introduced himself. 'You won't remember me, but we did meet in that hellhole. By God, it's good to see you, Manton.'

Bill frowned, studying Charles carefully, but there was no sign of recognition. 'I'm afraid you are right, sir. I don't remember meeting you, but I do know you are the man who helped Vicki when she was desperate. I thank you for that.'

'I should have done more, but all has turned out well. What do you think of our school?' he asked proudly.

'A place like this is badly needed, sir. It will give a few children a good education and a life away from abuse.'

'Just so. There's no need to call me sir, my boy; we are not in the army now. Everyone here calls me Charles. Not only are we helping needy children, but we have been able to employ ex-soldiers who would otherwise find it difficult to find employment.'

'I had noticed.'

'I saw too much suffering, Manton. Can't turn

my back on it. Now, I hope you are a good judge of horses because I've brought over two more animals. Come and have a look at them and tell me what you think.'

Vicki watched them walk over to the truck where Fred was already unloading the animals. 'That went well, Harry.'

He nodded. 'Next step will be to bring Peter here, and then Bill's parents.'

'In the meantime, we've got to decide where to put the tennis court.' Edward rubbed his chin thoughtfully. 'Needs to be well away from the house and stables, don't you think, Harry?'

Seeing that all the men were occupied and Pearl had already left to prepare the room for the new arrivals, Vicki went in search of Dave and Alfie.

She found them with the other boys. Dave had already told them about her, so they were quite open and friendly towards her.

The afternoon was spent roaming the country-side around the school with eight lively boys who were eager to show her their favourite places. They also asked a lot of questions, wanting to know how she had survived on her own, and, in turn, she learnt a lot about them. By the time they got back for their tea, they were talking freely and joking with her.

Jack was one of the boys who had been the most difficult to handle when he'd arrived, and as Vicki was about to leave, he asked, 'When you coming down here again?'

'Next Sunday, if I can manage it. It's the only day I have free.'

He glanced around to make sure no one else was listening. 'Er . . . Can I see you when you come?'

'Yes, of course, Jack. Is there something you want to talk about?'

He shrugged. 'I had a sister, older than me, but she died. She stuck up for me, but things got real bad after she'd gone. I ain't told no one about this, not even Mr Harry, so don't say nothing.'

'I won't say a word, Jack. You can trust me.'

'Dave and Alfie trust you because you are one of us. My sister would have been about your age. You're like her.'

With that declaration, he turned and ran into the school, and she was disappointed. She had hoped to get him to talk longer. There were so many troubled youngsters, she thought sadly. Next time, she would try to spend some time with him alone.

'Enjoy your long walk?' Pearl asked when she came into the kitchen.

'Exhausting.' She sat down. 'I'm gasping for a cup of tea.'

'Coming right up. Ah, here are the men at last.'

Charles stayed with them for tea and left immediately after.

'Our train leaves in an hour, Vicki,' Flo reminded her. 'We must say goodnight to the boys.'

'I also want to see Bill before I leave. Do you know where he is, Harry?'

'In the staff lounge or the library, I expect.'

'Thanks. Boys first, though.' The school had a large sports hall where the youngsters could play before bedtime, and that's where they all were. Vicki went round to everyone she had spent the afternoon with, and made a point of saying to Jack that she would see him next time. That seemed to please him. Dave and Alfie hugged her as they always did, and then she went in search of Bill.

He was in the library, surrounded by open books and writing. 'Sorry to disturb you, but we are leaving now.'

'I didn't hear you approaching.' He stood up and smiled. 'It's been an eventful day. Although I didn't show it at first, I really am pleased to see you again. You've made a good life for yourself, and that couldn't have been easy.'

'It wasn't, but I took your advice and studied that little book diligently. Harry said you are an excellent teacher, and I hope you will be happy here. Harry and Edward need men like you and John.'

'This school is an ambitious undertaking, and I would like to see it succeed.'

'It deserves to.' She noticed the English book on the table and picked it up. 'I am so pleased to have been able to return this to you at last.'

'I gave it to you, Vicki. I never expected to see it again.'

'I couldn't keep it. It belongs to you.'

'I had about three books with me at that time, and that was just one of them. It didn't mean anything to me. I like books and pick them up cheaply wherever I can.'

'It meant a lot to me.' She smiled up at him. 'I must go now or I'll miss my train. Bye, Bill.'

His only reply was a nod of his head, and Vicki walked away. When she had seen him writing, she had hoped he was looking into the origin of the book, but he had been preparing lessons. He hadn't appeared to have any interest in finding out about the crest. As far as that was concerned, his mind seemed to be a blank, and yet one thing was clear: he had known all the time that he was a teacher.

Two days later, when they had finished clearing up after the evening meal, Bob made Vicki sit down with them. 'We've been discussing your future, my dear, and realize we have taught you all we know about hairdressing. You are good and need another teacher now.'

Vicki's heart gave a lurch. Where was this leading? Were they going to send her away now? The old fears came rushing back. 'But you both know all there is to know about hairdressing.'

'Things are changing fast, and your talent needs a more advanced teacher now.' Flo caught hold of her hand. 'Don't look so upset, Vicki. We want the best for you.'

'That's right.' Bob leant forward. 'I saw Don James yesterday. His salon in Knightsbridge is favoured by the wealthy and famous. I told him about you, and he is willing to take you as a student for the next two years. After that, you will have all the necessary qualifications to work in a high-class establishment. With Don's name behind you, there will be no limit to what you can achieve.'

Vicki looked from one to the other in dismay.

'But I'm happy here. Don't send me away, please!'

The desperation in Vicki's voice brought Flo to her feet in alarm. 'Oh, my darling, we would never do that. We were so excited about giving you this marvellous opportunity that we haven't made the arrangements clear. You will go to Don James only two days a week, Tuesdays and Wednesdays. You can travel by train and come back here at night. This is your home, Vicki, and always will be. When we've gone, all this will be yours. We've made legal wills.'

Shaken and stunned, Vicki couldn't speak.

'I'm going to employ another girl just for those two days each week, and then you can show me what you're learning.' Flo sat down again. 'We can try the new things out on our customers. That will be fun, won't it?'

'Of course, if you really don't want to do this,' Bob told her, 'you don't have to. We wouldn't force you to do anything you didn't want to. It's a rare opportunity, but think it over and let us know what you decide.'

'I don't have to think about it,' she told them. 'It would be foolish to turn down a chance to improve, and I'll do my best to be a worthy student of Mr James.'

'We know you will be. If we'd had any doubts about your abilities, we would never have approached Don. Flo and I talked about this a while ago but knew we had to wait for the right time. You've found Bill at last, and we hope you are now ready to move on with your life. You have a talent, Vicki, and that needs to be developed by someone more qualified than us.'

'I understand you want me to become a skilled hairdresser, but I must admit the thought of working with someone else is rather frightening. And the salon sounds posh!'

'You don't need to worry about that.' Flo smiled encouragingly. 'Your manners are impeccable, and your speech excellent. Do you know your accent is very like Bill's? How did you manage that when you only met him once?'

'I liked the way he spoke and I kept that sound in my head as I practised.' A worried expression appeared on her face. 'I do hope he's going to be all right.'

'If you mean is he going to regain his memory, then no one knows that. My concern is that it has been too long since his injury, and if his memory was going to return, it would have done so by now.' Bob gave her a sympathetic look. 'But you mustn't worry about that. He is with Harry now and he will do all he can to help him.'

'You are right, of course,' Vicki agreed, and then changed the subject. 'So, when do I go to this posh salon?'

'Next week.'

Twenty-Nine

'I got your message.' Peter ran up to Harry. 'Are you sure it's him?'

'Certain.'

'Oh, that's marvellous! How is he?'

Harry studied the excited young man. 'He's taking a class at the moment; you can see him during the break. As to how he's doing, Peter, the answer is he's struggling. This is going to be difficult for you – for both of you – but you must let me introduce you. Try not to overwhelm him by rushing in and greeting him like the old friends you really are. To him, you will be a stranger.'

'But we grew up together. Is his loss of memory that bad?'

'I'm afraid so. When I first met him, there were a couple of things that made me believe his memory would return if prodded – now I'm not so sure. A doctor in the village is keeping an eye on him and trying to find out where he was treated, but he hasn't had any luck so far.'

'Oh, Lord, that's terrible.' Peter's eyes clouded with sorrow for his friend. 'But at least he's alive. I'll do whatever you say, Harry.'

'How much we tell him will depend on how he reacts to meeting you.'

'I understand.'

'Ah, there goes the bell. Follow me.'

Bill was still in the classroom cleaning the blackboard when they walked in. He turned his head, showing no recognition of Peter. 'Hello, Harry.'

'Here's someone who wants to meet you. Peter Harmond.'

Dusting the chalk from his hands, Bill nodded and shook hands with Peter. 'Are you a teacher?'

Harry could see Peter was having difficulty containing his emotions. When he shot Harry a quick beseeching glance, Harry nodded, and the young man turned back to his friend.

'No, Will, I am what you always said I would be – a gentleman farmer.'

Stillness came over Bill as he looked intently at Peter. 'You know me?'

'Yes, we grew up together. There were three of us, we were inseparable, and our greatest pleasure was riding. We used to gallop around the estate trying to beat each other. You always won,' he said, a touch of a smile on his face. 'Ah, they were good days before the damned war came and ruined everything.'

'Three of us?'

Peter nodded. 'You don't remember?'

Bill shook his head. 'Sorry.'

'Oh, God, Will!' Peter's composure began to crack. 'I am overjoyed to see you are still alive! We were told you were dead, and it's like a miracle to see you standing here. You obviously don't know who the hell I am, so can we start over again, as if we have just met?'

'I have a free couple of hours, so would you like to ride now? We have horses in the stables.'

'I'd love to!' Peter's face lit up in a broad smile. 'I'll beat you this time.'

'I wouldn't bank on it.' Bill winked at Harry to let him know everything was all right. 'I've got a special horse.'

When they walked out of the classroom, Harry let out a silent breath of relief. Bill had handled that well. He had seen how distressed Peter was becoming and had done exactly the right thing. They had been firm friends once, and there was no reason why they couldn't be again. Bill was going to have to get to know the people from his past all over again, including his parents. That meeting was going to be the hardest of all, he suspected.

It was late in the evening when Bill sought out Harry. 'Can you spare the time to have a talk?'

'All the time you need, Bill. Sit down. Would you like a drink?'

'A whisky, if you've got it, please.'

'A double?'

Bill's smile was wry. 'Definitely.'

'Who won the race?' Harry asked, handing Bill a large tumbler of whisky, and watched him take a good swig.

'I did. It felt right racing over the countryside like that. It's a mess, isn't it, Harry? What the hell have I been doing for the last few years? I haven't even tried to find out if I have any family.'

Harry topped up the glasses. 'Your past has been completely wiped out. You've had nothing to go on – no idea where to start looking – and you did what you had to do by trying to make a life for yourself. The situation you were faced with must have been devastating, but you didn't crumble or sink into despair. You held yourself together and reached for as normal a life as possible for you in the circumstances. You have nothing to reproach yourself for.'

Bill took another swig of the drink and shook his head. 'I should have tried! You didn't have anything to go on, but you found me.'

'Vicki wouldn't give up, even when every step we took ended nowhere. It was one disappointment after another, but that lovely girl was determined. It was only by chance she saw a photograph and insisted that one of the young boys was the stranger she had met. Even when everyone said you had died in the war, she would not accept it, declaring that you were alive, much to everyone's disbelief.'

'She's a very determined young lady and I'm glad everything has turned out well for her.'

Harry nodded. 'She has blessed us all.'

Draining his glass, Bill ran a hand through his hair and drew in a deep breath. 'It was hard seeing Peter so distressed when I didn't recognize him. He said we have been friends since we were children, and it meant nothing to me. It was as if we were meeting for the first time.'

'You handled it well, Bill. Inviting him to ride with you was the kindest thing you could have done. Have you arranged to meet again?'

'Yes. He's part of my past, and I've got to piece it together somehow.' He put the empty glass on the table with a crash. 'When I met Peter, I tried to remember him, but it was like looking into a thick fog. There's nothing there! I think all along I have feared meeting someone who knew me, knowing I would have to put myself through this torture.'

'Tell me the first thing you remember.' Bill was opening up, and Harry wanted to keep him talking. He poured a little more whisky in their glasses and waited.

'I was in a boat – a fishing boat, I think. They

283

dropped me off on a beach. I don't know where it was. When I walked into the town to get something to eat, no one understood me. I wasn't speaking the same language as them.'

Harry's head shot up. 'What language were they speaking?'

'English. I was speaking French.'

'Ah, so you were in this country. What time of year was it?'

'I saw daffodils growing, so it must have been spring.'

'Was the war over?'

Bill nodded. 'While I was having a meal, I heard someone say that it was a relief that terrible conflict was over.'

'So you had lost months. Where on earth had you been all that time?'

'I haven't the faintest idea, but it must have been France. And I had obviously been used to speaking that language, because for a while there I thought I was French.'

Harry was astounded by what he was hearing and desperately tried to fathom out what it all meant. 'You were badly injured – we know that – so someone must have been looking after you. But why didn't they take you to a military hospital? When you regained consciousness and your memory was a blank, you obviously knew the language and, hearing it spoken all the time, you did the same. Carry on. What did you do then?'

'I changed to English.'

'Just like that?'

Bill gave a wry smile. 'I was hungry, and I

soon realized that I understood what people were saying to me.'

'Did you have any belongings with you?' Harry was probing, he knew, but Bill was talking freely. 'What were you wearing?'

'A suit. It had been cleaned and repaired, but it had once obviously been quite good, and it fitted.'

'Quite likely your own, but why you weren't in uniform is a mystery. You said you had a meal; how did you pay for it?'

'There was English money in my pocket, enough to buy me food for a while. I used some of it to buy a ticket to London.'

'That's extraordinary! Can you remember anything else that happened before you came back to this country?'

'I'm afraid not.'

'From what you've just told me, it would appear that someone in France nursed you back to health and then brought you back here.'

'That seems possible, but who they were and why they did it, I really don't know. And I can't confirm that your hypothesis is correct. My memory only seems to start from the time I stepped out of that boat.' Bill sat back and closed his eyes for a moment, then opened them again, his mouth set in a grim line. 'What about my parents? Do they know I'm alive?'

'Yes, they know. They live in Yorkshire, and Charles has invited them to stay with him. They are on their way now. I've held them off because I wasn't sure how you were going to react, and your first meeting with Vicki didn't fill me with confidence. When I was certain you were going to stay with us, I told Peter he could meet you.'

'I appreciate you trying to introduce me to my past a little at a time, Harry. It would have been overwhelming to be faced with this all at once. I hope you have made it clear that it is unlikely I will recognize them.'

'I've explained that to them.'

'Thanks.' Bill finished his drink and began to stand up.

'Before you go, something is puzzling me. When Peter mentioned that there had been three of you growing up together, you didn't ask who the other one was.'

'I didn't want to know. If he had been alive, he would have come with Peter.'

'Now that's interesting. You knew that without being told. I think you ought to know his name.'

With only a slight nod of his head, Bill waited.

'James Ashington.'

A momentary look of anguish crossed Bill's face, and then his composure was back.

'That means something to you?'

'The crest on the book Vicki returned to me is that of the Ashington family.'

'That's right, and I'm pleased to see you have looked it up. James probably gave you that book. You served together in France.'

'No wonder I didn't want to know his name.' Bill sat down again. 'I think I need another drink, Harry.'

'Just a small one, then.' Harry poured the

drinks, smiling encouragingly. 'That fog in your mind might not be quite as impenetrable as we thought.'

'I'm not sure I want you to be right! There could be things there I don't want to relive.'

'I'm sure there are. If that fog starts to clear, there will be pain – I won't deny it. But there will also be joy as well – remember that.'

'Do you know I was living a peaceful life until you walked into that classroom, Harry? Now you and that little girl have turned my life upside down. I don't know whether to thank you or punch you on the nose.'

They looked at each, smiled, and downed their drinks.

It had been such a busy week that Vicki hadn't had time to visit Harry, but they had seen Charles, and he had given them all the news. The boys were fine. Bill was fine. Harry, Edward and Pearl were fine. The school was doing fine. There wasn't a thing to worry about.

Taking a look in the mirror, Vicki grimaced. It was all right for Charles to say that, but she did have something to worry about, and that was starting her training today at the posh salon. Why on earth had she agreed to this?

'Ah, you look lovely.' Bob nodded his approval. 'We had better go. It wouldn't do to be late on your first day.'

She managed a smile. He was taking her the first time to introduce her to Don James, and show her how to get there.

When they reached the salon and looked inside,

she wanted to run. It was all glass, chrome and pink leather! She thought it was appalling. The man she was going to be working with was tall and thin, wearing tight black trousers and a pink shirt.

'Oh dear,' she murmured.

Bob laughed at her expression of horror. 'Comes as a bit of a shock, doesn't it? But he's a first-class hairdresser, with a reputation for excellence. He's considered one of the best in the business, and his client list proves that.'

'Really? If he's that good, why is he going to train me? He's never seen me before.'

'I told him you were gaining a good many faithful clients who always asked for you to do their hair. He said he had a vacancy at the moment and would be interested in training you.'

'Really?' She couldn't take her eyes off the salon.

'Is that all you can say, Vicki?' he laughed. 'You'll enjoy the challenge. Come on, let's go inside.'

She followed reluctantly, muttering, 'I hope he doesn't expect me to wear that shocking shade of pink!'

'Ah, good morning, Bob. I see you've brought my pupil.' He studied Vicki from head to toe, and then back up again. He stepped forward and ran his fingers through her hair. 'Beautiful, but let it grow longer.'

'I like it short,' she said defiantly. 'It's the fashion.'

'I'm well aware of that, young lady, but very

few women have hair as lustrous as yours. It needs to be shown in its full beauty, and that can't be done if you keep chopping it off.'

Chopping it off! 'We don't *chop* hair, sir; we *style* it.'

He studied her for some moments, and she waited for him to show her the door. This couldn't have been a worse start, but she wasn't going to put up with his pretentious posturing. She always tried to please Bob and Flo, but this was going too far!

Suddenly, he laughed out loud. 'I like her, Bob. You leave her with me, and I'll make a hairdresser out of her.'

Vicki seethed. She thought she already was.

'Would you like me to come and collect you?' Bob asked, a broad smile on his face.

'No, thank you. I can find my own way home.'

When he'd gone, the salon owner said, 'Stop scowling, Victoria. You don't have to like me – just do as I say.'

'Yes, sir! What would you like me to do?'

'Try smiling for a start, then stay by my side and watch. I'll explain what I'm doing. You may ask intelligent questions, but apart from that I don't want a word out of you.'

Oh, this was going to be a long day.

'Jennifer!' He called to a young girl. 'Get a gown for Victoria. Everyone to your places – it's now time to open the salon.'

The girl hurried over to Vicki with a gown, and she was relieved to see it was cream and not pink. When she looked around, it was clear that only the stylists wore pink; everyone else was in cream. The clients began to arrive. The salon was soon filled with talk, and all the staff had permanent smiles on their faces.

As ordered, Vicki stayed close to Mr James and watched carefully to see if he was as good as everyone said. It didn't take her long to realize that he was, and she became fascinated.

Without being asked, she began handing him the tools he needed. He took them without comment, devoting his whole attention to his client.

The day flew by, and she was the last one of the staff left when the shop closed. She was putting on her coat when Mr James walked into the staff room.

'Make me a strong cup of tea before you leave, Victoria.'

'Yes, sir.' She was talking to his back as he left the room.

The tea was made by the time he returned, and she just stared at him in surprise. He was wearing a very smart navy blue suit and a white shirt. He looked like a different man!

'Ah, lovely.' He sat down giving a huge sigh, and waited while she poured him a cup. 'Thanks. You did well today, Victoria.'

'Thank you, sir. I found it interesting. Many of the procedures you used I had never seen before.' She studied him, confused. Was this the same man she had been working with all day? There wasn't a sign of the flamboyant stylist with his exaggerated gestures.

He looked at her puzzled expression and held out his cup for a refill, an amused glint in his eyes. It was then it dawned on her, and she laughed. 'It's all an act, isn't it?'

'I wondered how long it would take you to work it out. Showmanship is what the clients expect. Must give them value for their money.' He sat back, sipping his tea. 'Are you going to come again?'

She pursed her lips, giving it some thought. 'I'll give you another chance.'

He tipped his head back and laughed. 'Oh, Bob was right about you. I'll try not to disappoint you.'

Thirty

By Sunday, Vicki couldn't wait to get on the train. She was anxious to know how Bill was and looking forward to seeing the boys again. The last time she had been at the school, Jack had started to talk to her about his past, so she must see him on his own if possible.

John Steadman met her at the station and had brought Dave and Alfie with him. They had so much to tell her that she hardly managed to get a word in during the ride to the school.

'Where's Harry?' she asked Pearl when she came out to meet her.

'The men are off somewhere with Charles. I've just made a fresh pot of tea. Would you like to join us, John?'

'No, thank you, Pearl. I've promised to take some of the boys riding.'

'Ah.' Pearl smiled at Dave and Alfie. 'So you don't want tea either?'

They shook their heads and followed John to the stables.

'It's just us, then, Vicki.'

'How's Bill?' she asked the moment she sat down in the kitchen.

'He's been spending quite a few evenings with Harry. They've been talking late into the night – and drinking whisky. Don't ask me what they've been discussing because Harry hasn't said anything. What Bill is telling him he considers confidential.'

'I understand. Is he with Harry now?'

'No, he went riding with Peter early this morning, and now they've gone to lunch with Peter's parents.'

'Oh,' exclaimed Vicki. 'That sounds good. Did he recognize Peter when they met?'

'I'm afraid not. His mind still appears to be blank, but Peter is spending as much time with him as he can, so Bill can get to know him again. It's hard for both of them, but they are getting on well.'

'I can't imagine what it would be like to meet people who have known you all your life and not be able to recognize them. Has Harry done anything about Bill's parents?'

'Yes, they are here and staying with Charles. They are going to meet Bill at the Harmonds'. It could be a difficult meeting.'

'Isn't Harry going to be there? He ought to be there!' Vicki was alarmed.

'Don't worry, Harry will be taking Bill's parents

to see him at the Harmonds'. Charles is going as well.'

'Thank goodness!' Vicki breathed a sigh of relief. 'Does Bill know?'

'Of course he does, my dear. Harry wouldn't have arranged this without Bill's permission. Now, what are you going to do while the boys are out riding?'

'I want to find Jack. The last time I was here, he began to tell me what had happened to him, and I promised to see him when I came again. Would he have gone riding as well?'

'Unlikely. He'd rather play football or roam the countryside.'

Vicki stood up. 'I'll see if I can find him.'

Jack was alone on the playing field, kicking a ball about. As she walked towards him, he looked up, ignored her and carried on playing. 'Hello, Jack.'

'You didn't come last week.' He looked up then.

'I couldn't make it, but I'm here now. Didn't you want to go riding with the others?'

'Don't like horses.'

'That's a good enough reason not to go, then. I'm not too keen on them either. Would you like to go for a walk?'

He shrugged. 'Why not.'

It was obvious she was going to have to work hard to gain his trust again. He was quite upset she hadn't come last Sunday.

They strolled along, and she told him about her first two days at the posh hairdresser's. By the time she had finished, he was grinning.

293

'I'm surprised he didn't throw you out.' He burst into laughter. 'Are you gonna keep going there?'

'Oh, yes. He's very good and I'll be able to learn a lot from him. I'll just ignore his funny ways.' She studied Jack carefully. He was relaxed and smiling now. 'So, what have you been learning this week?'

'How to write properly and do sums.'

'Do you enjoy the lessons?'

'I do.' He sounded surprised to hear himself say that. 'I like Mr Bill the best. He don't shout or tell you off if you don't get something right. He goes through it with you until you understand. Do you know what he did the other day?'

'No, tell me.'

'Well, one kid kept hitting the boy next to him and calling him names. Mr Bill stopped the lesson and propped himself on the desk, all casual like. Instead of giving the bully a thump, he asked him why he was acting like that. Was it because it made him feel big to pick on someone smaller than himself? Well, the kid didn't know what to say, so Mr Bill kept talking to him – quietly like. He didn't tell him off or anything, just talked, and soon the kid was crying and saying he was sorry. He's been much nicer since then.'

'It sounds as if it was a good lesson for everyone.'

Jack nodded. 'Made us all think, I can tell you. After the class, I asked him if I could talk to him. He took me to the dining room and we had a cup of tea. I told him about my sister and how she died because she had tried to protect me.' Jack looked up at Vicki. 'I always blamed myself, you see. We talked for a long time, and Mr Bill made me see it wasn't my fault. He was right, and the same thing would have happened to me if Mr Harry hadn't got me away from there.'

'I'm so pleased you went to him. He's a very understanding and clever man. If it hadn't been for him, I wouldn't be where I am today.'

'Dave told me about that. Mr Bill's good at helping people. He took me to see Mr Harry, and, do you know, it was easier to talk about it again. It's like a weight has gone off me. I wanted to tell you, but you didn't come.'

'I'm sorry, Jack.'

'That's all right. You explained and I understand.' He grinned. 'Race you to the trees!'

They sprang into action, laughing, both happy to be running free in the open countryside.

By the time they arrived back at the school, the other children had finished their ride, and Jack happily joined them for a game on the sports field.

Harry and Charles appeared and came to greet Vicki. 'I thought you were at your place, Charles?'

'We came back to see you,' Harry told her. 'I saw you with Jack.'

'He was telling me how he talked to you and Bill.'

'That was a big step forward for him, and he knows now he can come to us any time and we'll listen to him.' Harry looked at his watch. 'We had better get going, Charles.'

'Pearl said you were going to the Harmonds'. Could I come with you, please?'

'Are you sure you want to?' Charles asked. 'This could be a distressing and difficult meeting for Manton and his parents.'

'That's exactly why I would like to be there. Mr and Mrs Manton have met me, and I might be of some help.'

'You could be right.' Harry nodded. 'But Bill has asked that he meet his parents in private, and that's the way they want it as well. Mr and Mrs Manton have been very good by agreeing to wait until their son asked to see them.'

'That must have been hard for them.'

'Very, but they understood it was for the best.'

They drove first to collect Mr and Mrs Manton, who were delighted to see Vicki.

Mrs Manton kissed Vicki's cheek. 'We must thank you, my dear, for giving us back our son. If it hadn't been for your determination, we might never have known he was alive.'

Vicki didn't know what to say. The Mantons were obviously very emotional about seeing their son again.

'Don't look so concerned,' Mr Manton told her when she remained silent. 'Harry has explained that our son is unlikely to recognize us, but the fact is he is alive and well, and that is enough for us.'

'Is everyone ready?' Charles glanced at the clock. 'The car is waiting outside.'

When they arrived at the Harmonds', Vicki held back, allowing the Mantons to enter the house first with Harry.

After quick greetings, Harry took Bill's parents to the study, and five minutes later he came back with Peter. Vicki took the chance to ask Peter how Bill was.

'He's doing fine.' Peter smiled at her. 'He might not remember us, but I've spent a lot of time with him, and he is the same person I grew up with.'

'That's good to hear.' Vicki relaxed a little then, and for the next hour joined in the general conversation.

When Mr and Mrs Manton came into the drawing room, they were smiling. Mrs Manton had been crying, but they had been tears of joy by the look of her happy face.

'Everything all right?' Harry asked.

'Yes, thank you, Harry.' Mr Manton took the drink being offered to him. 'He didn't know us, but that is our son. He hasn't changed in any other way.'

'Where is he?' Peter wanted to know.

'He's gone out the back for a walk. I think he wants some time on his own.'

'I'll go and see if he's all right.' Peter stood up and began to make for the door, but Harry stopped him.

'Peter, if you don't mind, I think Vicki ought to go to him. They do share an experience that isn't from his past.'

'All right. If you think that's best.'

'I do.' Harry guided Vicki out of the room. 'What I want you to do is just go and stand beside him. Talk if he wants to, or come back if he needs to be alone. Will you do that?'

'Yes.' Vicki went to the study and out of the doors leading to the garden. She saw Bill's tall figure immediately. He was leaning on a fence, watching horses graze, head bowed.

He didn't hear her approaching, and, without a word, she rested her arms on the fence beside him. He looked at her. The strain on his face tore at her heart, but she managed a gentle smile. 'Tell me to go if you don't want company.'

Draping an arm across her shoulders, he said, 'Walk with me.'

They strolled in silence for some time, and when they came to a large open area, Bill stopped and swept out his hand. 'That's what it's like inside my head. Empty. It's a terrible thing to be told by two distressed people that you are their son, and you don't even remember seeing them before.'

Vicki reached up and clasped the hand resting on her shoulder. 'I can't imagine how painful that must be; no one could who hasn't experienced it. But they are overjoyed to know you are alive, and by seeing them today you have given them the greatest gift possible – the son they thought lost to them for ever.'

'A son who doesn't remember them!'

'You will.'

'I wish I could believe that.'

'Take another look at the view, Bill. You said it was empty space, but that isn't what I see. It is full of wild flowers, birds, insects, rabbits and many other small animals. That space is teeming with life. I don't believe your mind is an empty space. For some reason, it has shut down until you are ready to deal with whatever is locked in there.'

Bill gazed at her. 'Do you know, Vicki, what you've just said has made me feel better. I'm so glad you came today, and I'm wondering how someone so young came to have so much wisdom.'

Seeing the tension leave his face and a slow smile appear, she said jokingly, 'I've grown a bit since we first met. I'm seventeen now.'

'Really? I don't know how old I am.'

'Twenty-nine or thirty.'

'I'll take the twenty-nine,' he laughed. 'We had better get back now.'

As they walked towards the house, he kept his arm across her shoulders, but now she could feel that he was relaxed. In a small way, she had been able to help him today, and that was good to know.

Thirty-One

The weeks from summer to autumn had flown by, and there was a hint of the coming winter in the weather. Working with Mr James was now interesting and enjoyable. She was a quick learner, and he was even allowing her to assist him instead of just watching. There were two girls he used as models and he let her practise on them. Her skills were growing and it was exciting.

'You are an excellent pupil,' he told her as they shut up the shop.

'Thank you, sir.' Wrapping a scarf around her neck to protect her from the cold wind, she hurried to the station, pleased with the compliment. He didn't hand them out lightly.

When she arrived home, Charles was there. 'Oh, it's lovely to see you. How is everyone?'

'They are fine.' He kissed her cheek.

'Had a good day?' Bob asked her.

'Very, and I've learnt a few more things we can try out on our customers. As long as they will let me, of course.'

'Jeannie Baxter is coming in tomorrow and she's quite happy to try new hairstyles.' Flo put a cup of tea in front of her.

Vicki smiled her thanks, and then turned her attention to Charles. 'Are the Mantons still with you?'

'Yes, I've told them they can stay for as long as they like. They are all coping well, and Bill is spending time with them and Peter. I've arranged a big firework display for this Sunday, Guy Fawkes Night. The boys have been helping to build a huge bonfire, and we will be disappointed if you don't all come and enjoy the fun.'

'We'll be there.' Bob told him. 'Wouldn't miss it for anything, and we can stay the night because we have decided not to open on Mondays in future.'

'Perfect. Come on Saturday evening if you can.' He looked at his watch. 'I mustn't miss my train. Sorry I can't stay for one of your excellent meals, Flo.'

When Charles had left, Vicki asked, 'Why did

you decide not to open on a Monday? Is it because it's a slow day?'

'That's one reason; the other is that it will give us a longer break, and when we go to see everyone at the school, we won't have to rush away. We can stay longer with the boys. They are like family to us now.'

'Yes, they are.' Vicki smiled, pleased about spending more time at the school.

They did as Charles had suggested and caught the train on Saturday evening. They hadn't stopped for a meal, but had sandwiches with them to eat on the way. Vicki couldn't wait to get down there. The school was turning out to be a huge success and it was always so lovely to see everyone.

There was great excitement when they arrived, and Dave and Alfie were allowed to stay up a little later for once so they could see them. 'My goodness, how you've grown in the short time you've been down here,' Flo said as she hugged them.

'That's plenty of good food, love and exercise,' Pearl told her, ruffling Alfie's hair affectionately.

He giggled, a broad grin on his face. 'We're going to have a bonfire and lots of fireworks tomorrow when it gets dark.'

'So we've been told. That's why we've come early,' Vicki told him, 'and we won't be leaving until Monday afternoon.'

This news was greeted with howls of delight.

'Mr Harry said we can have Monday as a

holiday,' Dave declared. 'So we'll have lots of time together.'

'And now it's time you were in bed, boys.' Edward held out his hand to Alfie. 'You need your rest before the excitement of the bonfire party.'

After they had given everyone a hug and a kiss, the boys went obediently.

None of the boys had ever seen anything like the fireworks shooting into the sky, bursting with a loud bang and spraying out many colours, and neither had many of the older people gathered in the field. The doctor was there with his family, the Harmonds and Bill's parents were also there, and, of course, Charles and every member of the staff and their families. It was a huge gathering and they had been busy all afternoon preparing the food to feed so many.

The light from the bonfire was flickering over smiling faces as they watched the fireworks exploding above them. All the children were being watched carefully to make sure they stayed at a safe distance.

Vicki was totally absorbed in the display when something caught her attention. Jack was rushing through the crowd towards them, panic on his face. Then she heard what he was shouting: 'Matron! Doctor! Mr Harry!'

'Come quick!' he gasped when he reached them, tugging at the doctor's arm. 'Oh, please, you gotta come!'

Harry caught hold of the distressed boy. 'What is it, Jack?'

'Mr Bill's sick! He fell down and I couldn't pick him up. He's bad. Please!'

Checking to make sure Dave and Alfie were safe with Pearl, Vicki hurried after Harry and the doctor, her heart thudding.

Jack ran into the school dining room, with the rest of them on his heels. The sight that met them stopped Vicki in her tracks. Bill was on his feet, gripping the edge of a table for support, head bowed and perspiration streaming down his face.

'What's happened?' Peter rushed in, took one look at his friend and tried to get near him, but the doctor kept him at a distance.

'Shut the door, Vicki,' Harry ordered. 'We don't want anyone else bursting in here for the moment.'

She did as asked, but she doubted anyone else had noticed. There was too much noise and excitement going on out there.

Jack had thrown his arms around Bill's waist, trying to support him.

'Leave this to us, everyone,' Harry ordered gruffly, making them all move back. 'Don't get in the way.'

Vicki nodded and watched anxiously as the men eased Bill into a chair. Elsie already had flannels and was wiping his face, talking quietly. When he tipped his head back, Vicki could see he was ashen and trembling. She stifled the urge to cry out in distress. What had gone wrong? Was it that head injury causing pain?

'I got the doctor for you,' Jack told him, still holding tight.

303

Dr Saunders moved Bill's hair out of the way to examine the injury to his head, making Jack gasp when he saw it and bringing tears to his eyes. 'How'd he get that? Make him better! Please make him better!'

Bill reached out and put an arm around the distressed boy. 'I'm all right, Jack. Just give me a moment.'

Just then, Mr and Mrs Manton rushed in a side door and went straight to their son. 'What's happened? What's wrong? Shouldn't he be taken to a hospital, Doctor?'

'That isn't necessary, Mother.' Bill's voice was raw with pain.

Dr Saunders finished his examination and, hearing how Bill spoke, moved to help him out of the chair. 'Harry, help me get Bill to his room. He needs rest and quiet. Jack, you can let go of him now. We'll take good care of him.'

The boy released his grip, but stayed close. 'I'll help too. Please let me come with you.'

'We'll be glad of your help, Jack.' Harry held a glass of brandy in his hands and, after a nod from the doctor, gave it to Bill. 'Drink that first.'

The drink disappeared in one gulp, and Harry put the empty glass on the table. 'How much of your memory has returned, Bill?'

'All of it,' he rasped. 'Those damned fireworks crashing and banging brought it all back in one massive wave. Get me out of here, Harry!'

Vicki covered her mouth with her hands in shock, not wanting to make a sound. She watched as the doctor and Harry lifted Bill to his feet,

304

with Jack determined to help and Peter hovering close by. Her legs were trembling. Mrs Manton had tears flowing down her face.

'He called me Mother. He knows us.' She grasped her husband's hand the moment the men had left the room. 'We have our son back.'

'But at what price?' Mr Manton ran a hand over his eyes. 'It tore me apart to see him suffering like that. I can't help wishing his memory hadn't returned. He didn't know us, but he was happy.'

'And he will be again.' Harry said, walking back into the room. 'It was a massive shock, but he's sleeping now. The doctor and Elsie are going to stay with him, through the night, if necessary.'

'Oh, that's a relief,' Mrs Manton said. 'Thank you, Harry.'

'No need to thank me. Bill has gained a lot of friends here.' He smiled as Jack joined them. 'Like Jack, here. You did the right thing, and we are all grateful for your help, young man.'

'I was frightened,' he admitted, 'but doctor said he's going to be all right.'

'He will be, he's a strong man, but he might find things hard for a while, so we will need to give him our support and understanding. You know what's happened to him, Jack?'

The boy nodded vigorously. 'Doctor explained it to me. Terrible thing to happen, and he's a brave man. He helps us when we have troubles. Now we can help him.'

'Good boy.' Harry looked around. 'It sounds as if the fireworks are over. Open the doors, Vicki, and let us enjoy the rest of the evening. We have a feast laid on.'

As soon as the doors were opened, everyone began to file in. Charles came straight up to them. 'I saw Jack running to the doctor, but I thought I had better stay with the children. Is everything all right?'

'Bill's memory has returned,' Vicki told him, 'and it hit him hard. He's sleeping now.'

'Ah, if it came back all at once, that will be difficult for him to handle; nevertheless, that is good news.' Charles smiled at the Mantons' strained faces. 'Don't worry about your son. I saw him in action in France, and, believe me, he will handle this in his usual calm, efficient way.'

Pearl and her helpers appeared bearing trays of piping hot sausages, bowls of soup and plates laden with all sorts of goodies.

'Eat up!' Charles called loudly to be heard above the chatter. 'There's plenty more, and I want to see empty plates!'

Pandemonium broke out as everyone crowded round the tables to help themselves, and Flo came over to Vicki and put her arm around her shoulders. 'Have something to eat, my dear. Don't worry too much. He'll be just fine – you'll see.'

'I'm sure he will, but he was bad.' She leaned on Flo, glad of the comfort being given. 'Thank goodness only a few of us know what has happened. Charles has gone to a lot of trouble, and I'm pleased the evening hasn't been ruined for everyone.'

Jack came over with a plate full of hot sausages

and held it up to Vicki. 'These are smashing. You must have some. Mr Bill wouldn't want us to be miserable. That doctor's looking after him good.'

'You're right, Jack.' Smiling, she took a sausage and bit into it. 'They are good, aren't they?'

Harry had been talking to the Mantons for a while, and he came over to join them. 'I've persuaded Bill's parents to go back with Charles; if they are needed, I will come for them myself. They naturally want to stay near their son, but there isn't anything they can do. He's still sleeping, and that's what he needs at the moment. Ah, food.' Harry took the last sausage from Jack's plate.

Seeing the empty plate, Jack said, 'I'll get some more sausages and ask Mrs Pearl to save some for Mr Bill. He'll be hungry when he wakes up.'

They watched the boy hurry away, and Edward smiled at Harry. 'He was very troubled and difficult to manage when he first arrived here, but he's turned the corner now. And that's thanks to the way Bill has handled him.'

'I've often wondered,' said Bob, 'but never asked before, why do the boys use Christian names like that, Harry? It's rather unusual.'

'Dave started that and we haven't tried to change it. It seems to make us more approachable to the boys, and that's what we want. Our aim is to make them feel that this isn't just a school, but we are all now their family.'

'Well, from what we've seen so far, I would say you are succeeding,' Bob told him.

'We've got a way to go yet. Gaining their trust

is the first step, and the most difficult, but we're making progress.'

With the fireworks over, the bonfire doused, and the food enjoyed, the gathering began to disperse. Tired out and happy, the boys all went willingly to bed, until the only ones remaining in the school dining room were the original gang, as Edward called Vicki, Harry, Flo, Bob, Pearl and himself.

They sat round the table talking until late, not wanting to retire.

Dr Saunders joined them, and, much to their surprise, Bill strode in right behind him. He nodded and sat down with them. Vicki's breath caught in her throat. He was relaxed and all the pain and anguish had left his face, but there was something different about him. There was a strength emanating from him that she could feel more than see. This man now knew who he was, and confidence showed in his eyes.

'I hope you've still got some food left, Pearl, I'm very hungry.'

'Jack made sure I kept some for you. What would you like, Bill?'

'Anything.'

'Coming right up.' Pearl glanced around the table. 'Anyone else hungry?'

When every hand was raised, Vicki stood up. 'I'll help you, Pearl.'

They soon had eggs, bacon, sausages and fried bread served up, bringing smiles to their faces.

'Where are my parents?' Bill asked Harry.

'They've gone back with Charles. I didn't think you would wake up until the morning.'

'I'll go and see them tomorrow, then, and Peter as well. Can I take a couple of hours off?'

'Take all the time you need.' Harry finished the last of his fry-up and sat back. 'Do you feel up to telling us what happened to you, or would you rather not talk about it yet?'

Bill took the tea Pearl was handing round. 'Thanks, that was just what I needed. It's a long story, but I'll give you a brief account. Because I spoke fluent French, I was asked to go to the nearest village and see if I could find out anything about German troop movements. A patrol came with me, and the plan was they would leave me at a certain point to make my own way. I was in civilian clothes, without identification of any kind. The only personal things I had on me were the English grammar book and another one in French. They could be explained away by saying I was studying the language. Unfortunately, we ran into concealed guns and all hell broke loose. There was a blinding flash, and the next thing I knew I was in a bed and everyone around me was speaking French. They told me they had found me in a ditch covered in debris, only aware I was there because they heard me groan. When they asked me who I was, I didn't know. I was badly injured, and in and out of consciousness for a long time. When I began to recover, they told me the war was over, and because I was strong enough they would take me home, wherever that was. The book was on the table beside the bed and I had looked at it often, so I said I wanted to go to England.'

Bill gave a wry smile. 'I didn't know why I

said that because I thought I was French, and so did they. Like them, I thought I had probably been hit by a lorry and left in the ditch to die. Anyway, they said that if that was what I wanted, then a cousin of theirs had a fishing boat and would take me across the channel. Once ashore, I headed for London and that was when I met Vicki.' Bill looked across the table and smiled at her. 'And she threatened to hit me with an iron bar if I came anywhere near her.'

Everyone turned to stare at her, smiling broadly.

'Well, he's a big man, and I had to protect myself,' she explained, trying to keep a straight face. 'Anyway, I soon changed my mind. He gave me a lecture on improving my speech, gave me the book and bought me breakfast.'

'And then I walked away to continue my aimless wanderings.'

Thirty-Two

Christmas was only two days away and Vicki was really looking forward to it. With Flo and Bob, she was spending the holiday at the school. There was going to be a huge gathering, including the Mantons, Harmonds and the boys, now numbering twelve. Charles was in his element planning everything. He had chopped down a large tree on his estate, and it was standing in the corner of the school dining room,

310

brightly decorated, with parcels heaped beneath it. All the food was coming from his farms. He was thoroughly enjoying himself, determined that the school and the boys had a Christmas to remember.

Over the last few weeks, Vicki had gone down there as often as she could, anxious to see how Bill was coping and what he was going to do now he had his memory back. She knew Harry had been worried in case he decided to return to his teaching post at Harrow, but, to everyone's relief, Bill had just told them that he was where he wanted to be. Harry was elated. He now had two men capable of taking over the school in the future.

'How are we going to carry all this?' Flo exclaimed when she saw the piles of luggage they wanted to take with them.

'Edward's thought of that,' Bob told her. 'He's bringing the bus for us tomorrow.'

'Oh, thank goodness for that. It means I can pop out and get a few more presents.'

'Tie her down, Vicki!' he laughed. 'We've already got enough.'

'Not if the bus is coming for us.' Vicki laced her arm through Flo's. 'Let's go shopping.'

On Christmas day, the tables had been arranged in a square, and Charles had engaged a top chef and his staff to do all the cooking, leaving Pearl free to join in the fun. The pile of presents around the tree was enormous, and they would be opened after lunch, but all the boys had woken up to find big stockings at the end of their beds. This had caused great excitement as none of them had ever experienced anything like this before.

During lunch, crackers were pulled and paper hats worn, causing much laughter. Once the tables were cleared, it was time to hand out the presents. Charles and Harry took charge of this. The children were given theirs first, and each child had a great many. Everyone had bought presents for them, and all the boys were wide-eyed with joy at the number of parcels they had to open. Soon the floor was littered with wrapping paper and boxes as the presents were ripped open. The noise was deafening with squeals of delight.

Vicki knew exactly what they were feeling because she had come from the same sort of home as these youngsters, where there had never been presents or any Christmas celebrations.

By the time the presents had all been handed round, Vicki, like everyone else, had a lot of parcels in front of her. She was about to start opening them when Bill came and sat beside her.

'Thank you for the books by Shakespeare and Dickens, Vicki. I shall enjoy reading them.'

'Are they what you like?' she asked, feeling sure he had already read these books. 'I didn't know what to get, but you did tell me you liked reading.'

'They are perfect. I am going to start putting together a library of my own, and these will be a lovely start to the collection.'

She smiled with relief and watched as he pulled a brightly wrapped present from his pocket.

'This is an extra little present from me. Happy

Christmas, Vicki.' He kissed her on the cheek and put the package in her hands.

She opened it and gasped when she saw the leather-bound book she had treasured so much. 'Oh, Bill, I can't accept this. It's yours and must mean a lot to you.'

'I want you to have it as a reminder of our first meeting. I don't know where I would be today if you hadn't been determined to find me. You have given me my life back, and so much more.' He gazed around the room full of happy people. 'This is beyond price.'

'Bill, I don't know what to say?' her eyes misted over.

'"Thank you, Bill" will do nicely.'

She smiled. 'Thank you, Bill; I will treasure the little book on English grammar.'

'Mr Bill!' Jack ran towards them, his face glowing, quickly followed by Dave and Alfie. The three had become firm friends. 'We've got trains! Can you show us how they work, please?'

He stood up, smiled at Vicki, and then turned his attention to the boys. 'We'll have to clear a space on the floor first.'

Vicki watched the excitement going on all around her. She had never seen Charles so happy. Flo and Bob were laughing with the Harmonds and Bill's parents. Peter and John were crawling around the floor with a couple of the younger boys. The presents in front of her remained unopened as she took in the scene. All this had come about because two men had helped her. The school would continue to give some youngsters a chance of a better life.

And that wasn't all. Charles had never mentioned any family, but he wasn't alone any more, and Bill was no longer drifting, not knowing who he was. Like her, they were now happy and part of a huge family – *her* family. They had reached out to her, and the thought that their kindness had been rewarded made her so happy. Her affectionate gaze went from Charles to Bill.

The blessings had started with two strangers and had rippled out to touch so many lives.